"PREPARE TO MEET YOUR DOOM," ANN SAID.

She stooped, grabbed a handful of snow and tossed it at him so quickly that he did not have time to duck. It knocked off his hat and spattered over his face. Raising a gloved hand, he wiped it out of his eyes.

"Oh no, you don't!" Lord Robert cried, laughingly. Grabbing onto her cloak as Ann tried to flee, he spun her about, circled her arm with one strong hand, pinning her in place—and saw that laughter lighting up her face quite transformed it. She looked almost pretty. His own expression was arrested as he looked down at her.

Her smile faded as he stared at her from mere inches away.

"You should learn to laugh more, my dear. You are lovely when you laugh," he murmured, flicking her cheek with a gloved finger.

She stilled and looked up into his eyes. He gazed steadily back. She could not seem to look away. Or move. Or breathe. They stood motionless as the tension built. A flame kindled deep in his eyes, heating her blood and sending a sizzling current of physical awareness crackling between them. Then they were both in motion at once. Ann was trying to wriggle out of his hold by kicking at his shins with her sturdy boots, but as his own boots covered his legs almost to the knee, she only succeeded in hurting her toe.

"Ha-ha! I have you in my power now, my dear."

Other Zebra Regency Romances by
Meg-Lynn Roberts

AN ALLURING LADY

A PERFECT MATCH

A MIDNIGHT MASQUERADE

CHRISTMAS ESCAPADE

LOVE'S GAMBIT

LORD DIABLO'S DEMISE

Meg-Lynn Roberts welcomes comments from her readers.
You can write to her c/o Kensington Publishing Corporation
850 Third Avenue, New York, NY, 10022-6222.
If you desire a reply, please include a SASE.

RAKE'S GAMBIT

Meg-Lynn Roberts

Zebra Books
Kensington Publishing Corp.
http://www.zebrabooks.com

ZEBRA BOOKS are published by

Kensington Publishing Corp.
850 Third Avenue
New York, NY 10022

First Printing: June, 1997
10 9 8 7 6 5 4 3 2 1

Printed in the United States of America

"And you must love him, ere to you / He will seem worthy of your love."

William Wordsworth, *A Poet's Epitaph*

"[He] Had sighed to many, though he loved but one."

Lord Byron, *Childe Harold's Pilgrimage*

Author's Note

Those of you who have read *Love's Gambit* will see here the full story of Lord Robert Lyndhurst and Miss Ann Forester that was first glimpsed there. For those who have not read that book, *Rake's Gambit* stands on its own.

The distinguished music critic Heinrich Friedrich Rellstab christened Beethoven's Piano Sonata 14 in C-sharp minor the "Moonlight Sonata" a few years after Beethoven's death in 1827. For the purposes of my story, which takes place in 1819, I have allowed Herr Rellstab his observation that the music reminds him of moonlight reflected on water a few years earlier.

Fanny Burney met Germaine, Madame de Staël, and her lover Louis de Narbonne-Lara, the former French minister of war, when they visited England in 1793. She wrote of her impressions of them in a letter to her father.

Passages from the poets include Byron, *Childe Harold's Pilgrimage;* Congreve, *The Mourning Bride;* Keats, *Endymion;* and Wordsworth, *It Is a Beauteous Evening, Lines Composed a Few Miles Above Tintern Abbey, Personal Talk, The Prelude, The Solitary Reaper, The Sparrows' Nest, Strange Fits of Passion Have I Known,* and *The Tables Turned.*

One

"Touch me," a low, husky voice invited. The man's breath caressed Ann's ears, sending shivers down her spine as she reached blindly in front of her. She was still feeling dizzy from being spun around when she was first blindfolded.

She despised playing childish games when she could be ensconced with a book or be spending an extra hour at the pianoforte practicing the difficult new Beethoven piece she was working on. But she was a guest at a Christmas house party, after all, and could not mew herself up all alone. That would not be very polite to her hosts, Lord and Lady Abermarle, and was certainly not the purpose for which she had been invited to spend the festive holiday at their country estate.

So here she was with a handkerchief bound tightly over her eyes, playing Blind Man's Bluff with a group of the houseguests that included both children and adults. It was her turn to be the blind man.

Instinctively, she turned away from the dangerous voice so near to her ear, drawing her elbows protectively against her breast. She made a quarter turn, took two tentative steps, and reached out again. A child danced near, giggling and shrieking, ducking under her outstretched arm, then flitting off again as her arms swooshed at the empty air. Several other people came close, staying just out of reach of her outstretched hands, then swerved away laughing as she neared them.

"You must be bolder, Ann," Patrice, Lady Praxton, one of the

Abermarles' daughters, called out laughingly. "You shall never catch anyone, if you do not give chase."

"Patsy is undoubtedly right, Miss Forester," Sir Everard Praxton chimed in. "After all, that's how she caught me."

"Oh, of all the conceit! If you think for a minute I was chasing you, you are all about in your head, Everard Praxton!"

"Papa's all about in his head! Papa's all about in his head!"

Ann heard Lady Praxton's cry of amused outrage and the singsong taunt of some children, undoubtedly the Praxton's brood of three. The children began to shriek with laughter as it seemed their father chased them or tickled them; she could not tell which.

"But I did not run very fast, my love," she heard Sir Everard say when he could get the words out around his laughter.

It was all very well for them, Ann thought. The Praxtons had had no difficulty catching someone else quickly when they had taken their turns at the start of the game. Nor had Lord and Lady Newberry, the Abermarles' eldest daughter, Madelaine, and her husband Stephen, when they had been blindfolded.

Ann bit her lip in frustration and growing panic. Would she be trapped behind this suffocating blindfold for an hour? She refused to lurch blindly this way and that, as some of the other participants had done—her reserve, her dignity would not allow it. Instead, she took halting steps in one direction, then another. It had become quite clear she would never catch anyone that way. It seemed she had to take chances and make a fool of herself. A fold of the material covering her eyes came down and tickled her nose. She tucked it up impatiently and made a renewed effort, walking forward more boldly.

Her hand met soft velvet. She grasped the material thankfully. Reaching with her other hand for the person's face, she realized in disappointment she had only caught one of the green velvet drapes hanging beside the long windows. Her knee bumped painfully against the protruding windowseat and she drew in a sharp breath through her nostrils.

"Touch me," the same male voice whispered again, closer this time.

Her fingertips brushed against the fine woolen material of his jacket sleeve. Tired of making a fool of herself, she reached quickly and grasped him. He had made a game of taunting her and she was angry with him. Reaching to hold him more tightly, to make an end of the game, her fingers encountered a hard muscular arm, then quickly lifted. She drew back as if burned.

The man's hand caught the underside of the sleeve of her plain woolen morning gown, holding her in place. "I am fair caught, Miss Forester," he murmured in a strangely accented voice, trying to disguise his identity to make her task harder. "You must now try to identify me in the time-honored fashion."

"No! I—"

The back of a long finger brushed over her cheek as gently as a soft summer breeze, then slowly traced down her neck, sending hot and cold shivers over her exposed skin. Could everyone see how he teased her so boldly, she wondered in a panic.

"She's caught someone! Miss Forester's finally caught someone!" the children chorused excitedly. "There! There! Behind the curtain. Look! Oh, look!"

"Can she guess who it is?" another voice chimed amid much exuberant laughter. She recognized Lady Newberry's voice urging her on to the next phase of the game—identifying her captive.

Ann was almost certain of the gentleman's identity, but what if she were wrong? What if it were one of the other gentlemen? Lord Newberry, or even Lord Abermarle? She had to make certain, for a wrong guess would free her captive and she would have to go on with the nerve-wracking game. Anything was better than that. Even—even touching the man she held.

Quickly, to put an end to the absurd game—and to the gentleman's intolerable teasing—she raised her hands and pressed them to the material of his jacket, covering his chest. Forcing herself not to draw back, she continued her exploration. Working quickly up, way up, her hands went to his wide shoulders, then to his face.

Under her fingertips, she outlined firmly arched eyebrows, skimmed over long silky eyelashes that blinked under her feathery touch, touched an errant lock of silky hair falling over his forehead, and with difficulty resisted the absurd urge to push it back. She hesitated briefly, swallowed, and continued her progress, stroking quickly over a nose that was neither overlong nor overwide, felt sharp cheekbones, and the slight roughness of his closely shaved skin on his square jaw. She was disconcerted to feel his warm breath on her fingers as they explored his face. Gritting her teeth, she continued, brushing over firm full lips that she realized were curved up in a smile. Her fingers stilled there for a brief second, but moved quickly when she realized in shock that the tip of his tongue was flicking the pad of her fingertips, moistening them as they moved over his mouth.

"Oh!" she exclaimed in outrage. "You can be no other than Lord Robert Lyndhurst!"

"Yes, yes, yes!" cried the children. "Lord Robert is *it* now! Lord Robert is *it!*"

"Sarrie can't catch me!" one bold youngster boasted, dashing headlong across the room. He tripped over a cushion that was strewn on the floor and was sent sprawling. Sarah, one of his young cousins, went dashing after him, screaming and throwing herself on top of him. The parents of the two youngsters busied themselves disentangling the overwrought pair while Lord Robert helped Miss Forester to remove the blindfold.

Everyone seemed to be speaking at once.

"I think we should have a rest now," Lady Praxton said, laughing. "The game is growing too wild. I had best take my trio back to the nursery for a quiet read."

"The *children* are growing too wild, you mean, Patrice," Madelaine corrected wryly. "We adults are behaving ourselves admirably."

"Um. All except Everard, you mean. I think *he* should be banished to the nursery," Patrice said, harking back to her husband's teasing comments.

"I would not mind going on with the game," Cynthia, the Abermarle's youngest daughter, said, casting her eyes in Lord Robert's direction.

"Nor I," chimed in Miss Felicity Kentwell, a schoolfriend of Cynthia's who had been invited for the holidays because she had nowhere else to go.

"Mama is planning to serve coffee in the morning room now," Madelaine told Cynthia and Felicity, in a voice that would brook no opposition. As the eldest of the Abermarles' daughters, she had always assumed an air of command.

"But Lord Robert has been just been caught and he has not yet taken a turn," Cynthia objected plaintively.

"Never mind, dear. Perhaps we can have another game tomorrow, and he can have first go," Madelaine consoled her. "Come and help me pick up these cushions that have been scattered about, tripping everyone up."

Everyone was milling about, setting the room to rights again while Ann and Lord Robert stood almost unnoticed to one side of the room.

"Here, allow me to help you," Lord Robert said, reaching behind Ann's head to untie the material that covered her eyes. "I know it is not pleasant to have one's face covered for such a length of time." The tease was there in his voice again and Ann bristled.

"Please!" she begged, awkwardly trying to push his hands away. "I can do it myself."

"Hold still, Miss Forester, and I will have this blindfold off your eyes in a twinkling," he insisted, grasping her shoulders firmly between his long hands. "It is knotted in the back. I do not believe you can remove it yourself without pulling half your hair out. And we would not want you tripping across the furniture and cushions littering the floor at the moment and falling across that tangle of children who are setting up such a screech in the middle of the room, and affording everyone a glimpse of your ankles."

"Oh!" She fought the quite natural urge to flee from his company as she had been doing for the past three days, and forced herself to freeze under his touch. She remained as still as a statue while he worked at the stubborn knot, reaching his arms around her head to do so. His breath was warm against her cheek as he worked. She caught a whiff of some woodsy male cologne and clean soap from his closely-shaved skin and swallowed. Standing rigidly in his near embrace, she tightened her hands and willed her nerves—and her heart—to settle down.

She had heard of Lord Robert Lyndhurst before she and her mother had arrived at the Abermarles'. His notoriety had spread from London even to her small corner of Hampshire and she was well aware of the rumors of his numerous petticoat affairs. He was a younger son of the Duke of Miramont, and had a shocking reputation as a rake. And when she met him, she had seen why he had had such success with women. With his tall, leanly-muscled physique, classically straight features, midnight black hair, and laughing green eyes, he was more than handsome—he was beautiful. And charming. Fatally charming.

She had wanted to run a mile the first time she saw him, and at the way her breathing had speeded up just *looking* at him, she felt she had!

Her mother had been most annoyed when she learned he was to be among the guests and had warned her to have nothing to do with the scamp. She would have been glad to comply with her mother's orders, but the gentleman seemed to have other ideas. Why he had decided to pursue such a plain spinster as herself she had no idea, unless word of the dowry that would be hers upon her marriage had somehow come to his attention. However it was, wherever she had gone, whatever she had decided to do during the past three days, she had found Lord Robert beside her.

"There! Now you can breathe freely again," he said, smiling down at her as he removed the handkerchief with a flourish, allowing his thumbs to trace her jawline as he did so. He did not move back, but stood mere inches away.

Feeling disoriented, Ann stood blinking, trying to refocus her eyes.

"Shall we join the others for coffee? Or shall I accompany you to the music room and turn the pages for you while you practice your piece at the pianoforte? You see, I have remembered after only three days of your acquaintance that at this time of day you are inevitably to be found in the music room. Am I not clever?"

She looked up at him solemnly and her lips tightened. His glittering, heavily-lashed green eyes held a devilish gleam she did not trust for a second. She backed away, but he caught her elbow, then slipped his hand down to her wrist. Glancing left and right, she saw that the room was now deserted as they stood near the window embrasure where a watery winter light was streaming through the glass, dappling the worn Aubusson carpet.

"Why do you fear me, Miss Forester?" he quizzed, his thumb rubbing in a circle on the exposed skin of her wrist at the unadorned edge of her long-sleeved wool gown.

"I do not fear you, Lord Robert. I dislike you," she said, meeting his gaze squarely.

Surprise replaced the mischief shining from his eyes. "Dislike me?" Frowning, he released her arm and spread his hands wide. "But why? What have I done to give you a dislike of me in so short a time, ma'am?"

"You think to flatter me with your attentions, my lord." She lowered her dark brows and glared at him, her slanting amber eyes sparking hazel and golden fire. "Perhaps you hope to encourage my admiration. But it is of no use. I do not admire you. It is said you delight in breaking women's hearts—"

"No, really, ma'am! I must protest! I do not delight in any such thing!"

"Can you deny that you are a gazetted flirt?" She was in a fine heat now and her tongue gave vent to her thoughts without consideration for the impropriety of her words.

"Indeed, I *do* deny it. Of course, I enjoy the company of women, but I hope I do not flirt!" He turned a boyishly innocent and hurt look on her.

"Do you take me for a fool, sirrah? You have been on the town for years and—" Hearing her own shrill voice in the quiet room, Ann blushed and came to an abrupt halt.

"And what, my little fire-breather?" He reached out and tweaked her nose.

She pulled away from him. "You are not irresistible, you know. You may as well know that you waste your time with me, my lord."

"Do I? That's a pity, then."

Ann was outraged by the humor she saw in his eyes and heard in his teasing words. "I am not to be flirted with or— or cozened by you!"

He threw back his dark head and laughed. "Miss Forester, you are the most refreshing woman I have ever met. No, no," he said, holding his hands palm up in front of him as though to ward off her scorn, "do not scold me by saying I offer you false coin. My words were sincerely meant." He sighed. "I see I must beg your pardon. I did not mean to offend you. Most women would be flattered by my attentions. But I see you are not 'most women'."

Curiosity got the better of her and Ann looked at him with her head a little on one side. "You sound as though it is *you* who scorn such women for taking your flattery seriously. Do you have no respect for a woman's intelligence?"

He quirked a brow at her. "An intelligent woman? Such a rare jewel has not come much in my way. However, I am willing to believe that I have at last met a woman worthy of that epithet. You are what is commonly termed a bluestocking, are you not, Miss Forester?"

"If you mean that I like to read and enlarge my mind and that I enjoy pursuits that involve some minimum of intelligent thought, that I enjoy poetry and music and painting and political discussions, and take an interest in the natural world around me as well as in the wider world, then yes, I suppose I am a bluestocking. I do not apologize for it." Ann drew herself up, squaring her thin shoulders, and looked him in the eye. She did not have that far to look up, for although Lord Robert was well above the common height for a man, she herself was quite tall for a woman.

Again his hands went up in front of him as though to defend himself from her vehemence. "No, no. No apology is called for.

I admire an intelligent woman, I believe. I have not had much opportunity to be in company with one whose mind is as accomplished as yours, is all, except for perhaps my eldest sister. But surely you cannot pursue such serious matters all the time. Does not that grow a little . . . dull?"

"*You* may think it dull," she riposted quickly.

His hand went to his heart. "Ah! A hit, a palpable hit! The lady thinks me a worthless fribble, interested only in fun and frolic and frivolity . . . Your tongue is a veritable rapier, my dear."

"No. I think you are interested in more than fun and frolic and frivolity, my lord," she replied seriously.

His eyes questioned her, still holding that detestable teasing gleam that was becoming all too familiar.

Grasping the sides of her plain grey woollen dress, she said, "I think you take an interest in drink and gambling and racing and cards and—" She sucked in a startled breath and looked stricken at her own outspoken impoliteness.

"And *what,* Miss Forester?" Lord Robert asked quietly, his green eyes narrowed and his face losing its habitual carefree, smiling aspect.

Her chin went up at his challenge. "And women, my lord."

"Ah, how perceptive of you. You, who have so much knowledge of the world, who have undoubtedly encountered men of my ilk many times and been subjected to their evil wiles, are well qualified to take me down a peg or two. I have been trying to become better acquainted with you, yet you fly at me. You seem to think me a loose screw of the worst sort. Knowing me so well, you wish to insult me and flay me alive? Is that what *intelligent* women do? Or perhaps you wish to reform me? Is that it, ma'am? I have heard that a lady cannot refuse the challenge of reforming a man of the world."

As he loomed over her, Ann saw bright anger burning like twin torches of green fire in his jewel-like eyes. She drew back, ready to flee should he reach out and grab her, as he looked ready to do.

"N-no. I did not mean—" She tried to control her shaking

voice and began again. "Forgive me, my lord. I do not know you at all."

His eyes became a little less challenging, and took on a speculative gleam. "We can remedy that. I will accept your apology, Miss Forester, on one condition."

How had he done that? Ann wondered, stunned. How had he put her so badly in the wrong and forced her to apologize to *him?* And now she was caught. As a gentlewoman, she would have to accept his condition, or look ill-mannered indeed. "What is that, Lord Robert?" she asked somewhat breathlessly.

He gave her a stern look. "That you will allow me to spend some time in your company, that I may become as puritanical and straitlaced and prim and good as you." At her look of consternation, his lips slowly curved up in a satisfied, and quite wicked, grin. "You can begin my reform, and in turn I shall teach you how to smile and relax and have a little *innocent* fun. You *should* learn to smile more, you know. We can start in the music room in—" he glanced down at his pocket watch, his dark lashes fanning his cheek "—half an hour."

His lips quirked into that slow crooked grin almost curled her toes. He was even more devastatingly attractive when he smiled like that, Ann thought privately. Yes, and the dratted man knew it, too! Well, if he wished to be reformed, she would have a good go at it, though she knew in her heart that he was only playing with her again.

"Good morning, Miss Forester," Miss Felicity Kentwell called in a friendly voice.

Ann halted briefly in her passage across the chilly black and white checkered marble hallway that led to the grand curving staircase. She turned with a smile toward the girl.

"Lady Abermarle says we are to walk in the snow that has already settled on the ground before luncheon. Do you think it will continue to snow and we shall be snowed in? What fun, if we are!"

"Well, it would certainly be a pleasant diversion," Ann replied, her expression wistful. She was remembering how as a child she had had no one to play with in the snow. It was one of the penalties of being an only child.

Miss Kentwell moved nearer. "Would it not be heaven to walk in the snow with Lord Robert?" she whispered conspiratorially. "Have you ever seen a more handsome man? So tall and slender and with that long dark hair that curls at the ends. And that smile that is enough to melt your insides! He is so handsome, I almost *die* when he looks at me." She giggled. "And you had the privilege of catching him and identifying him just now. How fortunate you are!" She sighed gustily.

Trying not to blush as she answered rather noncommittally, Ann continued on her way up the stairs to her room. Still shaken by her recent encounter with Lord Robert, she was glad to escape his disturbing presence for even a brief time. It seemed he planned to monopolize her company for the next few days. She had already promised to meet him in half an hour in the music room and then to walk in the snow with him later. He had suggested that they become luncheon and dinner companions for the remainder of the holiday as well.

Safe! she thought, when she reached her pretty little bedchamber at the back of the house and heard her door close behind her with a click. She rubbed her cold arms briskly over the thick woolen gown she had chosen to wear. It was not a fashionable garment, but it was warm. She walked to the small iron grate and held her hands out to the fire blazing there, gazing down into the flickering red and blue flames and thinking of her tormentor.

What had she done? Oh, what in the world had she done? she wondered in stunned disbelief.

She had promised to become better acquainted with him so that she could judge him from knowledge, not from hearsay. She bit her lip in agitation. Coming to know him would mean that they would spend a considerable amount of time together.

She did not want to spend time with him. She was already

disturbed by his threatening aura of masculinity. His fashionable coat and form-fitting pantaloons molded themselves to his tall, lean figure, doing nothing to disguise the muscles in shoulder, arm and thigh. His midnight dark hair turned up slightly at the ends and gave him an almost boyish look that caused her heart to turn over in her breast. Never had she seen a more gorgeous gentleman! But it was his undoubted charm—and his quite devastating smile—that disturbed her most.

How could she resist that charm, that package of vigorous masculinity, if she were in such close proximity to him?

She set her hands on her hips and frowned. Why had he singled her out for his flirtation, anyway? She could guess what that reason was. She was an only child, without much family besides her mother and an aunt in London to protect her—and her dowry was quite large enough to tempt any man.

But he could not seriously think to entice her into marriage, could he?

Marriage? Your imagination jumps from flirtation to marriage in a second. He is the son of a duke. He, who could have any heiress in England, would not choose you, my girl, she told herself, laughing rather bitterly.

Well, if she could not escape him, perhaps she could have a good influence on him. Perhaps she could reform him. How did one set about reforming a rake?

She had absolutely no idea.

Turning from the fire, she crossed the room and gazed at herself in the oval looking glass that was set above a charming little floral skirted dressing table. A plain, rather thin spinster of five-and-twenty gazed blankly back. Her straight dark hair was pulled back tightly from her face as usual. Her slanted amber eyes that she had always feared appeared somewhat odd were set under dark brows in her dark complexion. Her small mouth was pursed primly. She relaxed her lips and some of the strain eased from around her eyes.

She sighed. She was not much to look at, and her clothes did not help either, she decided, her eyes following the severe line of her plain morning frock as it fell to the floor in a severe line on her tall, slender figure.

"It does not matter," she whispered to her despairing image. "He is only playing some sort of perverse game with you." She straightened and a fierce light came into her eyes, making them glow.

"He shall not get the better of you, my girl," she told her image, "for no matter how handsome, how charming, he is, you undoubtedly have more brains than he does. You will outwit him at this game." A stiff finger pointed at herself in the glass. She nodded her head once decidedly and turned to find her music.

Two

Lord Robert smiled in anticipation as he watched Ann run away from him. She would not escape his company for long. He would see her in the music room in half an hour to continue their unlikely but amusing flirtation.

Pushing back the errant lock of dark hair that tended to fall over his forehead, he rested his foot on the window seat and gazed out onto the snow-covered lawn beyond. Lord, but this Christmas houseparty had been a dull occasion until the advent of Miss Forester. It was a family party for the most part, a hodge-podge of relatives, consisting of his Cousin Lydia, Lady Abermarle, her husband the viscount, their three daughters—two married with families and one only seventeen—and various friends, with more arrivals expected over the next several days. Their son, Rupert, was not in attendance. A widower of some three or four years, he was on the continent with the diplomatic corps, though his three children were there.

Miss Forester was in no way connected to his family, but it seemed her mother and Lydia had been bosom bows in their youth, thus accounting for the Foresters' presence.

Lord, but she was a bit of a prim spinster! With her dark hair and eyebrows set against her rather dusky complexion, she was too plain of face for beauty, and her too-tall, too-slim figure was definitely unalluring. She did have the most unusual eyes, though. He liked watching their ever-changing colors, and was learning to gauge her mood by their telltale expression. Their slanted almond shape gave her the look of an exotic Attic vase figure and their amber color was warm and lustrous.

Though unfashionably dark, her complexion itself was surprisingly soft and smooth when he laid his hand against it while he was untying her blindfold. He had wanted to leave his hand there longer, but knew he was already on the edge of offending propriety by flirting with her so openly in front of all the others.

He grinned. She was not in the usual style, he had to admit, but he had discovered that when he teased her, he could bring a fiery blush to her cheek and a dangerous glint to her eyes, in spite of her best efforts to resist him.

He did not like to be resisted. It irked him. He had always prided himself on his ability to charm any woman in his vicinity, with the possible exception of his mother, who had always been so distracted by her duties and by her large brood that she did not have time to be charmed by one or the other of them.

Lydia had told him that Ann Forester was a considerable heiress. His games were not designed to lure her into matrimony, however. Ever since he was a stripling of twenty, new come to London, he had enjoyed the company of many women, including several marriageable heiresses—and enjoyed more than the company of some of the more sophisticated ladies he had known, too. But he had never come close to being tempted to marry.

He was not interested in a marriage of convenience. He was not interested in any marriage at all for the moment. Despite his lack of financial resources, he had always supposed that if he ever did marry, it would be because he was so deeply in love that he could not live without the woman he wed.

He laughed at himself. It was a rather romantical notion for a man who had known a variety of women and who had fancied himself more than halfway in love a number of times. He supposed it was because he had grown up seeing one brother and three of his sisters marry with widely different degrees of success. Love and happiness and contentment *were* possible in the married state, but so too were strife and unhappiness and misery.

No. He was not interested in enticing Miss Forester into marriage or even into a serious flirtation. His game was designed simply to relieve his boredom. That, and to make her regret snubbing him.

She might be a female for whom he would not ordinarily spare a second glance, but she presented a challenge, and he had been drawn into a battle of wills that he could not resist. His vanity would not allow her to ignore him.

She should have been flattered and grateful for the attention he had lavished on her during the past three days. Instead, she opposed him at every turn, turning back his flowery compliments with a sharp word or look. Yes, if looks could kill, he would have been a dead man many times over these past few days after enduring her dagger-edged glares. And her tongue could slash, too. Deep biting wounds, like the one she had just delivered, calling him no better than an uncaring, frivolous libertine, if not quite a criminal sort.

Her recent criticisms had touched him on the raw.

Shoving his hands into his jacket pockets, his quirky smile faded into a hard line. Of course, he indulged in drink and cards, bet at the tables and the racecourse, and frequented the company of *chere-amies*. It was what was done when one was a young buck in London. He was no different than nine-tenths of the gentlemen who lived there.

Take him to task, think ill of him, would she?

Well, Miss Prunes-and-Prisms, we will see what you think about me at the end of the holidays, he thought, vowing to teach her a lesson in manners and in something else before their sojourn under the same roof ended. He would steal a kiss—more than one—before the fortnight was out. Yes, and he would leave her begging for more, too!

He turned and left the room with a purposeful stride, not pausing to consider the consequences of upsetting the staid existence of a plain, unfashionable, sharp-tongued spinster.

* * *

"Ah, there you are, Robin. We sent the troops out to find you, but they came back demanding sugarplums with no 'Uncle' Robin in tow." Madelaine met him in the hallway, greeting him with a friendly smile.

"Ah, well, you will remember how it was to be an excited child at Christmastime. After all, it was not so very long ago that you were their age yourself, Maddy."

Laughing, she linked her arm with his and led him to the morning room where coffee was being served. "Ah, I see you are still an excellent purveyor of fustian! I must be two or three years older than you, Robin, at the least. And the mother of a hopeful five-year-old, to boot."

He stopped just inside the room and lifted the hand that rested on his sleeve to his lips, saying in astonishment, "But my dear, how can that be? I am a sad old bachelor of eight-and-twenty and you are a fresh young thing who does not look a day over eighteen!"

Out of the corner of his eye, he saw Lord Newberry watching them with a dark look on his rather stern face.

"Oh, dear. Poor Robin! No one to flirt with but an old married woman?"

"The loveliest woman in the room, my dear," he said in the warmly caressing voice that he had found always raised ladies' interest. Not that he wanted to raise his cousin's interest, but the tone was habitual with him.

She laughed and watched as he accepted a cup of coffee from Patrice.

"Mama was pleased that you accepted her invitation this year, Robin, but she was surprised, too. Why did you come here and not go home as usual?" Madelaine asked.

"Change is good for the soul," he said flippantly, his eyes holding a teasing glint.

"Oh, Robin. I can see I shall get no sense out of you today. I had best go and placate Stephen, who is looking like a thunder-cloud for some reason."

Lydia's invitation had been a godsend, actually, he thought as he watched Madelaine walk away. Though he would miss the annual gathering with his eight siblings, he hadn't really wanted to go home for Christmas this year, where his younger brother James would be introducing his brand-new fiancée, Miss Anthea Fenchurch, and her family to his parents. There had been entirely too much between him and Miss Fenchurch before Jamie had decided to court her for Robert to be comfortable in her presence now.

In fact, Miss Fenchurch had given every indication that she would prefer to succumb to *his* charm rather than to an honorable proposal of marriage from the more worthy Jamie.

He had found her a silly chit, but it seemed Jamie was in love with the girl. He would never do anything to hurt Jamie. So he had taken himself out of the way.

"Come now, Robin. Why *did* you accept Mama's invitation?" Patrice asked in a straightforward manner that reminded him of his sister Frances, five years older than he and always bossy. "Dick has been pitching into you again, has he not?"

"My dear Patsy, how like you to hit the nail on the head at first try," he said with a wide smile, amused that she was indeed right on the mark. His eldest brother, Richard, the Marquess of Teignbury, heir to the dukedom when his father passed on, disapproved of him heartily.

"Dick has washed his hands of me, you see," he told her. "I am a blot on the family escutcheon—or perhaps a blip. His writing is atrocious, you know." He remembered the scorching letter he had received from his eldest brother only a fortnight ago.

"Papa is too easy with you. This year I have put my foot down," Dick had written in his usual brusque style. *"No more advances on your allowance from the estate coffers. We simply cannot afford it. My advice to you is to cut back on your expenses. Better still, go to Coniston and put your estate in order. Perhaps you can squeeze a few pounds from your sheep farm there, if you put your mind—and your back—to it."*

"How absurd Dick is! He acts like an old man, rather than a gentleman who is still in his thirties!" Patrice exclaimed. "Elder brothers are always like that, are they not? I well remember when Rupert forbade me to marry Everard. Can you imagine? Papa had already given his permission, but *Rupert* would not have it because Everard's estate was too small to suit *his* consequence. Well, of course I defied him. Would you not have done the same?"

"Er, in this case, I believe I would have obeyed Rupert. I do not think I would like being married to Everard."

Patrice gave a startled laugh. "Robin! Do not be so absurd! I do not mean that you should have married Everard. How ridiculous you are!"

"I hope not, my dear. And please do not let my valet hear you say such a thing. He would leave me in an instant, and then where would I be?"

"I am not talking about your clothes, you silly man!" she cried. "You are always in the height of fashion and put the rest of us to shame."

He grinned. Patrice always took everything so literally, but she was ready to laugh at her own absurdities, too.

"And how are they all? Your mama and papa, and all your brothers and sisters? Goodness! There are nine of you. There are only four of us, but sometimes I have trouble keeping up with everyone's whereabouts. Let me see." Patrice counted them off on her fingers, eldest to youngest. "There is Emily, then Dick, Catherine, Frances, Will, then you, James, Sarah, and lovely little Jane, of course. Have I that right?"

"Brava, Lady Praxton! All of us named and in the correct order, too! You have done better than even Mama on occasion. But to answer your question, Mama and Father are as well as can be expected under the circumstances, with nine children and almost a dozen grandchildren to worry about." He went on to tell her the latest news of all his brothers and sisters.

"And little Jamie is to be married! But he is just a child!"

"Six-and-twenty. Only two years my junior and just one inch shorter."

"Is he really? One forgets . . . And I suppose dear Sarah is still suffering the loss of her fiancé in the war . . . and poor Jane, not able to walk. I suppose Silena does nothing for them. I must confess, Robin, I have never liked Silena. Dick changed so much after he married her. And not for the better."

He could not but agree with her, but said nothing, only raising one brow quizzically. He often wondered if Dick's dissatisfaction with him stemmed in part because of Silena. Dick's wife had caused a rift between them with her strict ways and prudish manners. There was no fun and gig in her nature, definitely at odds with the fun-loving Lyndhurst clan. Privately, he thought Silena made Dick's life a living hell.

And of course Dick blamed him for what had happened to Will at Waterloo. Quite irrationally blamed him, but there it was. Will, his senior by three years, had joined the army and he had not. When Will had come home from the war minus his left arm and almost blind in one eye, Dick had blamed him.

He sighed. He would miss them all this year, especially Will and Jane, his youngest sister. But he would go home and see them after Christmas. After Jamie had left with Miss Fenchurch and her family.

Several of the children who had been so boisterous during the recent Blind Man's Bluff game raced through the room, shouting at the top of their lungs. He turned his head and watched them, grinning at their high spirits and excitement. One of the children called to Patrice and she moved away.

The antics of the children put him in mind of his own youth. He and Jamie and Sarah had been just such wild little savages. Jane had not been able to join in because of her feet, which had not formed properly, causing her to walk with a limp, but she had often sat nearby watching them, clapping and laughing at their antics,

Holidays had always been exuberant occasions at home, with much dashing about and laughter and high holiday spirits, fights and overwrought feelings and crying, good food and not enough attention from his parents to go around to all nine children.

Despite his father's exalted station, there was little money. Certainly none to spend on trips to London or even to travel about much, so it had been an exciting time when visitors came to the run-down ducal mansion for the holidays.

Children! He grinned. Little imps of mischief, the lot of them. They tended to crimp one's style, when one had a pretty pullet in view, as he had discovered to his chagrin when visiting his sister Catherine and her brood last summer. He had tried to flirt with Catherine's pretty friend, but the children had managed to thwart him time after time. However, there was no style to crimp here.

As yet, besides Miss Forester, there were only two other unmarried females above the age of twelve in residence, silly giggling chits fresh from the schoolroom both. There was not one dashing matron, not one widow or loosely married woman who knew how the game was played with whom to while away his time, though Lydia had promised that other guests would be arriving in the days just before Christmas and on the festive day itself.

He could not sleep away the hours until morsels more to his taste arrived, nor while away the time getting himself thoroughly foxed. He hated the way he felt the morning after he had overindulged in drink and for the last few years had imbibed only in moderation. He would have met even Silena's strict standards in that one area, had she known about it, he reflected with a wry smile. So he would have to make do with Ann Forester.

"We would like to ask your opinion, Robin," Cynthia addressed him archly, coming up with Miss Kentwell in tow. "Do you not think that Mama should have some waltzes played at our Christmas party next week?"

"The waltz is indeed a lovely dance, but I believe your mama knows best what will suit the company here."

Not entirely satisfied with his answer, Cynthia's lower lip formed into a pout. But in the next moment, she was looking up at him through her lashes.

"Well, whether Mama allows the dance or not, Felicity and I are anxious to learn it. We are to make our come-outs in another year, you know, and we wish to have all the accomplishments before we go to London."

His lips quivered.

"I am sure you are an expert dancer, Robin, and I want you to teach me. As you are my cousin, it would be perfectly proper. And perhaps Felicity could learn by watching."

"Not so much fun for Miss Kentwell," he said with a glance in the girl's direction. As soon as his eyes grazed her, her face lit up like a beacon and her eyes dropped to the floor. He hid his amusement by raising his coffee cup to his mouth.

"But *will* you, Robin?" Cynthia demanded rather petulantly.

Feeling trapped, he looked around and was relieved to see rescue in sight.

"We shall have to see what your mama says. Ah, Cousin Lydia," he greeted her. "Your daughter and her friend, Miss Kentwell, are anxious to learn the waltz before they go to London. They are importuning me—"

"Nonsense," Lydia said, "Cynthia knows that I will hire the same dancing master we had for Madelaine and Patrice when we get to London next year. He will teach her the *correct* way of performing the dance."

Lord Robert did not bother to hide his grin this time.

"Go along now, Cynthia, do. I wish you to take Rupert's children outside and build snowmen with them. Felicity can help you. You will enjoy it."

"But, Mama—Maddy or Patsy can help Rupert's three. I am too old for such childish games."

"Nonsense. Madelaine and Patrice have their own children to contend with. Run along now, my dear. The fresh air will do you good."

As the girls walked away, their shoulders slumped in disappointment, Lydia turned to him. "Have they been pestering you, Robin? If so, do not indulge Cynthia's whims. She is rather giddy at the moment."

"A lovely girl," he murmured before finishing the last of his coffee. "She will take the *ton* by storm next spring. But I have a bone to pick with you, my dear Lydia. Were you implying that I might teach her the *incorrect* way of dancing the waltz?"

Lydia chuckled. "I daresay that you know *how* to dance properly, but the waltz presents *such* temptations, does it not?"

His eyes gleamed. "Only when one is with a lady whose charms match yours, my dear."

"You are a wicked, wicked boy! I can't think why I should have invited you. I wonder why I did?" Lady Abermarle had been a noted flirt in her own day.

"To liven up the occasion, perhaps?"

She gave up matching wits with him and laughed heartily. "Oh, dear, but you do make me laugh." She looked around the morning room at the various guests still enjoying coffee. Many had left to don their outdoor clothes to take advantage of the weak sun that had come out. "I do not see Ann. Did she not want to join us for coffee?"

"I have no idea."

"A rather nice girl, do you not think? So talented. But reserved."

He replied nonchalantly and, dropping the subject, she left him to see to her other guests.

What *had* Lydia been about to invite him anyway? he wondered, disgruntled when he left the morning room after exchanging a few words with Paul, Viscount Abermarle, and some of the other guests.

Surely not for Cynthia, her youngest?

The girl could not be more than seventeen. She and her friend, Miss Kentwell, were two flighty chits, fresh from the schoolroom. He could see they had sized him up and decided to make him the object of their fledging attempts at flirtation, trying their newly emerging feminine wiles on him, fluttering their lashes and sending him inviting smiles.

He was not even tempted.

He shuddered as the jaws of a legshackle loomed open before him. No. Much safer to attach himself to the spinster than risk being caught in Parson's Mousetrap with one of those pretty, empty-headed infants.

He congratulated himself again for hitting upon the idea of teasing Miss Forester. At least he felt safe with her—and amused. Yes, it definitely amused him to deliberately provoke her.

Three

"The air you play is sublime. And you play it divinely, Miss Forester. Have you brought it with you from Mount Olympus where divinities such as yourself dwell?" Lord Robert murmured audaciously as he bent over Ann's shoulder to turn the next page of her music. He made sure that his arm brushed against her sleeve as he did so.

Ann's fingers crashed to a halt on the ivory keys and she looked up at him sharply. His face was inches away, his brilliant eyes glinting down into hers. "There is no need to patronize me, Lord Robert," she said indignantly, dropping her eyes to the mocking smile on his curving lips, then quickly looking away.

"Have I offended so grievously, Divinity, that now the warlike aspect of Athena sits darkly upon your angelic brow?" His hand smote his heart in a dramatic gesture while his eyes danced with devilish lights.

"As you undoubtedly hail from the other place and are accustomed to consorting with fiends, it is no wonder that you can so shamelessly utter such nonsense!" she riposted, but she had to bite her lips and look away from his eyes to prevent herself from smiling at his foolishness.

"A thousand, thousand pardons, my angel of music. Do not consign me to perdition by forcing me to keep company with those two schoolgirls—er, young handmaidens awaiting without this paradise."

"You are not afraid of Miss Kentwell and your cousin Cynthia, are you? I would have thought you would enjoy having two such adoring admirers who hang on your every word and are ready to indulge you in the nonsense you delight in speaking."

"Perish the thought!" He gave an exaggerated shudder and grimaced. "Fiendish woman to entertain such a foolish idea. I shall begin to think you are not of the angels after all."

Holding her eyes steady on his with an effort, she suppressed the urge to laugh.

Resuming his normal negligent posture, one elbow leaning on the piano, he folded his hands together and leaned toward her, saying quietly, "I am not patronizing you, you know. My compliment was sincerely meant, though you did not care for its delivery. You play well. More than well. Like a true artist. Perhaps I should have phrased it differently."

"Perhaps you should," she said primly. Seeing him draw back as if her words stung, she straightened her shoulders, trying to shake off the way her senses were responding to his disturbing presence. She took a deep breath and tried to ignore the small fluttery feeling in the pit of her stomach and calm her fast-beating heart.

"You play extraordinarily well. Truly," he said after a moment. "This is Beethoven you are playing?" His fingers flicked the sheets of music on the stand, then rested briefly on her shoulder.

Ann controlled her shiver. "Yes. One of his piano sonatas. It is quite difficult and I need to go through it several times before this evening, but I cannot concentrate with you hovering over me, my lord, and speaking to me while I am playing."

She needed to feel confident that she knew the piece perfectly before she played for the assembled company that evening, but she was utterly distracted with him standing so near. And that was an understatement.

"Could you find something else to do with yourself for the next half hour or so?" she asked, surprised and relieved that her voice sounded quite normal and not as breathless as she felt.

He eyed her consideringly. She was more attractive when her face was animated, with her eyes flashing amber lights and high color staining her angled cheekbones as now. He wished he had made her smile rather than frown, though.

"You would banish me from your presence for so slight an offense, Divinity? But what of your promise? We are to be the best of friends for the next sennight. How can we get to know one another better if we do not spend time together?" he asked reasonably, opening his eyes wide and his hands in appeal.

She distrusted his reasonableness more than she did his teasing. He sounded so sincere and looked so boyishly appealing that it was well nigh impossible to resist him. "I have promised to take luncheon with you, Lord Robert. Can you not take yourself off until then? Find a book to read or something. You do read, do you not?" she asked sweetly.

Something dangerous glinted deep in his eyes as Ann looked up at him. He lifted his chin and stared down at her as though she were an insect pinned to a board. Even the air vibrated between them. Had she gone too far? She squared her shoulders, bracing for a blistering setdown when they were interrupted.

"I s-say, Robin, is that you?" A young man's curly blond head peered round the door.

"Chubby! 'Course it's me, you idiot!"

"That's g-good. 'Cause I've been lookin' for you everywhere since we arrived upwards of an hour since," the young man said.

"Who did you think it was, the devil himself?" All the irritation instantly evaporating from his face, Lord Robert quizzed the round-cheeked young man as he came shyly into the room.

"I d-don't know how anyone would think you were the devil, R-Robin," Chubby objected stoutly. "G-got a face like an angel, leastways that's what my sister Kathy always says. D-don't see it m'self."

Robin cocked an amused brow at Ann to see her reaction to these words. Noting her flush with satisfaction, he introduced his relative. "Miss Forester, may I make you known to my gabby young relative here? Charles Harwood-Jones, otherwise known as Chubby."

Clasping his hands behind his back, the rotund young man smiled bashfully at Ann.

"Make your bows, Chub, old fellow," Lord Robert prompted, winking at Ann over his relative's curly head.

"How do you do?" Ann greeted the open-faced young man with a smile as he made her an awkward bow.

"You and R-Robin playing duets, Miss Forester?" he asked politely. "Wouldn't surprise me, in the l-least. Know for a fact he's always b-bangin' away on m'sisters' instrument at home when he comes to visit us."

"No. I have been practicing a piece I am to play for the company tonight. And I did not know that Lord Robert played. He has kept his talent well hidden." Ann turned on the bench to look at him, not bothering to hide the amusement in her eyes. "So you too have been visited by the muse, my lord?" she asked archly. She was interested to see a slight stain of red darken his handsome face.

He did not answer but occupied himself in brushing down his jacket sleeves and straightening his shirt cuffs while the heat in his cheeks died down.

"Yes," Chubby answered for him, "R-Robin always says beautiful music brings a tear to his eye."

"Chub, my boy," Lord Robert said, grimacing and clapping a hand on the young man's shoulder, "go and dunk your head under a jug of cold water."

"B-but, Robin. I've only just arrived. Don't want to b-bathe now!"

Ann burst out laughing. Lord Robert laughed, too, and released Chubby, cuffing him lightly on the arm as he did so. "Have I ever told you that—on occasion—you talk too much, old man?"

Chubby scratched his curly head and considered. "N-no, I don't believe you ever have, Robin."

Lord Robert raised his eyes to the coffered ceiling and gave a wry chuckle.

"I—I am sure Lady Abermarle will be glad to have you play tonight, my lord. As soon as I have finished practicing, I shall gladly relinquish the instrument to you," Ann said unsteadily, and gurgled with laughter again to see his chagrin. How good it felt to be able to tease *him* for a change!

"You are too good, ma'am." He bowed mockingly to her, then hissed out of the side of his mouth, "Now see what you have got me into, Chub. Do not be surprised to find yourself smothered in your sleep by a pillow one of these days."

Chubby grinned at him, unabashed by his threats. "You're teasin' me again, ain't you, R-Robin? Robin is a great tease, you know, Miss Forester. In fact, m'sister Kathy says—"

"Chub, old fellow," Lord Robert intervened, taking Chubby's arm and guiding him to the door, "you can regale us with Kathryn's words of wisdom at a later date. Miss Forester is attempting to practice a Beethoven sonata at the moment, and I am, er, assisting her. We need privacy, you understand."

Chubby's mouth opened in awe and he gave Ann a comical look over his shoulder at the door. "B-Beethoven, heh? One of those foreign chaps. Is Miss Forester a prodigal then, R-Robin?"

"Prodigy—and no, she is simply a very talented lady who needs time to perfect her art. Undisturbed time."

"B-but you are disturbin' her, Robin," Chubby countered unanswerably.

The helpless look that came over Lord Robert's face was ludicrous, Ann thought smilingly, but he recovered quickly.

"Disturbing her? You much mistake the matter, young Chub. I am inspiring her." To her eyes, the smile on his face was positively fiendish. However, she forgave him when he decided to have mercy and leave her in peace for a time.

"Until later, then, Miss Forester," he said, giving her a careless wave as he exited the room with his relative.

She watched them go with a smile. It was easy to see that an affectionate relationship existed between the two. Viewing Lord Robert through new eyes, her heart warmed toward him as she turned back to her music.

* * *

"My dear Lydia, I am not at all happy that Ann is exposed to the company of that—that *rakish* cousin of yours. If I had known Lyndhurst was coming, I would have thought twice about accepting your kind invitation," Mrs. Forester was saying to her dear friend over a cup of tea as they sat *tête-à-tête* in Lady Abermarle's flowery boudoir recovering from the morning's exertions.

"Nonsense, Sadie. Robin is a dear boy, really. He only needs to meet the right girl to bring out all the goodness in his character." Lady Abermarle opened her blue eyes wide and gazed at her guest with almost girlish innocence.

"Humph. Goodness in his character, indeed! Why, he is known far and wide as a shameless philanderer, and worse. I plan to keep a sharp eye on him, and I ask that you do the same, Lydia. For Ann's sake."

"Robin's reputation is much exaggerated—just because he is so extraordinarily handsome and virile looking, many women have sighed over him—and pursued him."

"Yes, I daresay the females all go mad for him—and he for them," Mrs. Forester said dryly, raising her cup to her lips.

"He is a healthy young man. I imagine he succumbs some of the time," Lady Abermarle said with understanding.

"Some of the time!" Mrs. Forester returned sarcastically.

"And do you think Ann susceptible to his charm, then, Sadie?" Lady Abermarle asked.

"My Ann has always been a sensible girl . . . but I do not know," Mrs. Forester said guardedly, setting her teacup down in the saucer with a pensive look. "He is so very . . ."

"Compellingly masculine?"

"I suppose you could put it that way, Lydia," Mrs. Forester allowed, clearly uncomfortable with such talk.

Lady Abermarle reached over with a soft white hand and patted Mrs. Forester's arm. "Do not fret so, Sadie. It will be fine. Ann will benefit from some male attention for once." A whiff of expensive perfume from her dressing gown sweetly scented the room. "I ask that you allow them to become better acquainted without any undue interference. Robin will not have the opportunity to seduce Ann under our very noses. And even if he did have the opportunity, he would not dare!" She laughed to show that she considered such a thing completely impossible, but Mrs. Forester was not convinced.

"Do you not have something else to do now, Chub?" Lord Robert asked. "Greet the Abermarles and the cousins, for instance?"

Ann bit her cheeks to keep from laughing aloud at the look of frustration on Lord Robert's face. She had accompanied him outside for a walk in the snow before luncheon as they had agreed. Unfortunately for him, Chubby Harwood-Jones had joined them. The young man seemed to have attached himself firmly to his relative's sleeve and she was amused to watch Lord Robert's unavailing attempts to shake him off.

Chubby gave them a guileless smile, "No. I like to walk in the s-snow. Reminds me of when I was a l-little lad."

"Fine. You go on ahead to the gatehouse. Miss Forester and I will catch you up," Lord Robert urged, putting a hand over Ann's that was resting on his greatcoat sleeve and bringing them to a halt on the snowy path that led from the front of the house down the drive.

Ann resisted the temptation to snatch her hand away from the pressure of his. The three of them were alone on the snow-covered front drive. All the other guests had walked at the back of the house and she suspected that her escort well knew it. However, his careful maneuvering to get them alone had been thwarted, temporarily at least, by his cousin's presence.

"Think I'll stay with you, if you don't mind, R-Robin. Got something important to t-tell you."

"Oh, Lord! What is it now, Chub? Are you in some kind of difficulty?"

"Well, you s-see, Robin, I've met a lady. I really like her, you see. She is pretty—and very nice. And I'm goin' to m-marry her!" Chubby announced proudly.

"What! You can't get married! You are a mere infant!" Lord Robert thundered. "What kind of female would engage herself to an infant, anyway?" A scheming hussy, his mind fairly screamed.

"B-Betsy is a very nice lady."

"Lady? She's a—" Lord Robert stopped abruptly when he intercepted Ann's warning glance. "Tell me about her, Chub," he commanded instead.

They listened while Chubby described his fiancée as a widow of one-and-thirty with two sturdy boys whom Chubby liked to play with. She lived not above a mile from the Harwood-Jones's country residence in Leicestershire and Chubby had met her at the local church fair where she was selling goods she had knitted herself at one of the stalls.

"I do not like it," Lord Robert said *sotto voce* to Ann, leaning his head nearer to hers. "The boy is too young to be married at all. And now some impoverished widow a decade his senior is taking advantage of his innocence. His mother, Cousin Adelaide, must put a stop to this nonsense."

"Perhaps it will not turn so badly as you think," Ann replied comfortingly. She could see that Lord Robert had a fondness for his cousin and did not like to think that he was being taken advantage of. She liked the young man, too, and found his slight stutter rather endearing.

Clearing his throat, Lord Robert said aloud, "Have you considered that this woman may be a fortune hunter, Chub?"

"Ain't got a fortune, R-Robin. An easy competence, mama's—I mean *my* man of business calls it. And even if I did have a fortune, B-Besty would like me anyway," Chubby said proudly, if not quite logically.

"I shall speak to your mother this evening," Lord Robert promised sternly.

"Mama's got nothing to say in the matter," Chubby said in quite a forceful manner, almost comically at odds with his youthful, open-faced appearance. "It's all settled. Want you to be m'best man, Robin."

"We shall see," was all Lord Robert said, his brows drawn together in a frown.

"Look, the sun has decided to come out at last!" Ann called to distract them from their near quarrel. "How lovely the snow looks in the sunlight, like a field of glinting diamonds!"

"Shall I gather a few to adorn your ears and fingers, Divinity?" Lord Robert said with a lopsided grin as he bent to scoop a handful of snow in his glove.

"You would not dare!" Ann cried, seeing the amused gleam in his eyes and slight uplifting of his lips that signalled his mischievous intent.

"I s-say, Robin. Shall we make snowballs like we used to do with Will and Jamie and your sisters?" Chubby asked enthusiastically, scuffing his feet through the new-fallen snow.

Ann glanced at her companion to see that he was looking down at her with a speculative gleam in his eyes.

"Why not, Chub? Why the deuce not? That is, if Miss Forester is game?"

"Yes, yes. Please, M-miss Forester," Chubby begged with childlike enthusiasm.

"No, no. That is, if the two of you wish to pelt one another with cold blocks of frozen water, do not let me stop you. I shall make my way back to the house alone."

"Afraid of a little cold snow, are you?" Lord Robert quizzed. "I am disappointed. I took you for an intrepid woman. Ready to take me on at our little, ah, drawing-room games, as well as in other things." He turned the full force of his appealing smile on her and Ann was no more proof against it than any other woman would have been. Sensation sizzled up her spine.

Dazzled though she was, she shot back defensively, "And I took you for a gentleman who delights in nothing so much as teasing us poor females with your wicked games."

"Did you? Well, perhaps you are right." He tossed the handful of snow he had concealed behind his back at her, then quickly moved out of her reach, a huge grin splitting his face. It splatted against her cheek, then ran down the front of her new red cloak.

"Ohhh!" she cried in shock, as much for the flush hit as for the unholy grin on her antagonist's face that accompanied it. "That was ungentlemanly of you, sirrah!"

He stood grinning still, feet spread wide apart, arms akimbo. For some reason, his cocksure posture irritated her even more.

"Prepare to meet your doom," she said, wagging a minatory finger at him before she stooped, grabbed a handful of snow and tossed it at him so quickly that he did not have time to duck. It knocked off his hat and spattered over his face. Raising a gloved hand, he wiped it out of his eyes.

"Hurray!" shouted Chubby, whirling about dizzily and grabbing fistfuls of snow that he tossed this way and that.

"Oh no, you don't!" Lord Robert cried, laughingly. Grabbing onto her cloak as Ann tried to flee, he spun her about, circled her arm with one strong hand, pinning her in place—and saw that laughter lighting up her face quite transformed it. She looked almost pretty. His own expression was arrested as he looked down at her.

Her smile faded as he stared at her from mere inches away.

"You should learn to laugh more, my dear. You are lovely when you laugh," he murmured, flicking her cheek with a gloved finger.

She stilled and looked up into his eyes. He gazed steadily back. She could not seem to look away. Or move. Or breathe. They stood motionless as the tension built. A flame kindled deep in his eyes, heating her blood and sending a sizzling current of physical awareness crackling between them. Then they were both in motion at once. Ann was trying to wriggle out of his hold by kicking at his shins with her sturdy boots, but as his own boots covered his legs almost to the knee, she only succeeded in hurting her toe.

"Here's for you, ma'am," he said, pressing a frozen fingertip against her neck that tickled and had her squirming and fighting against his imprisoning hand. She was breathless with laughter again.

"Ha-ha! I have you in my power now, my dear."

"No, no!" she got out between helpless giggles. "Oh! Oh, I beg of you, Monsieur L'Diable, do not treat me so cruelly."

"You must pay a forfeit for daring to assault this mug of mine," he said in a dramatically menacing voice. "My face is my fortune, you know. I have no other."

Feeling lightheaded and lighthearted, she recklessly entered the spirit of the game, responding in a quavering voice, "I will be your slave, pay your forfeit, do anything, if you will but spare me, sir!"

"My slave, is it, woman?" he growled close to her ear. "Then hear your punishment, slave. You must kiss your master one hundred times on the lips before you can win your freedom." Slipping his arm about her waist, he held her prisoner tightly against himself as he pronounced the fiendish forfeit.

Thinking he jested, she did not anticipate that he would try to claim the "forfeit." Looking up at him in confusion, she opened her mouth to demand that he let her go.

Giving her no opportunity for speech, he covered her open mouth warmly with his. And left it there for several endless seconds. His warm lips clung to hers while heat seeped into her cold cheeks and flooded her body.

Her hands went up to push him away. But somehow instead of pushing when they grasped one of the capes of his greatcoat, they stilled instead. Or perhaps they gripped him more tightly still. She did not know. She knew only that his lips were soft and moist, and slightly open over hers. Her mind was in a whirl, her body on fire, her knees alarmingly weak.

He was kissing her.

And she was kissing him back.

She never wanted it to end.

Chubby's voice rang in their ears. "I *say,* R-Robin! You are k-kissing Miss Forester."

Releasing her abruptly, Lord Robert jumped back. "Devil take you, Chubby! What do you think you are about to be dumping a bucketful of snow on us?"

Ann blinked as the shower of snow dripped over her head and face. She had had one brief glimpse of melting snow spiking Lord Robert's long silky black lashes—and the dismay on his face—when they sprang apart.

Her breath was coming painfully fast in her throat and her heart felt like it was going to pound right through her ribs. Her cheeks positively burned with mortification until the cleansing anger welled up and sprang forth like a glowing coal bursting into flame on the grate to save her from making a fool of herself.

"How dare you!" she spat, her slanted eyes shooting flames of amber fire. Her hands curled into fists at her side. She longed to strike out at him. If only Mr. Harwood-Jones were not standing there gaping at them as though at a raree-show, she would not have been able to restrain herself.

"I did not mean—" Lord Robert began placatingly, holding his hands out before him. He noted the deep flush on her face and the anger sparkling in her eyes, making her look catlike, and knew without a doubt that had they been in a more private location, he would have had his face smacked so hard it would have hurt for a week, despite the fact that the kiss had been the most innocent he had ever exchanged.

"Are you and Miss Forester going to be m-married, too, Robin?" Chubby asked excitedly.

"No, no. It's just something one does when playing in the snow at Christmastime," he said in a clipped voice as he busied himself scooping out wet snow that had begun to drip down the back of his neck under his collar, freezing his skin and cooling his unexpected ardor.

"Oh! Perhaps I should k-kiss her, too, then," Chubby said.

"No!" Lord Robert barked. But his order was unnecessary. Ann had already turned away and was marching back toward the house in high dudgeon, her shoulders and head held regally erect.

He frowned heavily. His determination to tease her by stealing a kiss was a little more stimulating than he had bargained for.

After he got his arm about her waist, he had been put off stride by the feel of her body under his hands. He had intended merely to peck at her lips in a teasing way, but he had been so distracted by the unexpected feel of her under the fine wool cloak she wore over her shapeless gown that he had lost his head. There was no disguising her small waist and the curves above and below. Not much above, it was true, but enough to make her feel womanly and to entice him.

And so what had started as a lighthearted attempt to steal a kiss had become something else entirely when she had turned all warm and laughing and soft desirable woman in his arms.

He was not sure when his intentions had changed. Or even if they had. But he had been kissing her seriously, and would have been kissing her more deeply still in another moment, if Chubby had not effectively cooled his ardor and brought him back to a sense of his surroundings by drenching them with cold snow.

Hell and the devil take it! he cursed under his breath. He would have the deuce of a time insinuating himself back in her good graces now!

Four

"Well, my dear, what do you think of my cousin Robin?" Lady Abermarle asked, seating herself beside Ann on a small brocaded settee in the drawing room. The ladies had gathered in the formal room to drink their tea and exchange gossip and confidences after dinner while they awaited the gentlemen, who remained behind in the dining room imbibing something considerably stronger and exchanging stories a little more robust.

The question startled Ann. "Why, I hardly know, Lady Abermarle. I have been acquainted with Lord Robert for less than a sennight," she replied, hastily trying to gather her scattered wits. She had been woolgathering, staring unseeingly at one of the painted cut-out figures that served as a firescreen before the grate and making no effort to converse with any of the other ladies.

"I was acquainted with Abermarle for less than a week before we became engaged," Lady Abermarle confided.

Unaccountably, Ann felt the heat rise to her cheeks and turned her head away briefly to hide her blush.

Lady Abermarle laughed at herself. "But I am being foolishly reminiscent about my long-ago romance, and that's nothing to the point at hand, is it?" She reached over and patted Ann's hand that was lying in her lap.

"Lord Robert seems a pleasant enough gentleman," Ann replied cautiously, trying to answer her hostess's first question as diplomatically as possible. "He is, ah . . . rather given to making provoking remarks, trying to put me out of countenance. I believe he finds it amusing to try to disconcert us poor females."

"Yes, in that Robin is a typical London gentlemen, I believe. They all like to engage in such light witty banter and put us to the blush. It is part of their charm." Lady Abermarle laughed gaily. "However, there is no danger in a little light flirtation. Do you not agree, my dear?"

"I am sure you are right, Lady Abermarle. I have no experience of London gentlemen, but Lord Robert does not seem so very dangerous as my mama has led me to believe. He seems just a rather wild boy at times," Ann blurted, then regretted her words. "But I should not say so."

"Heavens, whyever not?" Lady Abermarle leaned closer. "I think Robin is a perfect dear, and not just because he is my cousin. His reputation is much exaggerated, you know. If he *should* make you uncomfortable for any reason, do let me know, Ann dear, and I shall see to it that you have no further cause to be uneasy."

"Th-thank you, Lady Abermarle. But I am sure such a thing will be completely unnecessary."

Lady Abermarle smiled. "My dear, I am greatly looking forward to hearing you play this evening. Your mama tells me that you practice diligently and I understand that you are a superior performer. I hope that my request is not an imposition?"

"No, indeed. I greatly enjoy the pianoforte and thank you for your kind words. I hope I can live up to your expectations," Ann replied modestly.

"I am sure you will." Lady Abermarle patted her hand again. One of her daughters called to her and she excused herself to go and settle a minor dispute.

Ann leaned against the hard back of the brocaded settee and gazed absently at the grate, holding her almost empty teacup suspended in mid-air. Before the interruption, she had been thinking of Lord Robert and the strange contradictions in his character. He had been wickedly flirtatious during the game of Blind Man's Bluff, quite outrageous when she had been trying to practice her piece on the pianoforte, warm and affectionate with his relative, Mr. Harwood-Jones, playful during their snowball fight—before he boldly stole that kiss, anyway—then natural and relaxed and utterly charming at luncheon.

She contrasted the several Lord Roberts she had encountered that day and shook her head in confusion. Who was he? It seemed he had many facets to his personality. Some of which she could like, admire even. But not when he turned the wickedly teasing seducer, of course.

Guiltily, she admitted to herself that she was attracted to him even then and flattered by his attentions. It was those intensely green eyes of his, framed by the longest, blackest lashes she had ever seen. And that devastating smile, of course.

It was not fair! He was so beautiful, while she—well, she was just very plain. Too tall and thin with a dark complexion and nondescript brown hair. Just . . . plain.

She had taken special pains with her toilette that evening, choosing to wear her newest gown of dark blue silk which she had planned to save for Christmas, and having the abigail she shared with her mama dress her hair in a less severe style. Though she had told herself it was because all eyes would be on her during her performance that evening and *not* because she wished to appear pretty for Lord Robert Lyndhurst, now she felt remarkably foolish.

She feared all her resistance to him was crumbling. It had happened at luncheon. During their conversation then, she had seen him in an entirely new light—and it was an irresistibly attractive one. He had been utterly charming, unaffected and natural. She could no longer help responding to him.

She had still been upset, with high color in her cheeks and her eyes sparkling with anger, when she came down for luncheon and found him waiting for her.

Looking not a bit sheepish, he had grinned at her as though they shared some secret—as indeed they did. She was determined to ignore him, but he persisted in attaching himself to her side despite her efforts to snub him.

"I am sorry. I did not intend to embarrass you. Our little, er, game got out of hand, did it not?" he had whispered in a contrite tone, his compelling eyes gazing into hers.

She had felt herself weakening when Cynthia and Felicity Kentwell had come up and tried to engage his attention. He had ranged himself alongside her as though she offered some protection from the onslaught of the two energetic young ladies. That had amused her.

"Lord Robert, now that the sun has come out, Felicity and I have decided that it would be the greatest fun to go for a sleigh ride after luncheon," Cynthia had said.

"Er, have you, indeed? But I fear in order to achieve your ambition, you will need one essential ingredient, cousin," he had replied mischievously.

"Oh, what is that?" Cynthia had asked in a rather throaty voice, stepping closer to him and gazing up at him adoringly.

He had taken a step closer to Ann and set his hand on her elbow. "A sleigh, my dear young ladies," he had said, one side of his mouth tilting up mockingly.

Felicity had dissolved in giggles, but Cynthia was made of stronger stuff. "Oh, pooh! Of course we have one! And even though Mama says she doubts any one of the gentlemen would be willing to try out the old sleigh stored in the barn, Felicity and I wagered with her that there would be *one* gentleman, at least, brave enough to try it," Cynthia had challenged coyly. "Did we not, Felicity?"

Felicity, beside her, had nodded enthusiastically but silently, training her speaking brown eyes on him.

"Ah. You think that I might be such an intrepid gentleman?"

"Of course. You are a noted Corinthian, are you not?" Cynthia had smiled and fluttered her lashes, playing the coquette. "You could handle the team with ease and you would not care that the sleigh is not in first-rate condition. And we would not mind if we should come to grief, for there is certainly enough snow to break our fall."

"There you are wrong, my dear cousin. I am afraid that you have mistaken your man. I would mind very much. I find the prospect of overturning two such delightful young ladies, not to mention myself, decidedly alarming. Miss Forester will tell you that I have a strong aversion to rolling about in cold snow, soiling my clothes and all my valet's handiwork, with the dire prospect of a long walk back home through such inclement conditions ahead of me."

He had turned to Ann with an appealing look and shuddered comically.

She had had the utmost difficulty in keeping her voice steady as she told the girls, "I am afraid that Lord Robert objects to having his neckcloth disarranged to even the mildest degree or to the tiniest bit of snow under his collar, not to mention having his person subjected to the cold. It comes of his being such a slave to fashion, you see," she had said to his great indignation.

"Is this how you defend me, ma'am? I see I shall have to find a more partial champion."

The girls had given up in disappointment, Cynthia wrinkling her nose and decrying his spirit. "I would not have thought you would be so poor-spirited."

"Ah, the ravages of age, you see, dear cousin."

Ann had had to raise her fist to her mouth to stifle her laughter.

He had lifted his brow and looked at her innocently as the girls walked away and she had laughed aloud, calling him absurd. And then when he had extended his elbow to lead her in to luncheon, she had put her hand on his arm with no hesitation, her earlier outrage and embarrassment forgotten.

At luncheon, he had further ingratiated himself. He had given her the whole of his attention and she had been dazzled, not just by his looks, but by his warm smile, friendly way of speaking to her, and—yes, she had to admit—even entertained by the quality of his conversation and breadth of his knowledge.

She had not expected any such thing.

They had conversed on a variety of topics and shamefully neglected their other dinner partners. At first, she had tried to disconcert him by introducing the topic of literature. A man of pleasures of another sort, as he was reputed to be, would have no time for pleasures of the mind, she had thought.

He had surprised her. He knew more about literature and the arts than she would have thought. They found they shared a liking for Wordsworth's poetry and the new school of landscape painters and for Greek plays which Ann had read only in translation. She was envious when she learned that he had read a few of them at school in the original Greek.

"What I should be reading is Latin, Virgil's *Georgics* to be precise," he had said to her after they had argued over the rival merits of the three great Greek dramatists, Aeschylus, Sophocles, and Euripides, and the comedian Aristophanes.

"Oh? I do not know it. I know Virgil's *Aeneid,* his great epic poem about the Trojan hero Aeneas and the founding of Rome, of course, though again only in translation. What is the subject matter of the *Georgics* and why should you be reading it?" she had asked.

"Well, I am fated to become a farmer one of these days. But I'm trying to put off the fatal day for as long as possible . . . The *Georgics* will be my bible when I do turn myself into a rustic."

"What does a poem by Virgil have to do with farming?"

"It's about farming—a long poem devoted to the subject. *Ge* is Greek for earth, you see, and *georgos* is an earthworker. In other words, a farmer. The name George is derived from the word, thus our recently incarcerated mad king is sometimes known as 'Farmer George.' The epithet has not stuck to Prinny, even though he is a George, too. But Prinny has never been one for the farmyard."

"Oh, I see. The name George is an etymological pun . . . I wish I could read Greek," Ann said wistfully.

"It's a devilishly hard language to learn," he told her, shaking his head at his memories of struggling with the subject. "What with vocabulary, word order, noun declensions, and dealing with the many aspects of verbs—mood, tense, voice, person, and number, not to mention the horrors of athematic verbs—they are the worst. I never mastered them, though they tried to beat them into me at school. Why, it takes years of effort just to get beyond the second aorist—"

"The *second* heiress? I did not know you had got beyond the first one, my lord."

"Very clever, Miss Forester." He gave her his most charming smile, the one that started butterflies fluttering madly in her stomach.

"Well. Now that you have appreciated my humor, will not you tell me what it is?" she entreated smilingly.

He had gazed at her a moment with an odd look, then shaken his head as though to clear it. "A deuced nuisance—to learn that is. The second aorist is one of the verb tenses and a dam—dashed hard thing to keep straight. It looks like an imperfect verb, you see, but its stem has a different form, normally one that has undergone some form of vowel gradation."

"Oh, heavens. It sounds very difficult. I wonder if I should make an attempt to learn Greek, or even Latin?"

"Well, you must resign yourself to giving up the world, if you do so. You must mew yourself up for days at a time with moldy old volumes, spending your nights, too, by the fireside, ruining your eyesight, memorizing words and their various forms until you are conjugating verbs and declining nouns in your sleep!"

"I would not mind. I have nothing better to do with my time."

"Do you not? But I thought you already had a consuming passion to take up your time." His green eyes quizzed her.

Ann blushed as she knew he intended she should, but she recovered quickly. "Yes, the piano has been my great love since I was a little girl. If I practiced twenty hours out of the day, it would still not be enough to perfect my technique. However, we are talking of *your* future. You really intend to become a farmer one of these days?"

"Seems so." He let out a resigned breath and explained, "I was left a rather rundown sheep farm near Coniston in the Lake District by my maternal grandfather. I should be grateful there was enough land to go around when my turn came. I am one of nine children, you know, and the third of four boys. Papa and Mama have never been very frugal—with money or children."

Ann smiled, warmed by the affection she heard in his voice when he spoke of his large family. She regarded him sympathetically.

"I cannot picture it somehow. You striding across plowed fields, dealing with a herd of sheep, doing farm chores." Her eyes dwelt pointedly on his superbly tailored maroon velvet jacket, snowy white neckcloth, watered silk waistcoat with the pearlized buttons, and the gold watch fob hanging at just the right angle from the fob pocket. He was the picture of fashionable elegance.

"Can you not? To be frank, my dear, neither can I . . . But t'will be my fate, sooner rather than later. Unless I marry an heiress, of course." He had waggled his eyebrows suggestively.

Leaning closer, he had said in a low voice, "What say you to a bargain, Miss Forester? You take me on and I will teach you the little Greek and Latin I know. We could spend our evenings by the fireside translating the *Georgics* after a hard day in the fields doing our farming chores and then you could play the piano while I put my feet up to the fire and appreciate your music."

"Why, it sounds positively idyllic," she had returned, at which they both laughed. "Or with the interest from my dowry we could live in style in London. And we could do our translating and you could play the piano for me while I recline gracefully on a Grecian couch after an evening at the theatre or the opera."

"Now *that* sounds idyllic to me!" he had replied with a twinkle, making her laugh again.

"What are you speaking of that has provoked so much amusement, Robin?" Lady Abermarle had called to them from her place at the foot of the table.

"We are speaking of farming, cousin," he had answered with a droll look and a wink for Ann. "And translating Greek."

"Farming? Translating Greek? I did not know that those things were subjects for hilarity. Perhaps you can share the joke," she had invited.

Lord Robert had made a witty remark that had amused the whole assembled luncheon party. The conversation had become general after that, Ann remembered now with a reminiscent smile.

It had been so pleasant to speak with him without his usual flirtation discomfitting her. He had seemed completely human, not dangerous in the least. She had felt relaxed in his company and all her defenses had come tumbling down.

Not only did she admit she was attracted to him, but she found that she *liked* him as well.

He could be such an amusing and stimulating companion—when he was not making suggestive remarks and putting her to the blush, that was. As during their walk in the snow when he had behaved so badly—stealing a kiss like he had—there in broad daylight, when anyone might have seen. And indeed Mr. Harwood-Jones *had* seen, and then made those embarrassing comments.

She blushed at the memory of that kiss, remembering how she had run back to the house and up to her room, gazing at herself in the mirror to see that she looked positively tumbled. She had looked almost attractive—for the first time in her life. Her eyes had been shining unnaturally brightly, there had been high color in her cheeks and her lips had been rosy pink. She had raised her fingers to feel them and she found she could still taste him there.

Had she really dared to raise her hand to his crisply curling hair to see if it was as thick and silky as it looked? Had she actually kissed those wickedly curving lips of his?

She blushed again as she remembered the strange, delicious feeling of warmth that had gushed through her as his lips pressed against hers and . . . She became aware that Lady Praxton was standing before her, speaking to her.

"Are you feeling overwarm, my dear Ann?" Patrice asked. "Your cheeks are quite heated."

"Oh! No. No, not at all," she answered quickly. "I am a bit nervous about playing in front of all your mother's guests, that is all."

"Oh, please, try not to worry about that! From what I understand, we are all in for a treat."

Lady Praxton spoke to her for several minutes, assuring her the company would love her no matter what she did, then walked away just as the gentlemen entered the room. Lord Robert came straight to her, causing Ann to flush with embarrassment all over again. Hoping to resume the intimacy they had shared at luncheon, she smiled her welcome while trying to calm her racing pulse.

"Good evening, Miss Forester. It seems an age since I saw you last. What have you been doing in the intervening hours?" His eyes gleamed at her with a shared joke as he seated himself beside her.

"Do not be ridiculous, my lord. You saw me at dinner. Half an hour ago."

"Ah, but we were not seated side by side as we were at luncheon. I had Miss Kentwell on one side and Cousin Madelaine on the other. I would have traded them both for you," he said in a low, resonant voice, sending shivers down Ann's spine.

Oh! she fumed, biting her lip and looking at him in confusion. He was at it again. Using that seductive voice and making play with his eyes, allowing them to caress her intimately, to suggest things that were not quite proper in order to put her to the blush. Just when she had been feeling in such charity with him, too!

She was saved from an uncomfortable *tête-à-tête* when Lady Abermarle approached, saying, "My dear Ann, may I announce that you will play for us now?"

Ann agreed thankfully, turning toward the pianoforte with relief as Lady Abermarle hushed the guests. But a moment later, she was disconcerted to find that he had followed her to the instrument and fully intended to turn the pages of her music for her.

It seemed that there was no escaping him.

* * *

"Well, Robin, are you enjoying yourself? Or are you finding my family party quite dull for a young man used to all the liveliness of London society?" Lady Abermarle linked her arm with his the following morning. They were walking through the snow-covered back gardens and over the lawn to the frozen lake.

He had been quite at a loose end since he discovered that instead of practicing her music as usual, Ann had retired to her room to put the finishing touches on a watercolor she was doing for her mother's Christmas present. He had run into Lydia, and discovered that she too felt the need for postprandial exercise and fresh air.

"My dear Lydia, no party could be dull that included you," he said with practiced ease, taking up her gloved hand from his sleeve and planting a kiss on the exposed skin of her wrist.

She laughed gaily. "Shameless flatterer! You *must* be bored, to play off your tricks on me! . . . In truth, though, my dear, I am sorry there is such a sparsity of young people here for you to entertain yourself with, but several more parties will be arriving in the next few days . . . At least you have Ann Forester to talk with until then. What do you make of my goddaughter, by the way? You have been spending much time together these past few days, I have noticed."

"She is a lady of many parts. And quite puts me to shame with her learning and her accomplishments," he replied without hesitation, his face carefully neutral. He was an expert at foiling fishing expeditions.

"Yes, I have always found Ann a delightful girl, unspoilt and charming, if a bit serious and retiring. She is a brilliantly talented pianist and one of the most intelligent girls I have ever met. Some men would be put off by her reputation as a bluestocking. I am glad to see that you are more discerning."

Choosing to ignore this, he strolled on with her then asked abruptly, "Why has she never been presented?"

"Her father died of diptheria when she was eighteen and she

was in deep mourning for a year after that sad event. She was almost twenty when she emerged from her weeds, but her mother tells me she has refused to have a London season or even to be brought out in local society. I believe she finds the thought a waste of time—and perhaps a bit frightening for one of her retiring nature.

"And then there is the way her grandfather has left her a substantial dowry tied up in that strange way. She will see no more than a fraction of it in interest unless she marries. I believe," Lady Abermarle continued carefully, after stealing a glance at his impassive face, "that she fears if she were to put herself on the marriage mart, so to speak, she would find herself besieged by fortune hunters. She values her own attractions, physical and otherwise, very low, you see. And fears that men would be attracted only because of her large dowry. Her mother tells me that she expects never to marry. She is five-and-twenty already, you know."

He raised his brows. "No, I did not know. I took her for some three or four years younger."

Lady Abermarle was frustrated by this unhelpful reply.

"Robin?" She ran the tip of a gloved finger over her lower lip and looked uncomfortable.

He slanted her an inquiring look.

She pressed his arm with her other hand. "My dear, you will not practice any of your wiles on Ann, will you? For all that she is five-and-twenty, she is an innocent. At least, in the games you play. I do not know if she would be susceptible to your . . . charms, but promise me, my dear, that you will take care."

"My dear Lydia, all this fuss is most unnecessary, I assure you. Miss Forester and I are friends. Nothing more."

She gave him a questioning look.

"Well, if it makes you feel better, I will engage not to harm her or lead her astray. There. Does that satisfy you?"

She tapped his cheek with her gloved hand. "You are a good boy, Robin. Of course, I believe you. And I will also tell you, naughty boy, that I believe your stimulating company is good for

Ann. She needs to be brought a little out of herself. So continue your friendship, if you please. Even flirt with her a little. But nothing beyond that."

Lord Robert lifted his hand to his heart. "For you, dearest cousin, I promise."

Lord Robert was upset by Lady Abermarle's strictures. He regretted the promise she had extracted from him. He was not sure what he felt for Ann Forester, or what he wanted from her, but he did not like to have his actions restricted.

His interest in her had begun out of boredom, and he had decided to flirt with her, to tease her, because she rose so readily to the bait—and because she resisted him. Ordinarily, he would not have spared a second glance for a plain bluestocking, quite on the shelf, especially one who had a sharp tongue that she was not afraid of using to take him down a peg or two. For a lady not deep dyed in town bronze, she was quite good at parrying his sallies and depressing his attempts at flirtation.

For the most part he was amused by the barbs that flew at him from her sharp tongue, though occasionally they had the power to actually wound him.

Thank God she had no Greek or Latin and he could impress her with the little he had. It had been something, at least. He wanted her to think well of him. He was tired of being thought a heartless seducer, a devil-may-care philanderer, a reckless rogue with nothing on his mind but seduction.

Devil take it! He did not want to be bound by a promise not to take his acquaintance with Ann Forester to another, more interesting level.

He blew out a breath through his nostrils. As a gentleman, he must abide by his word to Lydia.

Strictly speaking, he had promised not to try to seduce her. Well, he did not plan to try. Did not want to.

On the other hand, he had unexpectedly enjoyed that kiss in the snow. It had been a warm kiss, but completely chaste—not seductive in the least. Indeed, he had wondered afterward why he had felt so aroused. He decided it must have been because he had not been near a woman for many weeks.

Still, he had an unaccountable urge to repeat the experience at the first opportunity, wanting to find out if he would feel the same stirring of his blood that had him wanting to deepen the kiss and hold her close without the encumbrances of coats and cloaks and gloves and scarves.

Five

"Where are the others?" Ann asked in some concern, looking behind her and not seeing any of their party.

She and Lord Robert had gone out with a large group of adults and children to collect greenery from the wooded area to the east of the house. Lady Abermarle had said that they had all been cooped up much too long in the house with little to do but get on each other's nerves. She sent them on their way, warning them that as the next day was Christmas Eve, they would all have to help festoon the house with the holly and pine boughs and mistletoe they collected. To do so before then would have been unlucky, she had explained, according to ancient tradition, at least.

"Lydia and your mother have stayed cozily at home, toasting their feet by the fire, and working on some Christmas decorations—bows for the kissing wreath, unless I am much mistaken," Lord Robert said, grinning widely and giving her a wink. "Chubby has ridden into town with Paul to escort Cynthia and Miss Kentwell on their shopping expedition—thank the Lord—and Patsy seems to have headed in that direction with all the children, her brood along with Rupert's trio and Madelaine's Henry." He pointed to their right. "I believe Maddy and Stephen wished to be alone for some reason. They were dragging back, or did you not notice?" he asked with a knowing look. "And they must have sent their son Henry on ahead with Patrice."

She looked puzzled at this. "But they have been married for some years. Why would they wish to be alone?"

"To settle a lovers' quarrel, perhaps. Married people do quarrel—and one presumes that some of them at least remain lovers."

His suggestion brought a hot blush to her cheeks.

"Or perhaps they have hung back to give *us* a chance to be alone."

Her blush deepened.

Oh, heavens! He was going to flirt with her today, instead of being companionable. She wished he would not. "Lord Robert, you had best be careful. What you are suggesting is highly improper and might be construed by some as scandalous," she said, giving him a reproving look and trying not to let his nearness disturb her so. "I know that *I,* and you too, would very much dislike being found in a compromising situation. Neither of us would like the consequences of that."

"You are tempting me, my dear," he said, dropping the large wicker basket he was carrying and moving toward her purposefully. Crumbled leaves and branches and icy snow crunched under his booted feet as he came nearer. "Perhaps it is you who should fear being trapped in wedlock with me."

The silence and isolation echoed loudly in Ann's ears. "Do not be ridiculous! You have no desire to wed me. You are just a wicked tease, sirrah," she said to fill the silence, but the sound of her own heartbeat was loud in her ears as he loomed over her. His suggestion set off a gush of warmth that spread through her breasts and down to her womb. Unconsciously she licked her lips.

In the week since he had kissed her, she had dreamed about his mouth covering hers every night and the warm, aching sensations that had flooded her. And now every time he came near, there was a heightened awareness of him that set her body humming. He seemed to deliberately create such occasions. Frequently she found his arm brushing against her, his hand touching hers or lightly going to the back of her waist whenever she preceded him out a door or into a carriage.

Just last evening they had gone for a ride with Patrice and her husband in the old sleigh that had been hauled out and repaired at Cynthia's insistence. Lord Robert had laughed and joked with the others as he climbed in and seated himself beside her, covering them both with the carriage rug that Patrice handed him. The whole side of him, from his hip to his muscular thigh, had been pressed against hers under that blanket. She had been so conscious of his body touching hers that she had found it difficult to converse with Sir Everard and Lady Praxton. She had been aware the whole time of her breath coming out not quite steadily.

"It is a gentleman's duty to tease pretty ladies," he asserted, looking down at her with a mixture of lighthearted mischief and some more intense purpose that glowed behind his emerald eyes. He reached out to tweak a lock of her hair that had somehow escaped the tight knot she had pinned up that morning and peeped from under the white fur edging the hood of her red cloak.

She clasped her hands in front of her. "Oh! If you have no wish to carry on with this task of finding mistletoe, then I shall go back and join the others."

She turned on her heel, but a yank on her cloak stopped her in her tracks. She uttered a low shriek as he reeled her backward and turned her about with strong hands on her shoulders.

"Foolish chit. I am only funning you." He ran his gloved finger down her cold nose and smiled into her eyes. "Let us get to work and find that mistletoe. I for one plan to put it to good use when the ladies hang that bedizened kissing bough they are expending all that effort on."

She stood her ground and looked at him warily. "Promise you will behave."

His smile was crooked. "Would you believe me, if I did? . . . Let us to our task, then, else Lydia will likely deny us a glass of Paul's rum punch when we get back frozen to the bone, with red noses and cheeks and numb fingers. Ah! I do believe that is mistletoe hanging in that oak tree over there. Coming?"

She followed him meekly as he pressed branches out of the way for her through a rather dense wooded area that led to the tree.

"Lady Abermarle believes it is unlucky to bring evergreens

into the house before Christmas Eve," she remarked, hoping to introduce an innocuous subject and take her mind off the fact that they were moving farther from the path and soon would be completely isolated from those ahead of them and those behind.

"Unlucky? Why?"

"I think the idea springs from the pre-Christian belief that plants such as holly, ivy, and mistletoe must be magical because they bear fruit in winter when everything else is dead."

"A magical plant, eh?" He led the way to an ancient, gnarled oak about ten feet away. "I hope it will perform some magic for me."

Ignoring his suggestive comment, Ann continued, "The Church will not allow such plants inside their precincts, you know. Indeed, mistletoe cannot be brought into churches at all because of its association with pagan practices."

"If it is so dangerous, why does Lydia dare have it brought in inside and chance ill fortune?"

"Well, Christmas is a such a holy time that all pagan influences and evil magic lose their potency and we are safe, for a few days at least. Actually, I think some of the pagan beliefs about mistletoe have been incorporated into our modern customs. Why hang it inside and allow it to override correct behavior else?"

He grinned at her. "Why indeed? . . . If I were of an age with those mischievous scamps of Patsy and Maddy and Rupert's, I am sure I would defy Lydia's injunction and smuggle some into the house, just to see what might happen." He laughed and she smiled, too.

"I remember going hunting for mistletoe with my brothers and sisters when I was a halfling. We often ended up in some sort of mischief that usually involved knocking off one another's hats and rolling about in the snow and coming home so ruddy-cheeked and runny-nosed and disheveled our nurse threatened that our parents would disown such ragamuffins."

"I imagine you gave them no end of trouble."

"Yes, I did!" He chuckled deeply. "How well you know me, ma'am." His eyes took on a reminiscent gleam as he stood of the bottom of the old oak tree. "There was the time when I was a scruffy schoolboy of about nine, home from school for the holidays, tasting freedom for the first time in months, full of high spirits and devilment."

A fond smile played over his face while Ann thought, *You still are full of devilment.*

"I persuaded Jamie, who must have been seven at the time, to sneak into the barn with me where we managed to move the Yule log that had already been cut and was just waiting to be carried into the house on the following day, Christmas Eve. We somehow managed to roll it a few feet, then covered it with hay. We had the deuce of a time shifting it. It was ashwood, the longest and heaviest log Papa and Dick and Will had ever cut—about ten feet long and wider than your waist. When my brothers and some servants went to get it, they were astonished when they could not find it. My sister, Sally, was convinced fairies had taken it." He laughed boyishly. "Old one-eyed Rufus was my undoing, though."

"One-eyed Rufus?"

"One of our many dogs. He sniffed out the log, pawed away the hay, and there it was! I was implicated, of course. Couldn't sit down for Christmas dinner that year!"

"Oh! That is too bad. I do not believe in spanking children, though I daresay you did deserve some punshment."

"I daresay I did, little moralizer. And I daresay *you* were a complete angel when you were a girl."

She sighed. "I daresay I was. I had no one to share mischief with, you see."

He sobered instantly. "You were a lonely child?" He did not look at her. He was measuring the distance from the ground to the mistletoe hanging from a rotted limb. He did not like the feeling of sympathy that had invaded his breast. He did not particularly want to see her as a person. It had been fun to tease her, to while away the time, to make her fall a little in love with him, but he did not want to be having any feelings deeper than friendship for her.

"I—I had my books and my paint and of course my music for company. And then there were the animals—my cats and dogs and horses."

He shrugged out of his greatcoat, then his jacket, and stood with hands on hips, looking for the best way to reach the mistletoe.

"Oh! You will be cold without even a jacket!"

"Not if I am quick," he said. Setting his boot in the forked crevice where two branches met, he heaved himself up in one fluid, athletic movement.

"Be careful, my lord!" Her hands went out to catch him, should he fall. She dropped them to her side immediately, realizing she was being silly. She could not catch him if he fell. He would bowl both of them to the ground if she tried to do anything so foolish.

"You had no siblings, Ann?" he asked, reaching above his head to dislodge the large sprig of mistletoe.

"No . . . I wish I had had brothers and sisters—or even just one—to share things like holidays with," she said, as she watched him stretched full-length there in the old tree, his long legs spread against two branches to brace himself.

"Yes, a large family has its advantages—and its disadvantages, too . . . If you have those nasty-looking secateurs concealed somewhere about your person, I suggest you produce them now. I have always been nervous of secateurs—I wonder why?"

"I have them here," she said, holding the secateurs at the ready, watching the play of muscles across his broad shoulders and back under his shirt when he reached above his head—and was disturbed by the sight.

She placed the secateurs in the hand he reached down to her.

"This stuff is dripping wet—and freezing," he said when he had managed to cut it. "Bring that basket nearer, would you? I will throw it down and there will be no need for you to get wet, too."

She did as he asked and he tossed the mistletoe into the basket she held up to him.

"I do not know what disadvantages there could be in having a large family," she said.

"Well, for a start, there is a great deal of bickering."

"Is that why you did not go home this year?" she asked curiously as he jumped from the tree and landed on the soft snow in front of her, brushing snow and twigs from his sleeves. Some leaves had caught in his hair too, and she had to restrain herself from reaching out to remove them.

His eyes became hooded. "Not precisely. Sometimes—sometimes one needs to be away from one's family, as much as one loves them."

"I see."

"No, you don't," he contradicted, his smile a little crooked. "It is a small matter, not a great scandal. I am here at Lydia's invitation and I am glad I came." He smiled fully into her eyes. "If you had had siblings, would not your fortune have been divided up among the lot of you?"

"I suppose. It was left to me by Mama's papa. He was the Baron Radcliffe, you know . . . But I would not have minded sharing. I do not know what good having a lot of money does anyway."

His brows shot upward. "Do you not? I do believe I would not have any such worries, should some fortune unexpectedly drop into my hands," he said, dragging on his jacket, then his greatcoat once again.

"Is that why men such as you spend so much time at the gaming tables? Hoping a fortune will drop into your hands?"

His eyes narrowed. "Men such as me, Miss Forester? Hardened gamesters, do you mean?"

She bit her lip. "That was unkind of me. I have never heard that you were a gamester."

His eyes burned into hers. "I am no gamester. I have seen the tragedy it can bring. A few years ago, my best friend, Lawrence Pritchard, killed himself after a disastrous night at the tables. He had lost everything. I avoid most games of chance. Anything more daring that playing whist for a pound a point is too deep for me, though I do like to place a small bet at the racecourse now and again."

"I am sorry," she whispered.

His jaw relaxed somewhat. "Make no mistake, my dear Miss Forester. You are right about one thing. I am a dangerous man. You are wise to keep me at arm's length."

"You are not!" she cried before she could stop herself.

"You do not think me dangerous?" he asked, his lips twitching.

"No. Not in the least," she said, her chin tilting up. "I think you are kind and witty and a good conversationalist and even gentle—except when you are being provokingly teasing, that is." She stopped when she saw the gleam of amusement in his eyes.

"I am glad to hear that you feel so, and I hate to contradict a lady, but I do not feel at all kind and gentle at the moment. Nor do I feel like engaging in any conversation. I shall be bold and take advantage of the situation that has been tempting me for the last quarter of an hour." Glancing upward, he put his hands on her forearms and moved her back a foot.

"What in the world?" Ann protested as she stumbled back under the pressure of his hands.

"It is not because I am dangerous, you know," he said as his lips whispered like silk against hers. "But because you are standing directly under the mistletoe, Ann . . . There must be a hundred berries up there."

His hands on her arms were pinning her to the spot, but she managed to move her head back from his questing lips and glanced upward. Indeed, the largest sprig of mistletoe she had ever seen was directly above her head. Her heart beating fast in her breast, she whispered back boldly, "It seems that you are indeed within your rights, my lord."

"Call me Robin," he said against her mouth and then he laid his cold lips against hers for a long moment. "Umm. You taste of fresh air and outdoors and Christmas . . . and honey!"

"I had honey on my toast at breakfast." She gave a low laugh and set her hands against his chest, realizing that she had stayed with him when they became separated from the others because she had wanted this, had wanted him to kiss her again. She had begun to think that he had no interest in doing so when he made no move to take advantage of the situation earlier.

He closed his eyes a fraction of a second before she did, but long enough to give her a glimpse of his dark lashes fanning out over his cheeks. Her stomach somersaulted.

And then he was kissing her, his warm mouth open over hers, sending a spiraling ache down through her breasts to her womb. And she was pulling him closer. Wanting to melt into his splendid male form that was pressed as tightly to hers as their outdoor things would allow. She wanted to be closer. She burrowed inside his open coat and wrapped her arms about his waist, pressing closely to his firmly muscled body. Opening her mouth slightly under the pressure of his, she felt the tip of his tongue outlining her lips. Her knees gave way under her and his arms were the only things holding her up.

"Halloo! R-Robin? Patsy? M-Maddy? Where are you all? Is that you under that tree, Robin? What are you doing there with M-Miss Forester?"

Chubby's voice forced them apart rather abruptly.

She was surprised to find herself not at all embarrassed at the disruption but disappointed. And all fluttery inside. Lord Robert was looking more than disappointed. He was looking . . . well, dazed, as though he was lost somehow, and utterly vulnerable.

"Dash it all," he whispered rather raggedly, "that's only five berries, by my count."

Robin went to bed that night far from satisfied, burning with anticipation for the morrow. His game was playing out to a more than satisfactory conclusion.

Trouble was, somewhere along the way the nature of the game had changed.

He was not quite sure how it had come about, but he found that he enjoyed Miss Ann Forester's company more than he had anticipated. And the more he was in her company, the more he admired her—her sweetness, her intelligence, and of course her musical talent. He had even come to admire her tall, angular figure which emphasized her proud, firm character.

He liked her, for God's sake, never mind that she was not a beauty. Not that she was so very plain as he had first thought. No. Her eyes, of that unusual warm amber shade and slanting like some Eastern houri's, were exquisitely beautiful by any standard. They melted his insides. Glowing with intelligence and, in the last few days, happiness, they seemed to see into his soul, making him feel naked. Vulnerable.

And when she smiled or coaxed beautiful music from the pianoforte, her face was transformed into something almost approaching beauty. When she had played that Beethoven sonata he had been entranced. No. He had been intensely moved.

He had watched waves of emotion pass over her face as she played, and he was moved. By the music. By her. She had looked almost lovely while she played with such abandon, as though possessed by the music. He had always loved music, but the passion that flowed through the music from her fingers seemed to invade his heart—and his very soul.

Enjoying her company as he had come to do, he wanted to be with her frequently.

He laughed at himself. That was an understatement!

He could not seem to stay away from her, could not seem to keep his hands off her. Whenever they were together, whenever he kissed her, something sparked between them that had him desiring her, wanting to take their embrace to a deeper, more satisfying, level. Not that he would act on his desires, though. But it was a heady feeling that he was not yet ready to relinquish, that he wanted to taste again. And again.

Yes. He anticipated the morrow with the greatest pleasure.

Six

Snow crunched under their boots as Lord Robert walked hand in gloved hand with Ann through the starlit night. It was just past midnight on Christmas morning and they were on their way back to the house from church services. Some of the others had chosen to ride back in the old sleigh, Mrs. Forester among them.

When he had asked Ann if she would walk with him, she had agreed instantly, despite the cold. There was no impropriety. Other members of the houseparty were walking ahead of them. Rather far ahead, now. He had deliberately slowed their steps, wanting her all to himself.

He could hear the older children scampering ahead, squealing their excitement in anticipation of Christmas morning and the gifts that would be awaiting them.

She was humming a soft lullaby, one of the ones that had been sung in church along with the more rousing carols. He smiled and squeezed her hand, remembering the couple who had sat in the pew in front of them whose baby had started to fuss, then cry, during the service. The child's mother, clearly embarrassed, had handed the baby to its father, who had held the infant close to his face and smiled down at the small bundle. The baby had quietened, then cooed contentedly as the whole congregation sang the lullaby, "O little one sweet, O little one mild, Thy Father's purpose thou hast fulfilled."

He looked down at Ann holding to his hand, her gloved hand tucked securely in his larger one. Her face, framed in her white fur-trimmed hood, with her beautiful eyes sparkling in the starlight, was quite transformed. She looked up smiling, and he forgot to breathe.

It was a perfect night under the stars. His throat tightened with emotion.

"It is a perfect night," she said dreamily, echoing his thoughts.

"*You* are perfect," he murmured.

"Oh! Please do not spoil this special moment with your meaningless flirtation again, Lord Robert."

He halted and turned toward her. "I am not flirting, Ann." His hand went up to press against her hood, forcing her to look into his eyes.

She gazed mutely back.

He bit his lip. Her eyes were wreaking havoc with his insides. "Ann, I—I love you. Will you marry me, my dearest girl?" he whispered.

"I—oh! I am sorry. *What* did you say?" she asked breathlessly as one of his gloved hands kneaded her neck warmly.

Both hands moved behind her head and his thumbs caressed her throat. He moved his head back slightly, while he cupped her face. "I am asking you to marry me, my dear. I know I am no bargain, but with you I feel as though I could be worth something. Will you consent to become a farmer's wife, and spend those evenings with me by our cozy fireside—a lifetime of evenings—while I teach you Greek and you teach me about poetry and music and all the other things that are dear to your heart? Will you take a chance on me? I think—I know we could be happy together."

"L-Lord Robert! I do not know what to say!"

"Then be guided by me. Say yes. And I wish you would call me Robin. It's my name, you know."

"Robin." She smiled dazzlingly, then raised her gloved fingers to her lips. "Oh. How can I answer you tonight? I have known you less than a fortnight."

"My sensible girl, trust to your feelings for once. Do you not feel as I do?"

"And how is that?" she whispered.

"That when I am with you, I am happy. Happier than I have ever been. That we belong together. For always."

"Yes—I mean, no! Oh! You have confused me so, that I know not what I am saying." She laughed in wonder, and in confusion. Her feelings were whirling like leaves in an autumn wind.

What did she feel? Did she love him? Her heart thundered *yes,* but her mind whispered caution. He seemed sincere. When she looked into his beautiful eyes, as changeable as the sea, she could believe anything. But he was an experienced charmer. He was notorious as a seducer of women—and quite likely a fortune hunter. Some of her excitement faded as doubts crept in.

"I want to see your face. To see what you are thinking." Reaching up, he removed her hands from her lips and took them in his, holding them tightly. He looked deeply into her eyes for a moment, then bent his head and pressed kisses on her gloved fingers, leaving his lips on them, his head bowed before her.

Ann could swear that she felt the warmth of his lips right through the thick wool of her gloves. That warmth radiated through her body right down to her toes. Daring greatly, she tipped her head and pressed a kiss on his bare head, on the shining disheveled locks that fell forward over his face.

"I think I *do* love you, Robin. But I must ask you for a little time. To—to be sure I know my own mind."

"Oh, Ann! Do you mean there is some hope for me?" He smiled at her and Ann could swear that she saw a mixture of gladness and fear, pleasure and anxiety, in his eyes.

"Yes. Yes, I do," she answered firmly and cried out a moment later when he crushed her to his chest and swung her round and round, lifting her off her feet for a few giddy moments before setting her down and sweeping her into an embrace of another kind. His mouth covered hers this time with a passion that took her breath away. She clung to him and kissed him back, not ashamed or afraid of showing him that she felt as much physical attraction for him as he seemed to do for her.

* * *

Dazed and giddy, Ann lived through Christmas Day in a perfect dream. She had never felt such happiness, such a welling of emotion that had her smiling continually, feeling that she was walking on air.

She had fallen in love. Fallen deeply in love with the most attractive, charming man she had ever seen. He had asked her to marry him and she was going to do it!

He was sincere. It was not her fortune. He swore he loved *her*.

She believed him.

All day, they made a delicious game of exchanging secret glances and finding opportunities to exchange kisses and embraces, sometimes brief, sometimes lingering. It was a different experience from kissing out-of-doors. Much more intimate. Much more dangerous. Now they did not have heavy cloaks and gloved fingers separating them. She could feel his bare fingertips on her flesh when he slowly reached out and cupped her face in his two hands. His skin was warm under her own hands.

She learned the power of a deep kiss, a kiss of more than lips—a kiss of mouths, and tongues, and bodies, and the heat it could generate, the way he could make her body ache for his touch and cry out for more. He was an expert. Oh, yes, he was an expert and she reveled in his expertise that was all for her now. He had sworn it.

It was almost midnight. She thought everyone had retired to bed as she walked quietly into the library. He was waiting for her there in front of a glowing fire, his lips curving up into a soft smile and his eyes lighting up when he saw her.

"Come here, my love," he commanded, holding out one hand to her.

She went to him, lifting her arms to his neck as his went round her waist.

"Do you realize that we are standing under the mistletoe again, my love? And it is my duty as a gentleman to let no lady remain unkissed who is so situated."

She smiled at him but did not answer, closing her eyes in anticipation. She felt the pads of his thumbs rubbing over her lips and his fingers moving into her hair, then his fingers moved down her jaw and caressed the skin of her neck as his lips whispered against hers. He brushed them back and forth several times, barely touching.

He was moving awfully slowly. Too slowly for her. She clasped his neck tightly, bringing his mouth down to hers. Her action seemed to release him from his trancelike state. Her mouth opened for him eagerly and he was kissing her as he had earlier, with his lips and his mouth and his tongue, rhythmically caressing her lips and exploring her mouth, at first gently, then more urgently. The hot breath from his nostrils fanned her cheeks while liquid fire produced by his kisses coursed through her body, speading a warm ache and turning her legs to jelly. She pressed closer to his hard length.

His hands were tearing at the pins in her hair, pulling them out, letting them fall to the floor. Combing his fingers through her loosened tresses over and over again, he kissed her lips, her eyes, her ears, her neck, her jaw, murmuring, "Beautiful, so beautiful, my love."

He drew back and looked down at her through smoldering eyes. "My God! It goes to your waist! Ann, Ann, why do you not reveal its glory, revel in its glory? I do." He picked up a handful of her hair and pressed it to his lips.

Then he was shrugging out of his jacket and drawing off his neckcloth, murmuring, "I can hold you closer without these encumbrances." Somehow her own fingers were unbuttoning his waistcoat and then that, too, was cast aside.

He covered her mouth and kissed her deeply. She pressed herself against him shamelessly, exploring his face, his neck, his shoulders, and his chest through his thin lawn shirt while he worked at the fastenings of her gown.

She gasped when his warm fingers caressed her bare skin. She could feel him against her. All of him. Though she lacked experience, she knew instinctively that he wanted her as badly as she wanted him.

"Ohh!" Her knees almost buckled under her while he kissed

her deeply again and caressed her flesh with warm knowing fingers.

Suddenly he stopped. Disappointment flooded her.

She watched him swallow.

"It is not private here, my love. We must wait until we are married before we continue this most pleasant exercise," he whispered unsteadily. "Though I suspect it will be torture for both of us." His hands were at her bodice, drawing up her gown, rearranging it over her shoulders.

She rested her head against his chest, trying to gain some control over her raw desire, making no protest as he pushed her hair aside and did up the tiny buttons at the back of her gown.

She had not wanted him to stop, but she caught herself in time from begging him. Just in time from embarrassing herself unspeakably.

His hands folded her to him gently. He was unwilling to let her go, though he knew he should. They risked discovery at any moment.

"Let us dance, my love," he murmured.

"Dance?" She pulled back her head and looked up at him, laughing slightly. "How? There is no music."

"Oh, yes. There is music in your heart—and mine. I will hum. You join in."

He circled her waist, took her hand in his, and began to waltz with her.

"Oh, I—I do not know how to waltz!" she protested, chagrined.

"Yes, you do. Just follow me."

And somehow she was following him as he twirled her around the furniture, from one end of the room to the other, becoming more inventive as she relaxed into the rhythm he was humming into her ear.

Laughter bubbled up as they narrowly missed tripping over a low stool.

"Oh, Robin. This is madness!"

"No. This is cool, calm and collected sanity. The other was

madness . . . We shall dance alone like this when we are married, living on our sheep farm," he said teasingly, but the idea delighted her utterly.

"A pity it is so gray and overcast for Boxing Day," Robin remarked as he and Ann set out for a walk through the still-frozen back gardens after luncheon on the following afternoon.

"Well, at least it is warmer. The snow has almost melted and I imagine the roads will be passable now."

"Except for the mud," he added, glancing back to make sure that they were out of sight of the house. Seeing that they were, he removed her hand from his arm and drew it around his waist as he put his arm around hers.

"Lady Abermarle is relieved. Her guests will be able to get through at last," Ann chatted, feeling the anticipation build as he led her farther away from the house. Any moment now, he would take her in his arms and kiss her, starting those delicious sensations coursing through her body once more. She looked up at him and saw that he was looking pensive rather than amorous. She swallowed her disappointment and took herself to task for craving his kiss at every hour of the day. She was far gone in love, indeed!

"Ann, I would like to speak with your mother when we return to the house. I suppose I do not have to seek her permission to wed you as you are of age, but for courtesy's sake," he said seriously, then added with his devastating grin, "I am afraid I grow impatient, my love. And I hope you will agree to settle on a wedding day not a month hence!"

She looked away, then back again, saying hesitantly, "I am not yet ready for you to approach Mama, Robin. I—I wish to wait until after New Year's Day."

"But why? That is almost a week hence!" he cried, a little hurt creeping into his voice.

He continued to protest the delay vigorously, but she would not change her mind. Something in her relished keeping their betrothal a secret. She did not wish to share it with anyone yet. All the secret kisses and meetings were just too delicious. If it were known that they were betrothed, people would be watching them like hawks. Their opportunity for such meetings would be severely curtailed.

Basking in the glow of his love, she felt happy—and attractive. And she did not want people looking at her askance and shattering her idyllic dream, whispering behind their hands, wondering how *she,* a plain spinster of five-and-twenty with nothing to recommend her but a large dowry, had attracted the attentions of the dashing, devilishly handsome Lord Robert Lyndhurst.

Robin was none too happy to let Ann have her way. He would have preferred that she allow him to approach her mother so they would have everything settled. He had never lived in such a state of unfulfilled desire. Ann was too innocent to realize how close they had come to anticipating their wedding night the previous evening. It was only his self control that had prevented them from making love to one another there behind the locked doors of the library. After he had gone to his own room, it had taken all his control to prevent him from going to her bedchamber.

Despite his torture, it was tantalizing to see her growing into a soft, desirable woman who was now aware of her own womanliness and wanted to fulfil it under his tutelage; exciting to see passion glowing in her eyes that he had put there.

He felt he was walking on air, his feet hardly touching the ground. He was in love, a state he had never experienced before and with an intelligent, desirable woman who would have been a prize for any man to win. He forgot about her dowry that would see both of them comfortable. He forgot that he had once found her unattractive. He no longer saw the old Ann. All he saw now was his love.

* * *

"It will not be a bad thing, Sadie," Lady Abermarle was saying to Mrs. Forester as they stood at a second-floor window watching Lord Robert and Ann disappear from view when they rounded a bend a long way down the back lawn. "Not a bad thing at all."

"Not a bad thing? To have my daughter seduced by a rake! Are you mad, Lydia?" Mrs. Forester asked in outrage. "You must send someone after them."

"Calm yourself, my dear," Lady Abermarle recommended. "Do you not see? They are in love. He means marriage."

"He means to get his hands on her dowry!"

"No, Sadie. I think not. I have known Robin from his birth. He has had the opportunity to pay court to any number of heiresses. Yes. Many of them were higher born than Ann and their dowries even more munificient than hers. But he has not followed up on his many opportunities. That tells me that he has been waiting for some special lady. One whom he could care for. One whom he could fall in love with."

"Humph. That is a high-flown romantic idea, indeed . . . Did you plot this, Lydia?" Mrs. Forester asked suspiciously.

Lady Abermarle laughed and there was a definite twinkle in her eyes. But she sobered in an instant, resting her hand on her friend's arm and looking at her out of huge blue eyes. "You will not try to prevent your daughter's happiness, will you, Sadie?"

"It is her *unhappiness* I wish to prevent. If in fact he does mean marriage, he will leave her once he gets his hands on her money and return to his raking ways soon enough. Mark my words, Lydia."

"You are so wrong, Sadie. The boy has a good heart. I grant you, his head has been turned by female admiration, but his principles are sound. He is a loving and affectionate son and brother. He does not play deep or spend much, other than on his clothes and his horses. Why, he does not even drink beyond a glass of wine at dinner, you know," Lady Abermarle pleaded his case. "I believe he is sincerely attached to Ann. Will you not give them a chance?"

Sadie Forester looked disbelieving but relented somewhat.

"Perhaps there is something in what you say, Lydia. But Ann has said nothing to me." She sighed. "I will wait and see if she broaches the subject. If she is determined to have him, I will not forbid the match, though I fear she will not have him dancing attendance on her for long after they are wed. And so I shall warn her!"

Seven

In her romantic daze, Ann hardly noted the arrival of several new guests that evening, including the doddering Sir Harold Stanhill and his stunningly beautiful young wife, Zara, Lady Stanhill, neighbors of the Abermarles.

After a late dinner, Lady Abermarle announced they were all to act charades, in keeping with the family custom. Some cheers and some groans from the assembled company greeted this pronouncement, but she would hear no protests. She insisted everyone must participate.

The men were not allowed to have their port in peace, but had to repair with the ladies to the drawing room where sides were quickly chosen up. Sir Everard captained one team and Viscount Abermarle the other. Unfortunately, Cynthia prevailed upon her papa to choose Lord Robert for his team, while Ann was snapped up by Sir Everard.

Lord and Lady Newberry were also on different teams and Ann could not help observing how much happier Lord Newberry had looked since the day they had all collected greenery. He was a rather stern-faced man until he smiled and his face was quite transformed into gentle attractiveness. She saw how Madelaine frequently gazed in her husband's direction and smiled and blushed—and how Lord Newberry smiled back. Perhaps Robin had been right; they had had a quarrel and now had made it up. It seemed likely.

She resigned herself to a long evening without much chance to talk with Robin, but she was a little cheered when she noticed how frequently he caught her eye and smiled at her, several times making her blush as brightly as Madelaine and once forcing her to stifle a laugh when he raised his brows and tilted his head, inviting her to find an excuse to step out of the room with him, and mouthing the word, "Later."

Classical themes dominated the evening with Sir Everard's team acting out Daphnis and Chloe, while Lord Abermarle's team performed Antony and Cleopatra with Cynthia as the Egyptian queen and Lord Robert as her Roman general.

Ann was pleased to remain a minor player on Sir Everard's team when she saw that he and his wife were past masters of the art of charades. Their Daphnis and Chloe was inspired.

As the game neared its hilarious conclusion, something ruined Ann's enjoyment of the evening. She couldn't help but notice how frequently Lady Stanhill, who sat close beside Robin, leaned over to whisper in his ear, taking advantage of the team's prerogative to consult among themselves.

The woman was garishly made up with a liberal use of cosmetics, Ann had noticed when she had seen her close up, and from the way she performed her part in the charades, it seemed likely she had been an actress at some point in her life. When Lady Stanhill boldly patted Robin's knee after he made a correct guess, Ann glanced at her sharply.

She did not like it. She did not like it at all. Soon after Robin caught her eye and smiled his secret smile. She frowned at him. His smile faded, one brow quirked up. His eyes held a question.

The game finished, with Sir Everard's team winning, and everyone proceeded to the dining room where an informal supper was laid on, with Christmas cake, plum pudding and mince tarts to tempt the guests.

"At last! Come sit with me, Ann," Lord Robert urged, coming up to her, plate in hand.

"Yes," she agreed. Her smile was slightly wobbly around the edges as she looked up at him, but as soon as he had found a place for them somewhat removed from the rest of the company, Chubby joined them.

"Chub, let me put a flea in your ear. Take yourself off, my boy. Go and sit over there where Cynthia is smiling at you and throwing out lures," Lord Robert said, blatantly hinting him away. But Chubby would not take the hint that they wished to enjoy a private *tête-ä-tête.*

"It's you she's winkin' at, R-Robin, not me," he said, calmly settling down in the chair next to them. "And I don't want a flea in my ear. Sounds dashed uncomfortable."

Ann laughed at the martyred look on Robin's face and began to relax somewhat.

As they finished their supper, Lady Abermarle approached them. "My dear Ann, would it be too much of an imposition to ask you to play a few dances for us?"

"Of course, Lady Abermarle. It would be my pleasure," Ann politely agreed. Her eyes turned back to Robin as her hostess bore her away across the room. She was somewhat mollified to see that he looked after her in frustration, grimacing and blowing a breath out through his mouth.

A few moments later, when she was seated at the instrument leafing through some music, she glanced up and saw in dismay that Lady Stanhill had joined him. His eyes sought hers across the room, full of apology. She could do nothing but stare blankly back, trying to give him no indication that she cared one way or the other. He shrugged his shoulders and turned to converse with the woman. The lump in her throat felt as though it had plummeted into her stomach and turned to lead.

She played stiffly, uncustomarily hitting several wrong notes, but no one noticed as they took to the floor in the country dance she played. Her throat was so tight she could scarcely breathe. When Robin actually stood up to dance with Lady Stanhill, she had to bite the inside of her lips to keep them from trembling.

Her eyes were filled with unshed tears when Patrice approached half an hour later saying, "You should have a turn to dance now, Ann. I will take your place. Though I do not play half so well." She laughed gaily. "Perhaps no one will notice, if they are busy dancing a country reel."

Ann relinquished her place, but she did not know where to go. She wished to leave the room without being seen, but that was impossible. The instrument was set near the French windows that led to the balcony, all the way across the room from the main doors that led to the hallway.

A strong hand grasped her elbow and turned her about.

"My sweet! I thought Lydia would keep you at the instrument all night, blast her!" Robin said next to her ear. "But here you are, free at last to dance with me."

One look at her face wiped the smile from his and had him demanding, "What is the matter, my love?"

"Oh, I am just tired, R-Robin."

"Ann." He shook her elbow slightly. "What is it? Tell me!"

"Nothing."

"It is not *nothing,*" he said with an anxious look. "Blast! We cannot talk here. Come. Something is bothering you. We will get to the bottom of this." He took her arm and began to walk toward the double doors that led from the drawing room out into the marbled foyer.

"Robin, stop. People will wonder at you taking me away like this," she whispered in a shaky voice.

"I do not care what they think. Something has upset you and I am concerned." Inexorably, he led her out the door and down the hallway to the library.

He closed the library door carefully behind them and guided her over to a large overstuffed chair set before the fire. He sat down and pulled her with him, settling her on his lap. She resisted, pushing against his chest with her hands, but he wrapped his arms about her waist and held her still until she stopped fighting him.

"Now. What is distressing you, my love?"

She played with a fold of his neckcloth, not meeting his eyes. "I am just tired, I suppose."

"Ann. Look at me." A long finger tilted up her chin. "Is it tiredness that has tears standing in your eyes? Or is it something else? Has someone said—or done—something to upset you? If so, they will answer to me," he declared fiercely. "I will not have my future wife made unhappy."

"Robin," she said, looking up quickly, then away again, her eyes not holding his, "I am not your promised wife—yet."

"What's this? You have not changed your mind, have you, Ann?" Panic welled in his chest at the thought that she had decided not to have him.

"No, no." She was looking down again, patting his neckcloth with an agitated hand. " 'Tis just that we are not formally betrothed yet." She glanced up and a smile flickered briefly across her ravaged features.

He sighed deeply and his tense expression lightened. "Well, I am glad that is all. But we can remedy that at one word from you."

She shook her head, still not meeting his eyes.

"Well, kiss me, sweeting, then I will see you up to bed. You do looked a bit peaked. A good night's rest will set you up again, right as rain." He lifted her chin with a gentle hand, but she turned her head away.

"Not tonight, Robin."

Allowing his hand to drop, he leaned his head back against the chair cushions and closed his eyes in defeat.

"Ann . . . please," he said after a long minute. "What the devil is it?" he demanded, none too gently this time, tightening his hands on her arms.

She hesitated, then drew a long breath. "You—you seemed to enjoy the company of Lady Stanhill tonight. You spent a long time with her."

His bark of laughter reverberated in the room. "You are jealous of an old crow like Zara—Lady Stanhill? Ann, darling . . . how foolish!"

"Oh, I am foolish, am I?" she cried, pushing out of his arms and jumping up from the chair. She stood before him, hands on hips, glaring down at him.

"Yes, you are, darling. But I must admit I am flattered." Still

sitting at his ease, he folded his arms over his chest and looke
up at her, his green eyes twinkling devilishly.

"You may flirt with whom you like and I am to sit by an
watch you do so. You flatter yourself if you think I will stand fo
such treatment for a minute." She was beside herself now. Sh
could feel the heat in her cheeks and hear the shrillness of he
voice, but she was in the grip of a strong emotion and powerles
to control her outburst.

He gave a great crack of laughter and got to his feet. "You *ar*
jealous, you little shrew. My, my, I see I shall have to hew to th
straight and narrow after we are married. I am sorry you though
I was flirting, but I assure you that I was not. Ah, I *have* me
Lady Stanhill previously, you see, and she was presuming o
previous acquaintance to renew our, er, friendship."

Seeing that she still looked angry and disbelieving and hi
words had not soothed her, he raised his hand. "I swear it, Ann
Zara Stanhill is nothing to me. She never was."

"How can I believe that? You are a rake. There have been many
women in your past."

"A *former* rake, dear heart. And, you know, we reformed rake
make the best husbands, after all, ready to settle down and stay
cozily at home with *one* woman . . . Come here, my love. Kiss
me before we must part for the night."

"No. I will bid you goodnight now and go to my room." Gripping her arms with her hands so that she would not be tempted
to reach out to him, Ann turned toward the door.

He reached out and took hold of her, preventing her retreat.
"Devil take it, woman, you shall *not* go until you have kissed
me and told me that you see you were mistaken," he insisted
through his teeth, angry now and a little frightened, but most of
all desperate to convince her.

"Let me go!"

Whirling her about, he imprisoned her in his arms and kissed
her fiercely. She fought him, putting her hands between them,
pushing against his chest and keeping her mouth firmly closed

while his lips pressed against her mouth and his tongue sought entrance.

He released her abruptly. "Go, then," he said angrily, pushing her away from him.

She stared at him out of wide eyes bright with unshed tears, her face pale and drawn.

His expression softened somewhat when he saw the hurt and vulnerable look on her face and the tears in her eyes. He spread his hands wide. "You are tired," he got out with an effort. "Perhaps after a good night's sleep, you will be more yourself. I look forward to seeing you tomorrow, my dear." He bowed formally, but did not dare reach for her hand to kiss.

"Good night, my lord," she replied stiffly, then turned and walked from the room, her back straight and her head held at a regal angle.

Robin pounded his fist into his open palm and growled. He was upset—and angry with himself for not handling her more gently and convincing her of his innocence where Zara Stanhill was concerned. He promised himself he would convince her tomorrow.

Ann paced furiously about her bedchamber for many long minutes, wiping away the tears that trickled unchecked down her cheeks. She knew she should beg his pardon. Tonight. She could not wait until morning with her apology. She wanted to go to him now. She could not sleep until she had done so. And she would give him permission to speak to her mother tomorrow so that they could announce their betrothal immediately.

Daring greatly, she stepped into the darkened hallway with her lighted candlestick, still fully dressed in the dark blue silk gown she had worn at dinner. She tiptoed down the hallway with her heart in her mouth. There would be a dreadful scandal if she were seen. With her own heartbeat sounding loudly in her ears, she lifted her hand to knock on his bedchamber door, then quickly dropped it again. She turned around and took a step away, her nerves on edge.

She could not do it.

Plain spinster, Miss Ann Forester, knocking on the bechamber door of the much sought after, incomparably handsome Lord Robert Lyndhurst in the middle of the night. It was too ludicrous for words. She smiled at her foolishness, bit her lip, stepped quickly to the door again and knocked lightly before she should lose her courage.

When his valet opened the door a moment later, she flushed red with mortification, and was thankful that at least she was fully dressed in her dinner gown, modestly covered by her woolen shawl.

"I—I have an urgent message for Lord Robert," she said awkwardly, keeping her voice low. "May I speak with him?"

"I am sorry, miss," the valet replied, eyeing her with undisguised surprise and something else that she thought was pity. "His lordship has not yet come up."

"I see. I am so sorry to disturb you," she apologized, dreadful embarrassment making her want to sink through the floor where she stood.

When the door was closed on her again, she stood still for a moment, thinking he must be still downstairs. Taking a steadying breath, she decided that it would be much better to speak to him there than in his bedchamber. Holding her candlestick high, she made her way down the main staircase as silently as she could. Coming first to the drawing room, she carefully opened the door, only to find it deserted. She glided along to the library. Hearing muffled voices coming from within, she pushed open the unlatched door and stepped into the semi-darkened room.

The sight that met her eyes in the dim firelight stopped her heart in her breast. A deadly coldness came over her and she felt as though she were viewing the nightmarish scene from down a long, long tunnel.

Robin was locked in a passionate embrace with Lady Stanhill.

"Oh!" A muffled cry of shock burst from her. She swayed, and put her hand to her mouth, as faintness and nausea overtook her.

"Ann!" Robin exclaimed, paling as he saw her holding to the door, looking like a ghost.

She gripped the door more tightly as she stared at him. His eyes were unfocused and his dark hair tousled, a lock falling over his forehead almost covering one eye. His dishevelment proclaimed his recent activity as loudly as words.

"What the devil are you doing here?" he growled, putting Lady Stanhill from him abruptly, his hands pushing against her shoulders while she protested loudly. As he did so, Ann could see that her gown was disarranged and that a good deal of skin was exposed at her neck and lower down her bodice. In fact, her bodice could hardly be said to be covering her at all.

"Good evening, Lord Robert, Lady Stanhill. I could not sleep and came down for a book. It is chilly tonight, is it not? I see you two have found a way to keep warm, however," she said in a voice of deadly calm. "But I would advise you to button up your gown again, Lady Stanhill, before you take, ah, cold."

With that Parthian shot, she turned and with careful dignity walked out of the room, her thin shoulders squared against the weight that now rested so heavily on them, feeling as though it were crushing her to the floor.

"Ann! Ann, wait a moment!" She could hear Robin calling to her and Lady Stanhill protesting, "But darling, we have not finished yet!"

As soon as she gained the hallway, she picked up her skirts and rushed toward the staircase, climbing the steps swiftly, her face twisted and her mouth open in a silent wail of agony. *I will not cry! I will not cry!* her mind screamed.

She could hear him running after her, calling in a low voice, "Ann! Ann, wait! Please!"

He caught her on the landing.

"Ann!" his voice was desperate. "It is not what you think.

Please, darling, let me explain," he pleaded, holding her arms bruisingly tight, holding onto her for dear life.

"I enjoyed your 'explanations' earlier, if you will remember, my lord. You sounded so convincing then. But your words proved so much insubstantial air . . . Let me go!"

"Ann, Ann. I love you," he whispered in a ragged voice.

She gave a low, disbelieving laugh. "No. You love my money. Well, you will never get your greedy hands on it now. I thank God my eyes were opened in time," she said bitterly, her eyes brimming with tears.

"It is not true! I will convince you." One hand grabbed her arm and the other her waist as he tried to kiss her. There was panic and desperation in his voice and in his face.

"Take your hands off me, you deceitful philanderer!" She jerked out of his hold and one of her hands flashed up. She cracked him hard across the cheek, so hard that she feared the sound reverberated through the sleeping house. But no one came out from their bedchamber doors to see their scandalous position.

Stifling her sobs, Ann turned and ran back to her room.

Robin watched her go, his hand held out helplessly. "God damn it all to hell!" he cursed, clutching his hair. He took several shuddering breaths through his nostrils as he tried to walk calmly to his room. *I will convince her tomorrow,* he kept telling himself, trying to convince himself, but he knew the task would be the most difficult—and the most critical to his future happiness—he had ever undertaken.

"Good morning, Robin my dear," Lady Abermarle greeted him brightly early the following morning as he came into the almost empty breakfast room.

"Good morning, Lydia," he replied in a subdued voice, gazing around the deserted room in disappointment. "Are we to be *tête-à-tête* over breakfast?" He attempted a smile.

"It seems so. Paul is out in the stables, checking on the horses as usual, but everyone else is still abed . . . Forgive me for saying so, my dear, but you look dreadful. Are you feeling quite the thing?" she asked, scanning his countenance and seeing that he looked almost ill, with dark rings under his eyes and a strained tightness about his mouth.

"I am afraid that I did not sleep very well last night. I daresay it was the thought of turning yet another year older in the new year that had me tossing and turning."

She laughed lightly. "Well, I can give you twenty years, but I do not let it keep me from my rest . . . Well, now that you are up beforetimes, are you planning to go riding now that the snow has all but disappeared?"

Waving away the hovering servant, he poured himself a cup of coffee. "No, I do not plan to go riding first thing. Perhaps later. I am hoping to convince Ann—Miss Forester to take an early morning walk with me."

"Oh, my dear! Did you not know? Ann and her mother left over an hour ago."

"Left?" He looked incredulous. "Where have they gone?"

"Home to Hampshire."

"I—I did not know." He turned away to the sideboard and groped helplessly for a spoon to stir his coffee.

Pity for him welled in Lady Abermarle's breast as she saw the stricken look that came into his eyes. "No, of course you did not. How could you? It seems there was some urgent problem that called them home."

"I . . . see." Still with his back to her, he set his coffee cup down on the sideboard with shaking hands, spilling coffee into his saucer.

"Do you, my dear? I wish I did . . . You would not care to talk about it, would you?"

He tried to smile, but his lips were so unsteady that he could not manage it. "Talk about it? What is it you wish to talk about, Lydia?"

"Robin, there was something between you and Ann, was there not?" She came straight to the point.

"No. Nothing at all," he said with a twisted smile, folding his arms casually across his chest and leaning back against the sideboard negligently. "A pleasant friendship for the holidays."

"I thought that you had fallen in love with her, and she with you," she said in a sympathetic voice, her blue eyes full of pity for him.

"Me? You are out there, my dear. I am afraid I am committed to lifelong bachelorhood." He essayed a smile that he could not hold.

"Oh, Robin . . ." She looked at him in appeal, but she could not force him to confide in her.

"If you will excuse me, Lydia, I find that perhaps I would like to go for that ride before breakfast, after all."

"Of course, my dear. Do enjoy yourself."

He left without answering, his cup of coffee sitting untouched on the sideboard.

Lord Robert left that afternoon for London. As soon as he left the house party, the rumor circulated that he had trifled with the affections of Miss Ann Forester, a previously sheltered heiress, and that he had jilted her and her considerable fortune for the charms of one of his old flames.

It was said that he had broken Miss Forester's heart, just as he had that of so many women before her.

Eight

"Ann, Ann, my dear, do you not hear what I am saying to you? I am reading your Aunt Jermyn's letter, yet you heed me not. You are gazing through that window as if the most interesting thing in the world is happening out there, when there is nothing to view but a bleak pond."

"I am sorry, Mama," Ann said, lifting her fingertips from the frosted glass and turning back to look at her mother across the cramped little sitting room. "I am afraid I was woolgathering."

"You have been *woolgathering,* as you call it, ever since we came back from Lydia's Christmas party more than two months ago, neglecting your music and your watercolors and spending hours in your room. I hope you are not still thinking of that scamp, Lyndhurst?" Her mother sent her a sharp, narrow-eyed glance. "I thought you had forgotten him after you were so wise as to turn him off."

"Still thinking of Lord Robert Lyndhurst? Good heavens, what do you think of me, Mama?" She laughed shortly. It sounded artificial to her own ears. "I hope I have enough intelligence to regret my acquaintance with that fortune-hunting rake." Hoping her blush was not visible to her mother's sharp eyes, Ann clasped her hands before her and turned away to stride about the room crowded with bits and pieces of furniture from their previous, much larger dwelling.

"I hope you do, too. You have always been a sensible girl. And you certainly spent enough time in his company at Christmas to have taken his measure."

"Yes. He singled me out for a flirtation as a way to pass the time, I suppose. And after he learned of my dowry, he led me to think his attentions were serious. But when his former . . . flirt . . . arrived, he revealed his true colors soon enough," she said bitterly.

"Oh, my dear . . . he has broken your heart!"

"No!" Ann denied vehemently. "I could not break my heart over such a worthless fribble. I am just . . . just tired of the same routine, the same neighborhood, the same faces, day in and day out here at home." She wandered restlessly to and fro, picking up a bibelot from her mother's cluttered whatnot table and studying it absently.

Mrs. Forester frowned in concern. "It has been difficult for us both living in reduced circumstances since your father's death. I believe you would benefit from a change."

"And what about you, Mama? Would you not benefit from a change, too?" Ann smiled slightly.

Her mother waved her hand dismissively. "The rheumatics will keep me close to home until the summer, I fear. But you do not need to stay to keep me company. Your Aunt Jermyn has written and is again offering to have you stay with her in London this spring. I think you would be wise to accept. Of course, with her peculiar notions of entertainment—literary evenings, musicales, trooping around art galleries—there will be little chance for you to meet any eligible men."

"Mama! I do not wish to meet any *eligible men,"* Ann protested.

"Well, your wish will undoubtedly be granted, for I do not see how any will come in your way. Henrietta is not proposing to take you about to *ton* parties or to procure vouchers for Almacks, as I would wish. She has offered to arrange music lessons for you with some German emigré or other, however."

"Has she? That would be wonderful!" Ann felt a spark of interest for the first time in weeks. "Perhaps I will go then . . . I wonder if the gentleman is acquainted with Herr Beethoven?"

Mrs. Forester glanced down at the letter lying open in her lap, studying it through her lorgnette. "She does not say . . . The man, Herr Müller, has come from Bonn to live in London. His wife appears to be English, at any rate." Mrs. Forester looked up at her daughter again. "But, my dear Ann, you must make an effort to meet a gentleman to your liking when you are in London. You know you will never receive more than a competence from the fortune your grandfather left you if you do not marry. Merely the interest from the capital. It will hardly be enough for you to live on after I am gone."

"I do not worry on that score. You will live for many years yet, Mama . . . Such a foolish way for grandfather to leave me his fortune, though! The entire capital to be given into the hands of my husband and controlled by him from the moment I marry—as though women are not perfectly capable of looking after their own financial affairs!"

"However, he *did* leave it to you that way. You *must* marry if you are ever to receive the benefit of your large dowry . . . There are no men in this neighborhood who have captured your interest. And I fear that your aunt will only encourage your bluestocking ways while you are with her," Mrs. Forester despaired. "At least it will be a change of air for you. And perhaps—" She gazed at her daughter over the folded letter she was holding with a considering look on her face. "Perhaps there may be *someone* at one of these dry, dull literary or political meetings Henrietta is so fond of."

"Perhaps, Mama." Ann smiled slightly and excused herself to go and dress warmly for her daily walk.

A quarter of an hour later she was tramping up the muddy lane in the direction of the little town of Chilcomb, intending to call on her friend Miss Lorna Stewart, the rector's daughter.

She had been trying to overcome her lowness of spirits since returning to Hampshire from the Abermarles' houseparty, but it had been a miserable winter, cloudy and gray and damp—no sunshine at all—and she had been unable to regain her former equanimity. The little copse to the side of the house was leafless and dreary and it had been so muddy from the continual rain that she had not walked into Chilcomb to visit Lorna above two or three times in the last month.

She was lost in thought as she walked. Should she accept her Aunt Henrietta's invitation? She would not refuse to go to London because *he* would be there. That would be cowardly. If she ever encountered him, she intended to show him that she did not care a fig, as she had by returning unopened the two letters that had come from him since she had returned home.

They would not move in the same circles, so perhaps she could avoid him altogether. But she would know in her heart that she had gone to London in spite of the fact that he was there.

He had been far above her touch, of course. Elegant. Sinfully handsome. A man of the world. And charming, of course. Charming enough to have captured her heart and broken it in less than a fortnight.

How foolish she had been! To believe that such an exquisite creature could have conceived a tendre for *her*—a twenty-five-year-old bluestocking spinster. He was nothing but a rakish fortune hunter who had used his considerable experience to make her believe he was in earnest when he told her he loved her. He had probably been laughing up his sleeve at her gullibility.

She who knew she had no beauty, had always prided herself on her intelligence, her accomplishments in music and painting—and her sense—had lost that sense when she was near him, flattered by the attentions of such a nonpareil who knew how to curve his lips up into a slow, sensual smile that heated her insides so that they melted into a liquid fire that consumed her body. Where had that intelligent, sensible woman gone when a handsome face set atop a pair of broad shoulders, trim hips, and muscular legs took some notice of her?

She was chagrined, furious that she had allowed herself to become his victim. He had hurt her. She had fallen in love, quite against her will, and now she was suffering the painful repercussions.

Well, she had left behind the unfortunate episode, and with it her naive girlhood. She was a woman now, one who had tasted the first intimations of physical passion, and one who had experienced the deep hurt of disappointed hopes and broken dreams. One who had learned that a man who was attracted to many women could not mend his rakish ways—and that handsome, charming men and plain girls did *not* live happily ever after.

Robin sat on the side of the sagging bed clutching his head. He eyed the cracked basin, full of dirty grey water, in the corner of the room and his stomach heaved. There was activity behind a filthy, rickety screen in the other corner where the girl was dressing.

"Damnation! Never again!" he swore, swallowing his revulsion and closing his eyes to stop the spinning. He shivered. There was no heat in the appallingly squalid room.

Rising carefully from the rumpled bed, he stepped into his equally rumpled pantaloons, trying to ignore the smell of gin and damp sweat and recent carnal activity that assailed his nostrils and gagged him. He walked to the window, hoping for a breath of fresh air.

Pushing back the threadbare curtain with one long finger, he gazed out onto the murky stews below. Where in the devil had he ended up last night? he wondered, appalled at his carelessness—and stupidity. It looked like the depths of hell out there. All light was blocked by the press of smoke-encrusted buildings and the low overhanging clouds. The air at the window was no better, for the fetid smell of the middens borne on the morning's fog from the river rose up and curled in the narrow passageway between the blackened buildings.

"H'I were a good girl, last night, h'I were." A high-pitched female voice assailed his ears, sending a fresh wave of pain through his throbbing head. "Expects payment for me wares, h'I does," she insisted. "Jacko be waitin' below. 'E don't like it, if h'I don't come back with some of the ready—*sir.*"

Good God!

"Take my purse. Take the whole thing. There. In my jacket."

The girl moved to his jacket thrown over a chair, the only item of furniture in the spartan room apart from the bed, which was nothing but a straw mattress stretched over some boards. He heard her behind him rummaging in his pockets, and did not doubt that her quick fingers would soon latch onto the purse.

" 'Oy! Ain't nothing in 'ere, ye bloody cheat. You flimflammed me, you did!" She came toward him with fingernails extended, ready to scratch his face. "H'it's Jacko for ye, me dandy boy. 'E'll do yer pretty face for yer!"

He closed his eyes briefly. "Here. Take my ring," he said, jerking the signet ring that had belonged to his maternal grandfather over his knuckle and thrusting it at the girl.

He sneered at the look on her face. "It's gold . . . I have nothing else."

She snatched the ring, bit on it with her decayed teeth, then flounced from the room, her swinging hips radiating anger.

He winced at a pain in his shoulder. Bloody hell! The wench had bitten him!

Snatching on the rest of his clothing with lightning speed, he gritted his teeth and prepared to run the gauntlet below, with his fists, if need be.

"Two sugars, my dear?" Miss Lorna Stewart asked her visitor as she poured the tea. "And please have some of the macaroons. I baked them this morning."

"Yes, two please. Thank you, this is lovely," Ann said, accepting the cup of tea and taking one of the macaroons. "I have always loved this room, Lorna. It is so charmingly decorated and the view of your garden is so soothing," she said, relaxing back against the wide chair near the window that looked out over the back garden. They sat in a little sitting room off the rector's dining room. It faced a pretty garden that was not yet in bloom, but the outlines of its carefully laid-out beds made a pleasant view through the mullioned window.

"Yes. I often sit in here to do my sewing so that I can look out from time to time. We have a cock robin who likes to perch just on that overhanging branch of the apple tree. It is *his* garden as much as ours, I often think . . . Oh, Ann, shall you really accept your aunt Jermyn's invitation and be off to London in a few weeks time?"

Ann stirred her tea. "Yes, I have quite determined to do so. At last." She smiled at her friend. "I have a desire to visit this teeming metropolis of ours and see for myself some of the places I have only read about in the history books."

"How exciting! I wish I could accompany you."

Ann reached out impulsively and covered her friend's hand with her own. "Oh, do come, Lorna! I am sure Aunt Henrietta would not mind. I understand that her house is quite large and there would be plenty of room."

"It is tempting, but I cannot. Papa has too much need of me here. But you will write and tell me *everything,* will you not, Ann?"

"Of course, I shall, goose. Instead of 'Dear Diary,' I shall write 'Dear Lorna,' and tell you all."

"I shall like that. You are such a wonderful writer, your descriptions of people and places and events are so thoughtful and fresh and full of detail that you bring them to life. I shall feel that I am there with you seeing all the sights, meeting all the people . . . Have you . . . have you considered that you might see *him* while you are there?" Lorna asked tentatively, fully aware of Ann's recent broken romance.

"I expect we shall move in quite different circles," Ann responded carefully. She had told her friend much of what had passed at the Abermarles'. Having a confidante to whom she could unburden her heart had soothed that sore organ. "Aunt Jermyn does not frequent *ton* parties, nor gaming hells, nor visit fashionable impures," she said dryly, lifting her teacup to her mouth.

"But surely he attends functions in polite society, too. After all, he is the son of a duke, if an impecunious one. Perhaps you shall see him at the theatre or the opera," Lorna suggested hopefully.

"Perhaps. If so, at least he shall see that I am not such a coward that I would stay away from London forever just to avoid him," Ann declared fiercely.

"Oh, Ann, my dear." Lorna leaned across the table to look more closely into her friend's face. "Is it indeed all over? You are certain there is no hope?"

"None. He is a scoundrel of the first water. I am very fortunate that my eyes were opened in time."

Lorna sighed as she raised her cup to her mouth. It had all started so romantically, she wished that it could end happily. No one deserved happiness more than Ann. "I shall miss your help at the village school, Ann, especially with the girls. And your free music tuition will be sorely missed by all those who are trying to learn to play the piano and the organ."

"I shall miss the children, too. Especially Jane Ford and Lilly Ashdown. They are most promising scholars. Promise me that you will see that they are included with the boys when your father takes the Latin class, Lorna."

Lorna smiled. "You have always insisted that females are just as capable as males and should be educated equally. No, no. You do not have to convince me. I agree with you. And I promise to see if I can bring Papa round, but do not expect miracles."

Robin stepped from the path and captured the lady's bonnet that was being tossed and tumbled across the grass in Green Park by the fierce March wind. Another few seconds and it would have blown into the water of the reservoir and been quite ruined. He looked down at it for a moment and smiled fleetingly. It was a frivolous confection of yellow straw and bright blue ribbons and bows—and no protection at all from this wind.

Glancing up for a sign of the owner of the pretty but almost useless article, he was immediately rewarded by the sight of a small young lady with short red curls running toward him, the wind blowing her skirts above her trim ankles.

"Oh, sir, I thank you for rescuing my bonnet," the girl was saying, stopping breathlessly in front of him. "I am afraid the wind lifted it quite off my head."

"Pleased to be of service, ma'am. A very pretty confection, but quite useless in this wind, I fear."

The girl laughed up at him, her turquoise eyes twinkling. "La, sir, you know we females must strive to be fashionable despite the wind and rain and cold—or the scorching sun in summer. Though perhaps something sturdier and warmer would serve us better, such a practical bonnet would not flatter us half so much," she said with a droll look.

"I believe we are all slaves to fashion, ma'am," he riposted, gesturing to his curly brimmed beaver that he held firmly to his head with one hand.

She laughed gaily once again as an elderly maid came puffing up to stand behind her, offering some chaperonage. "I am Miss Georgiana Carteret." She looked at him expectantly.

"Lord Robert Lyndhurst, at your service, Miss Carteret." He bowed slightly.

"Lord Robert Lyndhurst?" she cried. "Why, I have heard of you! You are quite well known to several of my acquaintances."

He raised his brows haughtily, sure that she had heard all the worst gossip.

"Oh, do not poker up so. I have heard that you are nothing if not charming," she said saucily. "And you have certainly come to my rescue today. Would you like to come home with me to tea as a reward? I am sure my grandmother, Lady Carteret, would welcome a gentleman who has done me such a kind service. That bonnet cost her ten guineas just last week." She laughed merrily again.

Robin was slightly stunned at the incautious words that tumbled from Miss Carteret's wide, smiling mouth. She seemed to give no thought to proper decorum. "Er, my dear Miss Carteret, I fear that your grandmother would *not* welcome me. Our acquaintance is quite irregular—and of such *short* duration." His own eyes gleamed mischievously.

"Stuff and nonsense," she said, placing her hand on his arm. "It is just a step. We live in Half Moon Street just across Piccadilly along this side of the park. Come along, my lord."

Feeling cheered for the first time in months by the lady's friendly smile and equally friendly manners, Robin allowed himself to be persuaded, hoping that Lady Carteret would not take umbrage at her granddaughter's having befriended him in such an unorthodox fashion. He smiled to himself. If the old lady *were* a stickler for propriety, he might find himself tossed out on his ear in next to no time for daring to cross her threshold without a formal invitation and the equally formal introduction that would have preceded it, if her granddaughter had more properly observed society's strict rules.

Nine

"Yes, indeed, I am enjoying myself enormously, Aunt Henrietta." Ann smiled brightly, trying to banish the feeling of heaviness that had overtaken her after sitting in the ill-lit, overheated room and listening to the *third* aspiring poet read from his as yet unfinished work in progress. This time it was an epic poem on the beauties of some blond, blue-eyed young woman who had inspired him to such high-flown rhapsodies.

She stifled a groan. It was hard to summon much enthusiasm for work of such poor quality and to look impressed when her aunt informed her in an awed tone that the current reader was living half-starved in a cold and lonely garret for the sake of his art.

This was what she had come to London for, she told herself: to enjoy serious discussions about literary and political matters, and to meet aspiring poets and novelists and essayists and playwrights and musicians. Here these young men were being encouraged and appreciated by an admiring audience—perhaps they would acquire a wealthy patron or two to support them in their literary endeavors.

She did not know why she was so dissatisfied.

Her mind wandered from the sing-song voice of the young poet. Earlier, she had been taken aback when she overheard a rather pompous clergyman explaining that he had left his living in the "benighted" north to a curate so that he could reside in the "more refined metropolis." His snobbery had offended her.

And for a man of the church to shrug off his duties in such a fashion was scandalous.

Another time she had noticed a young lady with a squint trying to flirt with the wavy-haired blond gentleman whose poetic efforts were so poor that Ann had been hard pressed to hide her smile of amusement at some of his tortured rhymes: woe and doe, church and besmirch, fodder and ladder, true and through, armor and amour.

Flirtation and pomposity, snobbery and pretense at being better than they were . . . well, she supposed this *petit monde* was only a pale reflection of that grander society, that London *beau monde,* with its greater pretensions and foolishness and misuse of wealth.

"Young Mr. Henderson is quite serious in his efforts, do you not agree?" Mrs. Jermyn whispered, jarring Ann from her reflections. "With a little more work, he will have a truly first-class poem on his hands."

"Perhaps," Ann hedged.

"And he is young and not bad looking, either. Poor as a church mouse, of course. He needs patrons. Perhaps I should give a small dinner and invite him. What do you think, my dear?"

Ann's heart sank. "Oh, not on my account, please, aunt. That is, if you wish to invite him, by no means let me dissuade you."

"We shall see, my dear," Mrs. Jermyn said with a scheming smile, moving away to join the group around Mr. Henderson.

"Deadly dull, is it not, Miss Forester?" Lady Emily Gwent commented in a quiet aside. "You must come to my salon next month. I promise you a more lively evening. I even dare to hope that Miss Burney will put in an appearance, but I cannot promise."

"Thank you, Lady Emily. I should like that. That is, if my Aunt Jermyn approves," Ann qualified.

"Leave Henrietta to me, my dear," Lady Emily said, patting Ann's arm and giving her a conspiratorial wink.

Ann's spirits lifted. She liked the fashionable, dark-haired Lady Emily whose green eyes sparkled with intelligence and a lively sense of humor. Earlier Ann had been part of a lively discussion on the merits and drawbacks of formal education for women. Lady Emily had contended that women were equal to men in every way, and that they should be entitled to the same education.

"My brothers studied Latin and Greek and so did I, after I demanded of my father that I be tutored in the classics along with them. In the end, he agreed, but only because it was more economical than sending me to an expensive and quite useless finishing school," Lady Emily had concluded humorously.

"I agree with Lady Emily," Ann had chimed in. "Women's minds are no less capable than men's. We can learn and understand the same things."

The discussion had become heated after that. Lady Emily had looked across at Ann and they had shared a smile of deep understanding.

It had been the brightest moment of the evening for Ann. It seemed she had found a new friend whose taste marched with hers.

"Our engagement calendar is quite full for the remainder of the week, Ann dear," Mrs. Jermyn said in the carriage on the way home. "You are not feeling the strain of becoming a London gadabout, are you?"

"No, indeed, aunt," Ann replied, thinking that attending three literary evenings and one organ recital at church in the past two weeks had hardly taxed her strength. "I am not tired in the least."

"I am glad to hear it. I was afraid now you are visiting Herr Müller three mornings a week for lessons upon the pianoforte and then practicing above three hours every day when you return home, you might not like to go out much in the evenings."

"Oh, no. I enjoy the break from my music. I go back to it refreshed after we have been out."

"Then you will not be alarmed when I tell you that we go to a musicale on Wednesday and the theater on Friday!"

"I shall look forward to them, aunt."

Ann froze. She feared for a moment that her eyes had deceived her, that the tall, dark-haired man dressed in severe black and white standing to one side of the doorway was not Lord Robert Lyndhurst, but some other gentleman. But when she looked again, she knew that it was indeed Lord Robert standing there looking dashing and exceedingly fashionable . . . and quite impossibly handsome with a lock of his dark hair falling over his forehead in that heartstoppingly familiar way.

"This way, my dear," Mrs. Jermyn directed. "The refreshment room is this way. We want to stretch our legs and have some punch to quench our thirst before the next performer delights us." She grasped Ann's arm to prevent her from retreating from whence they came, puzzled by her niece's hesitation in walking on. "I wish to introduce you to some of my friends. Come along, Ann."

Ann had no choice. Blind panic had her turning back to the music room when she saw Lord Robert standing outside the refreshment room speaking with a small, red-haired young lady. "I am surprised Lady Woodson's butler let you in the door, arriving so very late as you did, Robin," the young lady was saying in a lively manner, taking him to task for being late for the musicale.

Robin, the girl called him. Robin.

That "Robin" hurt her.

The spritely young lady laughed gaily up at him, laid her hand on his arm briefly, then sailed away with a saucy grin over her shoulder as she went.

Lord Robert gazed after the lady with a lazy smile, then looked up and saw Ann.

Her heart did a somersault as her eyes met his. She watched

as his smile died abruptly and all the color drained from his face. She saw his lips silently form her name. "Ann."

She clenched her hand tightly to prevent herself from reaching out to him and dropped her eyes from his.

"Come *along,* Ann," Mrs. Jermyn urged. "Do not stand there gawking at London's greatest rakeshame. If he hears of your dowry, the rogue might take it into his head to pursue you, then we would be in the soup," she muttered in a low voice, hurrying Ann past Lyndhurst, who stood unmoving as they passed him.

Ann kept her eyes averted and did not acknowledge his presence by so much as the flicker of an eyelid. But her heart was beating painfully against her ribs and the ache in her throat was so raw she did not know how she could bear remaining for the rest of the program.

Robin stood as though turned to stone, his thoughts well concealed behind his polite half-smile as some of the guests exchanged greetings with him on their way into the refreshment room. Others shepherded their charges past him as though he were a carrier of the plague. One high-nosed matron in a purple turban frowned heavily and kept her platter-faced daughter carefully shielded as they hurried past.

He did not note them.

Well, he thought. Well. Ann had come to London—and cut him dead. He had seen her again and the earth had not stood still.

Or had it? he wondered, as the chill in his blood thawed and the hurt of the wound she had just dealt him penetrated deeply.

Why had she come to town? He thought she was adamantly opposed to putting herself on the marriage mart. It seemed she had changed her mind, he thought cynically.

She would see what she had turned down, he decided, vowing to flirt with every personable woman at the musicale, young and old, married and not, who did not shrink from his presence. Turning on his heel, he strode purposefully into the refreshment room.

* * *

"You are very popular tonight, Robin," Georgie Carteret said as he accompanied her back to her seat when Lady Woodson gave the signal that the performances were about to recommence. "I believe you have paid court to every woman in the room."

He glinted down at her. "Are you jealous, my heart?"

"I am not one of your court, sir," she answered tartly.

"No? I must be failing in my technique, then. Must be old age creeping up, lining my face and graying my hair."

"La, sir, but you do seek for compliments, do you not? As if you had any need of them! Should I see a face like yours gazing back at me from *my* looking glass, I would swoon with delight."

Robin's lips twitched. "If you saw a face like mine looking back at you from your glass, it would be a deuced miracle. It would mean you had changed your gender, my girl."

Georgie's peal of happy laughter rang out and had several heads turning in their direction. "That was not my meaning, sir, and well you know it! I meant if I were as beautiful as you are handsome, I should be in heaven."

"Alas, my dear, one cannot be in love with oneself."

"Hmm. I do not know if you are correct about that," Georgie replied, thinking of one rather smug beauty and a certain toplofty gentleman of her acquaintance. "Tell me, Robin. Who is that very prim, dignified young lady over there whose stiff back tells me she is ignoring you for some reason? I have not seen her about before tonight. She seems to be the only female in the room not smitten by your charms." Georgie pointed to Ann with her fan as she and Lord Robert took their seats in preparation for the evening's central event, the performance of the noted soprano Signóra Carla Cellini.

All the light went out of his face. "I presume you refer to Miss Ann Forester," he answered bitterly, a harsh note in his voice. "She is new come to town, I believe."

"You have previous acquaintance with Miss Forester?" Fairly

Exploding with curiosity, Georgie turned wide inquiring eyes on him.

"She was a guest at the Christmas house party I attended this past winter," he admitted warily.

"Then she is the one—! Oh!" Georgie cried, clapping a hand to her mouth and giving him an apologetic look over her fingers. Leaning closer, she whispered, "What happened, Robin? Can you not tell me the whole story? I promise to lend a sympathetic ear."

"There is nothing to tell. Nothing at all." He turned his attention to the front of the room where Lady Woodson was introducing Signóra Cellini.

Georgie looked at his closed, unhappy profile and resolved to have the whole story before the week was out. She had heard all the gossip that swirled about Lord Robert Lyndhurst since she had become acquainted with him. The son of an impecunious duke, he was said to be a callous heartbreaker, a philanderer, a fortune hunter—a man of handsome face, fatal charm, and many vices. A rake, in other words.

Georgie dismissed the catalog of his sins. She had met the so-called cad for herself and had found him a charming friend. Darkly handsome enough to turn the head of any woman, of course.

She had sensed that he was troubled about something almost from the day she met him. As she became better acquainted with him, she noted how often he sighed or lost the thread of the conversation and gazed off into space with a look of sadness on his handsome countenance. She recognized the signs. And had heard the *on dit* being whispered about. On the brink of the announcement of his engagement to an heiress, he had abandoned her, leaving her with a broken heart.

It was *he* who had had his heart broken, if she were any judge.

And this Miss Forester was the cause of his distraction, she guessed now. Well, she would not have her friends suffering. It was her nature to see them happy. She would make the acquaintance of Miss Ann Forester, and if she found that the lady would do for Lord Robert, then she would do her best to see the rift healed.

Paying no attention to the soprano, Georgie studied Miss Forester's back, for the girl and her chaperone were seated to the side and in front of herself and Lord Robert. She was tall and thin and dressed in an unfashionable gown of pale blue muslin that did not suit her olive complexion.

She had certainly not made the most of her appearance, Georgie thought. With her dark hair pinned tightly to her head, without ornamentation of any kind, she seemed very plain, which fact astounded Georgie. She had expected Lord Robert would pay his addresses to a gazetted beauty. If he was interested in the unprepossessing Miss Forester instead, she must have hidden depths, Georgie thought hopefully, deciding once she had befriended the lady, she would learn the truth of the matter for herself.

She hoped she would like Ann Forester, but then she supposed she would. There was hardly a soul she disliked. And anyway, if Robin had fallen for Miss Forester, she must be a very special lady indeed.

"So good of you to give us a ride home after our carriage horse went lame, Mrs. Gleason," Mrs. Jermyn said to the woman seated across from her. "Ann and I are very grateful."

"As we live in the same general direction, it is no trouble," Mrs. Gleason answered discourteously. She had no opinion of the shabby genteel bluestocking Henrietta Jermyn whose standing in the *ton* was lower than the Thames when the tide was out, but she could not leave the woman and her niece standing on the pavement, wringing their hands when their limping carriage horse was unharnessed and led away just in front of her own vehicle.

Though the last thing she wanted to do just then was make polite conversation, Ann tried to dispel the rather strained atmosphere left in the carriage after Mrs. Gleason's ungracious remark.

"It was a pleasant evening. Some of the musicians were outstanding, though I thought the soprano was a bit out of tune. Do you not agree, Miss Gleason?" she asked the young lady seated opposite her.

"Oh, I hardly know," Miss Elspeth Gleason answered with a giggle. "I was too busy ogling the handsome gentlemen and looking to see what everyone was wearing to listen much. I did not think that pink and gold gown suited Lady Woodson, did you, Mama?"

Lady Gleason returned a critical remark and Ann stifled a sigh. Miss Elspeth Gleason was very young and very giddy. She seemed to be interested only in fashion and flirting.

"Look, Mama! There is Georgie Carteret," Miss Gleason cried, glancing out the window to see who might be milling about outside Lady Woodson's residence waiting for their carriage to be called. "She is on the arm of that gentleman everyone was whispering about tonight. Who is he, I wonder? He is ever so handsome!"

Leaning over her bulk, Lady Gleason bent her turbanned head forward a fraction of an inch to look out the window. "Humph. That's Lyndhurst. I know not what Augusta Woodson was about to invite that scoundrel to her musicale. He ain't fit company for decent society."

Ann almost jumped in her seat. Involuntarily, she turned to the window—and stared directly into Lord Robert's eyes as the carriage pulled away from the curb. He gazed steadily back, his eyes half closed and a rather sneering half-smile on his face. Drawing back quickly, she bit her lower lip and clenched her hands in her lap.

"Yes. I am afraid Lyndhurst has a most shocking reputation," Mrs. Jermyn was saying, distracting Mrs. Gleason's attention. "He is known as a reckless libertine."

"But he was the most handsome man in the room tonight! So dark. So tall. Such a manly physique. He cannot have need of buckram wadding for his shoulders and calves, I'm sure. And those eyes! Why, they are a heavenly emerald color! When he looked at me, I thought I would swoon! He cannot be so very bad, can he?" Miss Gleason objected, not wanting to hear criticism of someone's character when their lineaments were so gorgeously packaged. "Georgie seems on friendly terms with him."

"Elspeth! I forbid you to know that man!" Mrs. Gleason commanded. "As for Georgiana Carteret—that gel has no discrimination. Or caution. She will take up with anyone. Some say she is like a breath of fresh air, but it is *my* opinion that the gel is *much* too free in her manners. She should have a care, or Lyndhurst will give her a slip on the shoulder."

"What is 'a slip on the shoulder,' Mama?" Elspeth asked innocently, while Ann blushed in her corner and wished she could block her ears so that she could not hear this disparagement of him. She did not want to *think* about Lord Robert Lyndhurst—now or ever again.

"Something innocent girls should avoid at all costs. Or they will be outcasts from society," Mrs. Gleason warned darkly.

"I still do not understand," Elspeth complained with a pout. "And what has Lyndhurst done that is so dreadful, anyway?"

"Even I, who do not move in society's highest circles, have heard of his infamy, Miss Gleason. I am afraid that he has a wild reputation. He is a spendthrift, and a wicked libertine. It is said he seeks to find an heiress to fund his profligate ways. And I believe he is rather a philistine where the arts are concerned." This last was the worst of his faults in Mrs. Jermyn's opinion.

"But he is not a philistine, aunt. He went to Cambridge and studied Greek there!" Ann cried, then immediately regretted her outburst.

"What? How do you know this of Lyndhurst, Ann?" her aunt asked in astonishment.

"I—I know his cousin, Lady Abermarle. She speaks highly of him," Ann explained lamely.

"Does she? Must be family prejudice, then, for his reputation is quite besmirched in town," Mrs. Jermyn said decisively.

"He engages in all manner of evil, Elspeth," Mrs. Gleason

interposed, relishing the chance to tear someone's character to shreds.

"Yes, why I remember some rather clever satiric verses that appeared in the newspapers some years ago now that were said to catalog his vices," Mrs. Jermyn added.

"Oh, what did the verses say?" Miss Gleason asked with excited interest.

"He's a gambler and a womanizer," Mrs. Gleason said in her gravelly voice. "Courts ladies and leaves them with broken hearts. Consorts with the lower orders, too. Harriet Wilson and her ilk. Why, I remember the scandal when he was caught hidin' in a lady's wardrobe. The scamp was wearin' the lady's husband's nightshirt, no less—but that was some years ago now."

"Was there a duel?" Elspeth cried, clasping her hands to her breast in excitement.

"I believe the duke—ahem, that is, the wronged husband overlooked the matter," Mrs. Gleason said with a rumbling sound like coachwheels bumping over cobblestones.

"Lyndhurst is rumored to be an expert marksman and swordsman, you see," Mrs. Jermyn explained for the girls' benefit. "The gentleman in question did take his wife to the country and, as far as I know, they have not come up to London since then. But as I do not frequent *ton* circles, perhaps I am wrong?" She looked to Mrs. Gleason for clarification.

"No, no, you are quite correct, Mrs. Jermyn," Mrs. Gleason confirmed with a satisfied smirk. She was in her element, indulging in scandalmongering. "You are to stay away from him, Elspeth, and not give him a chance to look at you again. I won't have you swoonin' like some ninnyhammer, and encouragin' him to believe he has a chance at your fortune."

"I do not care what mama says, I think Lyndhurst is the most handsome man I have ever seen! Quite like Lord Byron's Corsair! What do you think, Miss Forester?" Elspeth whispered as the elder ladies took leave of one another outside Mrs. Jermyn's Seymour Street residence.

"I am sure I do not know," Ann answered coolly, thankful that

Miss Gleason could not be aware of her heated countenance and inner turmoil.

It hurt her to hear him spoken of in such terms, his character denigrated, to hear that he was held in ill repute by the whole of the fashionable world.

Yet not so, in truth! The ladies might talk about him as a dangerous rake, but that did not stop many of them from vying for his attention and courting his favor. Oh yes, she had watched him out of the corner of her eye at the musicale, laughing and talking with many women, individually and in groups. They had fluttered around him like so many gaily-dressed, adoring butterflies drawn to the lure of his overwhelming masculinity.

He had ignored her completely after that one shocked moment when she had seen his lips forming her name.

Though she thought she had prepared herself to see him while she was in London, she had been almost overcome with shock and a deep intense longing. She had not expected to see him that night, never dreaming he would attend so refined and proper an occasion as a musicale. He had been looking exceeding well . . . no, he had looked more devastatingly handsome than she remembered—and utterly lost to her now.

It had been more painful than she would have believed possible to see him again. She had ached to go to him. To put her hand on his arm and look up into his eyes. To have him smile down at her and tell her that everything would be well now.

But such a dream was pure fantasy. In all likelihood, he was embarrassed to see *her.* Yes, now that he was back among his fashionable admirers, she was sure he regretted paying her his attentions at Christmas.

How right she had been to turn him off before she made a complete fool of herself!

Ten

"Ah, there you are returned from your piano lesson at last, Ann dear," Mrs. Jermyn said, poking her head around the door and peering out into the front hallway.

"Yes, aunt," Ann replied, removing her bonnet and placing it next to her York tan gloves on the hall table.

"When you have removed your things, please come into my book room. There is something I wish to show you, my dear."

"I am sorry to be late, but Herr Müller insisted that I repeat one particular passage several times until he was satisfied that I had it right," Ann explained, entering the small first-floor room at the front of the house that her aunt was pleased to call her book room. "And then he asked me to take tea with him and his wife. I could not refuse. I met his wife's nephew, a Mr. George Allenthorp, who was there at the time. Mr. Allenthorp saw me home."

Mrs. Jermyn's looked at Ann with raised eyebrows.

"Saunders, your lady's maid, accompanied me as usual, so there was no impropriety, aunt."

"What manner of gentleman is this Mr. Allenthorp?" Mrs. Jermyn asked with lively curiosity. "Is he well looking?"

"A pleasant man. And quite well looking, yes. He is an aspiring writer. Is not that a coincidence? When I spoke of the many readings we have been to this season, he expressed his surprise that we had not met previously, as he said he is frequently invited to read from his work at such occasions."

"Hmm. I shall ask my friends if they have heard anything of

this young man," Mrs. Jermyn replied thoughtfully, taking a long look at Ann's heightened complexion. "Has he published anything yet?"

"I do not believe so. He did not menton it . . . I—I have promised to allow him to accompany me home after my next lesson. I hope you do not dislike the notion, Aunt Henrietta."

"Hmm. Yes, you must bring him here so that I may meet him. We must be sure that he is not some hedgebird who has learned of your dowry. And you must be sure you always take Saunders with you when you go to your lessons. You cannot be too careful, you know."

"Yes, aunt . . . What did you wish to show me?"

Mrs. Jermyn held up a cream vellum card with a triumphant smile. "An invitation to an anniversary celebration for the Marquess and Marchioness of Benningham. The dowager marchioness is a good friend of mine, and her son is an upstanding young man, married these ten years now. It is sure to be a select occasion, for the Benninghams are quite well-connected."

Ann concealed her dismay. This sounded like one of those glittering occasions she had hoped to avoid, much more threatening than the salons and musicales they had attended thus far. "I thought you were not interested in London society, Aunt Henrietta."

"No, *I* am not, but your mother wishes you to be introduced to society, Ann dear, and this will give you some entrée."

"Oh no, please, aunt! I do not wish to make a come-out with the young ladies who have come to town for the season. I would stick out like a crow among swans," she protested in alarm as visions of encountering Lord Robert at every turn flashed through her mind.

"Oh, dear me, no. Not a formal come-out. That would not do at all for you. But we will attend some entertainments given by the more respectable and intelligent people whom I know. And perhaps we will meet someone of interest at the Benninghams'."

"But aunt—"

"Now, I know what you would say. And I agree with you. I

do not approve of much that goes on in what passes for high society—the frivolity, the interest in fashion and gossip and amorous dealings to the exclusion of things of more import—literature, music, drama, painting and so on.

"But I do see your mother's point. You should have a chance to mingle with young people, though it is to be regretted that many of the girls are foolish ninnyhammers. So many gilded butterflies, lovely to behold, but empty-headed and empty-hearted, flitting from one frivolous activity to another, with no idea of good conversation, and with no other purpose than to be admired for a brief span and contract an eligible alliance. And the young gentlemen are no better. An unsavory collection of coxcombs, rakes, rattles and over-dressed dandies, the lot of them. Perhaps somewhere among all the chaff there will be a young man of a more serious cast of mind who will take your fancy."

"I assure you, it is unnecessary, Aunt Henrietta. I prefer to concentrate on improving my technique on the pianoforte and, as soon as the weather is warmer, I shall take up my watercolors again. I—I have no wish to contract a suitable alliance." Ann tried to dissuade her aunt. But when that lady remained adamant, she found she had no choice. She would see him, then, she thought as her heart began to beat faster, whether in anticipation or dread, she did not know.

"I suppose we must get you some new clothes," Mrs. Jermyn said with a pained look.

"That will not be necessary, Aunt Henrietta. I had several new gowns made in Winchester before I left Chilcomb."

"Ah, Winchester. Miss Austen is buried in the cathedral there, I believe. You have read her works, of course?" At Ann's nod, her aunt continued, "But I digress. You believe the gowns you have brought with you will suffice? I must own, I have no patience for shopping. I am glad you are not one of those flibbertigibbets interested in all that nonsense, my dear."

Ann assured her aunt that her wardrobe did not need augmenting.

* * *

"Hello. You are Miss Ann Forester, are you not? I am Georgiana Carteret, but you must call me Georgie. Everyone does, you know."

Ann looked up in astonishment at the young woman who addressed her in such an informal manner. She was in the ladies' withdrawing room at the small dinner party she and her aunt were attending for a young lady who was making her come-out. "I—I am sorry . . . Miss Carteret, is it?" she answered in bewilderment, smoothing her hands lightly over her gown. "We have not met before?"

But Ann had seen her and remembered her well. She was the small, vivacious lady of the vivid red hair who had been chatting to Lord Robert when she had seen him at Lady Woodson's musicale.

"No, we have not met before. But I have heard of you," Georgie said with a twinkle in her eyes. "You are reputed to be quite an accomplished pianist and watercolorist. I have heard, too, that you prefer serious discussions about music or education to gadding about on the town."

"Well, I—," Ann faltered, quite at sea.

"Oh, dear, I have embarrassed you. I did not mean to do any such thing. I meant to compliment you, but my tongue runs away with me sometimes. Do forgive me?"

"Of course. I *am* flattered, not embarrassed," Ann responded generously. "But who has been telling you of me?"

"Was not that soprano dreadful at Lady Woodson's musicale the other night? I declare, my ears are still ringing after enduring half an hour of her screeching," Georgie chattered, ignoring Ann's question.

Ann smiled, intrigued but a bit bemused by her new acquaintance. "Indeed, I have heard better. Much better." At the face Georgie made, Ann laughed. "Abominable, was it not?"

Georgie agreed, then Ann said, "Perhaps this evening's performer is more talented and will soothe our offended sensibilities."

Georgie smiled engagingly. "Oh, yes. I know she will. She is my friend, Sarah McIntyre, and she is very talented. I have heard her play her harp several times. Have no fear. You shall enjoy it . . . Sarah is in love with Mr. Charles Blandford, heir to Earl Bicester, you know. They are both very shy, but I have a scheme to bring them together, and before you know it, they will be engaged!" Georgie laughed gaily and linked her arm with Ann's as they prepared to leave the ladies' withdrawing room.

Ann looked at her in alarm. Was Miss Carteret half mad? she wondered.

But when Georgie chattered on happily, commenting on many of the people at the small party they were attending, and smiling and waving to one and all—and receiving smiles and waves in return—Ann was reassured. Perhaps her new acquaintance was just one of those effervescent personalities whose easy manner enabled her to make friends with everyone.

A few days later, Ann found herself mingling with an even more select gathering at the home of Emily and Marcus Whaleon, the Marquess and Marchioness of Benningham.

"Good evening, Miss Forester."

"Lord Robert!" Ann turned from greeting her hosts to look into flashing green eyes boring down into hers. Her heart jumped into her throat. She could not seem to take a breath.

"Will you deign to know me tonight? Or will you pretend that I am an insect beneath your notice?" he asked in a voice that revealed the steel beneath his elegant exterior. His face looked dark with anger against the bright splendor of his intricately folded neckcloth.

She looked up at him in mute appeal, her hand going up to finger the topaz necklace at her throat. There was a fiery hardness in his eyes that had not been there when she knew him before.

Her eyes fell from the accusing glare in his and she took a step away, fighting for air.

"You shall *not* ignore me this time," he grated in a low voice, taking her elbow in his hard hand and forcing her to turn to him again. "We have unfinished business, you and I."

The feel of his hand pressing into the flesh of her arm had her almost shivering. He was so tall. So broad in the shoulder. So very masculine. She had forgotten.

Trying not to want to turn and run from him, she forced herself to speak calmly, "Please, my lord. Do not make a scene. Someone will see."

His lips twisted into the semblance of a smile. "Very well, I shall not make a scene, if you will grant me five minutes of your time so that we may exchange . . . pleasant nothings."

She nodded stiffly, still not meeting his eyes. He loosened his hold on her elbow and turned to walk with her toward the long windows where there were few people to overhear their conversation.

"Why did you leave me, Ann?"

There was a world of hurt in his tone, but she would not let that convince her that she had been wrong. It was all artifice. He was experienced at playing this sort of game.

"Why did you not answer my letters?"

"Don't." She flashed him one imploring glance, then bit her lip, feeling tears prick her eyes. He looked so very familiar—and so very dear.

She heard him inhale somewhat unsteadily. "Forgive me. I am grown into such a savage since Christmas that I have forgotten how to conduct myself with charming young ladies."

To her ears, he sounded cynical and unmoved by her struggle to bring herself under control, but she did not look up into his face and so did not see the misery there.

"Have you been well since we last met?" he asked in a strained voice.

"Quite well, thank you," she replied flatly, training her eyes on his stark white neckcloth and the small emerald pin winking there that somehow reminded her of the sparkle and color of his eyes. She looked up to check that her impression was correct. And immediately realized her mistake.

She could not look away.

She saw him draw in a sharp breath through his nostrils, but he only said, "The weather has been atrocious for this late in April, has it not? I expect spring to be in the air by now, yet this exceptionally frosty period lingers."

"I do not wish to discuss the weather with you, my lord . . . If you will excuse me." She was desperate to move away from him before she lost all control.

His hand shifted to her wrist. He tightened his fingers, circling her wrist, and bent his dark head near hers. "Ann. Why have you come to London? To see me?"

"No!"

"Why, then? No, do not turn away from me! We must talk. There is no privacy here. If you will give me your direction, I will call for you tomorrow morning."

"No! I have nothing whatsoever to say to you, and I have no wish to hear anything you might have to say to me. Good evening, Lord Robert," she said, pulling from his hold at last and not seeing the defeat on his face as his hands dropped to his sides.

Trying not to hurry, she walked away, holding her back regally straight, and her chin high.

Robin stared after her rigid back in frustration, his hands curled into fists at his side. Since he had recovered from his surprise at seeing her at Lady Woodson's musical evening, he had looked for her everywhere, almost sick with longing for another sight of her. He had taken to attending society entertainments he had long since scorned, and even endured the snubs of the gossipmongers with seeming indifference, using his playful flirtation with Georgiana Carteret as an excuse to put in an appearance at such high-toned events, desperately hoping he would encounter Ann again.

But he had been frustrated in his search. Until this evening. Dear God! He had hardly been able to credit his eyes when he had seen her walk into the room with the older woman she had been with before. He had gone to her immediately, vowing this time he would not let her walk right past him without speaking.

Hell and the devil take it! It was clear that she had no regrets in throwing him over at Christmas. She had sent back those two letters he had sent her full of apologies and explanations, begging her forgiveness. He had put his heart and soul into those letters and she had scorned them. Why should he expect that she would relent now? She believed the worst of him and had decided that he was not worthy of her love. There was to be no second chance for him. He should accept that fact and turn his attentions elsewhere. He did have some pride, after all.

A muscle tensed in his jaw, then he spied Georgie Carteret across the room with Viscount Sedgemoor at her side. The little redhead's company always served to distract him. He moved across to greet her and solicit a dance.

"Georgie. You are looking particularly lovely tonight. Dare I hope you have space left on your card for a dance with me?" he asked, noting Sedgemoor's disapproving frown out of the corner of his eye. They had had a confrontation over Georgie's favors in another ballroom recently. If Sedgemoor was spoiling for a fight, he was in a prime mood to take him on.

His wandering attention came back to Georgie. She was agreeing to save him a dance, but she was naming conditions. He had to promise to dance with two of her friends.

One of the "friends" she named was Ann Forester.

Good Lord! Since when had Georgie become friends with Ann? He could not gracefully refuse. Damping down his dismay, he gave the required promise. "You exact a high price for your favors, Georgie," he quizzed her, hoping to disguise how much she had disconcerted him.

"You are a good boy, Robin," she said, tapping him on the cheek playfully.

Only Georgie would be so innocently indiscreet, he thought,

giving her his best smile, slow and broad and full of the promise of things to come. Lifting her hand, he turned it over and pressed his lips to the skin on the inside of her wrist. With a challenging sideways glance at the glowering Sedgemoor, who was looking ready to do murder, he took his leave, promising to collect her for their dance when the pianist struck up the first waltz.

Devil take it! he thought as he moved away, he had just agreed to dance with Ann. As she did not wish to even *speak* to him, he did not know how he was to carry out his foolish pledge.

Eleven

"You are dancing with me under false pretenses, Robin," Georgie said as they waltzed down the room some little while later, after she had had the happiness of unexpectedly meeting some friends from home, Miss Susan Tennyson and Mr. Thomas Cunningham.

He cocked a brow and looked down at her as he twirled her about. "Am I, my dear?"

"I do not believe you have danced with Ann Forester, yet, sir."

He grimaced.

"Oh, you slowtop, Robin! Surely you have not failed to persuade her? Where is all that vaunted charm of yours?" She laughed at him, then cast a brief glance about the room. Her eyes gleamed suddenly. "I believe—yes, I fear that I have trod on the hem of my gown. Grandmama's French modiste *would* make it too long for me. I am such a dwarf. Alas, there is nothing else for it," she added with a gusty sigh. "I shall have to pin it up, if I do not wish to land on my face on Lady Benningham's floor—and you along with me. What a scandal that would be!"

"Now, Georgie, what mischief are you plotting?" he asked as she led him pell-mell from the floor. He realized what she was up to a moment later when he found himself face to face with Ann.

Georgie's words were pouring out, explaining about her allegedly damaged gown. "Ann, please be a dear and take my place in this set. I can recommend Robin as an excellent dancer and you are the only woman below the age of fifty who is not dancing at present."

"Oh, no! Please Georgie," Ann said in a suffocated voice, "I cannot possibly—"

"Certainly you can," Georgie insisted. "You must! I feel the veriest rudesby for deserting poor Robin so precipitously."

A moment later she was gone. They both stared after her, then Lord Robert put out his white-gloved hand.

Ann hesitated.

"We are being watched. Do not make a scene," he said under his breath.

She set her own gloved hand in his. And felt the shock of deliberately touching him again. Oh, it had been so long!

She could not bear it. She tried not to want to pull her hand away. He tightened his fingers around hers as though he sensed her intent. Aware that the eyes of several people were on them, she relaxed her hand, allowing it to remain in his. Palm to palm. Fingers curling around fingers. Heat beginning to seep through his glove into hers.

She concentrated on her breathing. Slowly in, then just as slowly out again.

She held herself stiffly, trying not to drink in the splendor of his correct evening attire, the way his dark green evening jacket sat tightly across his shoulders, the way his buff inexpressibles hugged his lean muscular thighs—and the way that lock of dark hair was falling over his forehead, making her long to reach up and push it back.

"Please bear in mind that I am quite unfamiliar with the dance," she said with cold dignity, not meeting his eyes as he slipped his hand to the back of her waist.

"I do remember—and you were coming along nicely under my tuition last Christmas when we last attempted . . . ah," he faltered. He swallowed, and tightened his lips. "When we last danced together."

Gingerly, she rested the tips of her fingers on his shoulder and he swirled her into motion without another word.

Grateful that he held her correctly and lightly as he guided her about the room, and made no move to converse, Ann tried to hold on to her composure, biting her lower lip to hold her emotions in check. *I will not allow him to affect me,* she vowed, trying to steel herself against the memories that flooded her . . . how he had hummed a tune in her ear and danced her round the furniture before the fire in the Abermarles' library . . . how they had—No! She would not think of *that.*

She missed a step.

His strong hand grasped her waist more tightly and kept her from stumbling.

"I told you I am no dancer," she apologized in chagrin.

"You are a gifted musician. Just relax, and allow yourself to flow with the music. The rhythm can guide you better than I."

She made no answer but tried to do as he recommended and soon found herself picking up the rhythm of the dance. Concentrating on the music served as a distraction from thinking about her partner.

"You look well, Ann," he said in a tight voice, filling the awkward silence that stretched between them.

"Do not address me so! We are no longer on intimate terms."

He looked down at her, his eyes half closed, searing anger radiating through his dark lashes. "No, *Miss* Forester, we are no longer on *intimate* terms."

At that look, scorching heat shot through her veins, leaving her mouth dry and her cheeks hot. She felt suffocated.

"Are you enjoying yourself in London, *Miss* Forester?"

"Yes." She forced herself to speak. She would not let him see the power he still held over her. "I have found much to interest me here, including many sites of historical significance in the city—the Tower, the Abbey, and St. Paul's among them. Then, too, my aunt is fond of literary salons and I have met several people whose views or work I admire. And I am studying the piano with a German master. I spend many hours practicing. It has been hard work, but I believe I have benefitted from Herr Müller's tuition." She glanced beyond his right ear as she spoke and was disconcerted by the sight of his crisply curling black hair at the edge of her vision.

"Ah. I am glad you have found much to occupy you . . . Have you been asked to play at any of these salons you attend?"

"Oh, no. My talent is inferior—"

"Nonsense! You play better than anyone I have ever heard! These so-called arbiters of taste you consort with are mere pompous philistines, if they do not recognize your superior talent. Your technique is strong and you have a gift for conveying deep feeling when you play that transports your listeners to a higher realm," he declared heatedly.

"Thank you. You are very generous," she whispered. His unstinting praise warmed her even as she distrusted it.

"It is no more than the truth," was all he said for some time.

Finally, "Ann—"

"Please. Don't."

"I was merely going to observe that this fawn-colored gown suits you. It brings out the amber lights in your eyes and the chestnut highlights in your dark hair."

She looked at him then, her eyes wide with disbelief. "Do not make mock of me, my lord. I am not some foolish chit who will be taken in by your practiced flattery. I can see that I am not as fashionably dressed as the other ladies here. My dress is plain. As am I. I wonder that you are not embarrassed to be seen with such a dowdy Maypole as myself, when you are rigged out in the first stare of fashion yourself."

"Hush! I shall not listen to you belittling yourself. Your bearing is elegant. You are a striking woman and do not need overly ornate gowns and ornaments and furbelows to disguise any weaknesses of face or figure as some ladies do."

Ann laughed ironically. "What fustian!"

"I do not lie. To me you look just as you ought. A different hairstyle, a different dress could not improve you. I admire you just as you are."

"I do not wish you to admire me in any way at all, my lord," she responded perversely. His blatant flattery was not soothing her. On the contrary, with every word he spoke, her ire increased. She had learned that she could not trust him. He was merely toying with her to suit his own ends.

The music died, but Lord Robert did not release her hand immediately. "Come driving in the park with me tomorrow?"

"I have an engagement tomorrow."

"The next day, then?"

"You waste your breath, my lord. I am busy for the remainder of my stay in London."

His jaw hardened. "So be it then." He gave her a small mocking bow, turned on his heel and strode from the room.

Ann did not see him again that evening.

"That did not go too badly, I think," Mrs. Jermyn was saying as their carriage rumbled over the cobblestones, wending its way home. "I had a most interesting conversation with Lord Benningham about Byron's *Childe Harold's Pilgrimage.* The fourth canto has been published recently, you know. Lord Benningham told me one noted authority has described the poem as all 'daring, dash, and grandiosity.' I thought that a marvelous description . . . Did I mention that his mother is a friend of mine?"

"Lord Byron's?" Ann asked in astonishment.

Mrs. Jermyn tittered. "No, my dear. Lord Benningham's mother, the dowager marchioness. That is how we came to be invited. Quite a decorous occasion overall, except for the inclusion of Lyndhurst, of course. I was astonished that he was invited, but it seems that one of his sisters is married to Lady Benningham's brother, Sir Myles Trent."

"Yes, I suppose that would account for it," Ann murmured.

"How came you to stand up with the scoundrel, my dear?" Mrs. Jermyn looked at her askance through the murky light of the carriage interior. "I was quite shocked when I beheld him twirling you down the room."

"Georgie Carteret was dancing with him, but she tore her gown. She presented him to me as she went off to pin it up. There was nothing I could do, aunt," Ann faltered. "To have turned him away would have been very rude."

"He did not say—or do—anything scandalous, did he?"

"No, of course not, aunt," Ann hedged. It seemed her mother had not informed her aunt of her dealings with the gentleman at Christmas. Ann was not about to enlighten her now.

"No. Well, you are hardly in his style, thank the Lord!" Mrs. Jermyn went on to relate her conversation with Lord Benningham at length. "And now, what do you think of this? I have received invitations for both of us to Lady Wycombe's salon next week. And who do you think will be the guest of honor? The Angel poet!"

"I—I beg your pardon, Aunt Henrietta. I was not perfectly attending," Ann had been hurt by her aunt's words—*You are hardly in his style*—and had not listened to her rambling discourse.

She was remembering how she had felt when she saw Lord Robert waltzing with Georgie Carteret. She had hardly been able to bear the sight. It brought back such vivid memories of her own waltz with him in front of the library fire at Christmas.

It had been agonizing to see him again, but she had been unable to prevent herself from following him with her eyes all evening. She had been on the point of excusing herself, finding her aunt, and claiming a headache when Georgie had dragged him scowling up to her and literally forced them to dance together. And then she was forced to touch him again and look into his eyes and listen to his false compliments as they danced.

"Ah, you are tired, my dear. I was telling you that we are in for a rare treat at Lady Wycombe's literary evening. Mr. Faris, the poet—the man they call the Angel—will be there to read for us!"

"The Angel?"

"Yes, indeed. His poetry is the very music of the spheres. Not only does he have the mien of a heavenly being, but one cannot but admire the beauty of his words, and his voice is quite divine, too!"

"Why, you are in raptures, aunt!"

"Yes, indeed. You will see why he is so admired when you glimpse him and hear him read. You will be in transports of delight, I promise you!"

Lord Robert went directly home from the Benninghams'.

Sprawling in his favorite overstuffed chair in the small room his valet cum manservant euphemistically called "the library," he rolled a glass of brandy between his hands, warming it. He had been toying with the same glass for half an hour as he lounged with his leg hooked over the arm of the chair gazing unseeingly into the glowing embers in the grate.

Why had Ann come to town? He was amazed that she had done so. From what she had said at the Abermarles', he never thought she would. Had she come to look for a husband? He winced. The thought was like gall on an open wound.

When he had seen her at the musicale last week, for one heart-stopping moment he dared to hope that she had come because of him.

But then she had walked past him, her eyes lowered, not even acknowledging his presence, and his heart had cracked all over again.

He raked his long fingers through his hair in weary despair.

How had things gone so badly wrong after such a promising start?

Instead of going to see his family after Christmas as he had intended, he had come to town directly from the Abermarles', where he had embarked on a round of wild excess for a few weeks, trying to dull the strange heavy ache and emptiness he had felt—trying to put Ann Forester from his mind and from his heart.

He had gamed away his quarter's allowance in an evening, then had sought to quieten his stinging conscience by drinking himself into a stupor. A deal of consolation he had got from that! He had awoken in a vile room to find that his purse had been stolen and that he had apparently "enjoyed" himself with one of the lowest doxies of the street. He had been celibate ever since and had given fervent thanks that he had not ended up with a case of the clap.

He had not succeeded in forgetting Ann through debauchery, but had only violated his promise to himself not to succumb to drunkenness and gambling fever ever again. He had seen only too well the disastrous results of those two deadly vices. His closest friend, Lawrence Pritchard, had ruined himself one night at the tables. The next day he was dead by his own hand, a bullet through his head.

And so he had sworn off drinking to excess and gaming. Again. And women—one of his last pleasures, one of his last vices. He meant to keep his vows this time, even though that would not influence Ann to take him back. One side of his mouth tipped up. She would not even know of it.

He shifted his position, leaned his head back against the well-worn cushion and contemplated the shadows dancing on the ceiling in the firelight.

How had he come to fall in love with Ann Forester in the first place? he asked himself. He had been in the middle before he knew that he had begun.

He had not found her beautiful, or physically alluring—at first. But he had been piqued by her resistance to his flirtatious games and her ability to stand up to him. He had been intrigued by her intelligence and her wit, and frankly envious of her musical talent.

What had started as a flirtatious game to pass the time had turned into something quite different when he had kissed her in the snow and had found to his complete astonishment that he desired her. For once in his life, he had been serious in his dealings with a woman.

He had felt she was someone he could anchor his life to and had been about to reform his ramshackle way of life. Do something right for a change. Even Dick would have approved.

But that was not why he had wanted to marry her—to redeem

himself in his family's eyes. No. There had been another reason. A stronger reason.

Damnation! He slammed his fist against the chair arm.

He damned Zara Stanhill to perdition, but that did little good. She had thrown herself at him because she had thought he would be receptive, as he had been previously. He had been pushing her away and trying to extricate himself from the embarrassing situation when Ann had walked in upon them and seen the woman half unclothed—and immediately jumped to the wrong conclusion.

Pressing a knuckled fist to his mouth, he closed his eyes at the memory of feeling absolutely helpless.

He had never experienced rejection before. And he had never experienced pain in his dealings with women. It was an entirely new experience, one that left him reevaluating the way he had lived his past life. Had some of the women he had known felt such misery when he left them? He had never considered it before, but he did so now. He did not want to be the cause of the kind of suffering he had endured.

Rejection hurt. This continuing pain and upset hurt.

It was over. He would just have to face the fact. Ann would never have him. Never.

Well, she was not the only woman in the world . . . But his heart whispered that she was the only one for him.

Oh, Ann! if only . . .

He gnawed on his knuckles. Lord! He was not going to cry again, was he? He took a sustaining gulp of the brandy and choked, sputtering at the fire of it, then impatiently flicked the moisture from his eyes with a long finger.

Twelve

"*Miss* Carteret, are you suggesting that I *pretend* to court your friend, Miss Tennyson, to make her country bumpkin of a suitor jealous?" Lord Robert asked in feigned astonishment.

"That is *exactly* what I am asking of you. I congratulate you, Robin. I can see *you* are not a slowtop like Tom Cunningham," Georgie said, tapping him on the wrist with her fan and smiling roguishly.

"Why me, Georgie? Why not one of your other friends? Sedgemoor, for instance?"

"I do not have to tell you that your face is masculine perfection, and your figure is the very height of manliness—"

His smile became a perfect leer at these words.

"—and though you are a conceited fellow, I think your heart is good, at base."

"Are you sure I am not simply base at heart?"

Georgie laughed. "Your rakish days are numbered, my lord. As are Gus's," she said, referring to Viscount Sedgemoor. "I have other plans for him," she pronounced with lowered brows and a militant gleam in her eyes.

They were standing a little apart from the company at a card party at the home of Georgie's friends the Greenleas.

"Ah. I assume that means you have plans for me, as well." He looked at her with a question in his eyes, wondering what she was up to.

"As to that, my lord, you shall just have to wait and see." She gave him an innocent stare that was nevertheless full of secret laughter.

"Little devil!" Lord Robert reached out his forefinger and tapped her on the tip of her freckled nose.

Her blue eyes danced with teasing lights and she smiled up at him dazzlingly.

"And how am I to be, ah, rewarded for my participation in this little farce, my dear?"

"In the usual way, sir," she answered, peeping up from under her lashes.

He looked his query.

"Virtue is its own reward, or so I have always believed," she said, then burst into laughter at his dumbfounded look.

It seemed to him there was a hazy nimbus around her red curls in the winking candlelight. But Georgiana Carteret was no angel. Managing little imp of mischief, more like, he thought with a crooked smile. And with the most damnably tempting pair of lips!

A very shy, and very young, gentleman came to claim Georgie as his whist partner for the game that was being set up, putting paid to their light flirtation.

"Goodbye, Robin. I shall see you later, perhaps?" she said.

"I believe not, my dear. I have promised my sister to look in on her this evening."

"Oh! I am glad then. Do enjoy yourself!" Georgie exclaimed with another of her dazzling smiles.

Lord Robert watched her dance away buoyantly, chattering nonstop to the gauche boy, putting the lad at his ease.

Since he had met Georgie, her friendly, unconventional manners and infectious gaiety had helped distract him from the blue devils that had plagued him since Christmas.

Now she wanted him to pay court to the lovely, but rather retiring, Miss Tennyson to make another man jealous. There was no danger that he would hurt the girl, if Georgie were to be believed. She had assured him that Miss Tennyson was deep in love with her childhood sweetheart, Mr. Thomas Cunningham.

Ready to be distracted from his own heartache, he was more than willing to become enmeshed in Georgie's madcap schemes and to fall in with the merry games she wished him to play.

He took his leave of the Greenleas and decided to walk to his sister's house. He frowned, remembering the previous evening when he had tried to speak with Ann during an interval at the theatre. It was the first time he had seen her since their waltz at the Benninghams'. She had rebuffed him yet again.

Well, he could not keep beating against a closed door, tearing himself up in the process. He would endeavor to console himself with Georgie's vivacious company instead.

He was sorry now that he had confided to Georgie almost the whole of his relationship with Ann. He had been in a particularly bitter, black mood one evening after overhearing some malicious gossip about himself—two old biddies had been talking of him as a callous heartbreaker and dissolute scoundrel of the worst kind—and somehow Georgie had wheedled the truth out of him.

Georgie had exclaimed that it was a case of true love between him and Ann. He had seen the sympathy in her eyes when she had urged him to try again. It had been too painful to continue talking of his own disappointed hopes. He had changed the subject, flirting with her instead.

Well, why not? He was a healthy male. He needed a woman in his life, now his raking days were over. Little Miss Carteret would certainly keep a fellow amused—and constantly on his toes with the mischief she got up to. And then there were those damnably kissable lips of hers to keep him distracted. . . .

"Oh, ye elfin sprites, ye nymphs of air on high and water deep.
Come. Come, sit by me while I tell a tale to make you weep.
Hear the trill of the river's quiet voice.
Pay homage, oh you despoilers of the countryside path.
Cease your depredations, you have no other choice,
Else you shall incur outraged nature's wrath."

The ladies gathered around Mr. Raphael Faris at Lady Wycombe's literary evening clapped enthusiastically as he came to the end of his long poem in praise of nature and the countryside and the dangers man, with his newfangled industrial ideas, posed to England's heritage, her "green and pleasant land."

Mr. Faris bowed and smiled at one and all, not neglecting to catch Ann's eye and give her a particularly sweet smile, undoubtedly aware that she was one of the few *young* women in his audience. He then modestly lowered his lashes and turned to one of his more elderly admirers.

Ann clapped, too, but mentally she rolled her eyes. The man was a charlatan with a clichéd style who had set himself up as a romantic poet. He had tried to copy the themes and poetic forms of Messrs. Wordsworth, Coleridge, and Byron, not singly, but all at once. He lacked the powerful imagery, subtlety, command of the language, and individual genius that characterized those other gentlemen. His poems were a dreadful hodgepodge as a result.

"Was that not marvelous, Ann dear?" Mrs. Jermyn asked, her eyes shining with pleasure.

"Why, I believe I enjoyed Mr. Allenthorp's essay quite as well as Mr. Faris's poetry," Ann temporized.

"Oh, do you really think so? His reading voice is very dull and his manner lacks all the charm of Mr. Faris's," Mrs. Jermyn said dismissively before turning to the fair-haired poet once more.

Her aunt had met Mr. Allenthorp and had given him a qualified approval. She had told Ann he seemed a polite enough gentleman, though after careful questioning, she had been unable to determine how he supported himself. He seemed to reside in his aunt Müller's household, but had no visible means of income. However, as he was reputed to be a serious writer, she had cautiously sanctioned Ann's continued acquaintance with him for the time being.

Mr. Allenthorp had accompanied them that evening. When Ann had spoken of the event in his presence, mentioning that

Lady Wycombe held open house and her salons were not by invitation only, he had asked if he could escort them. Mrs. Jermyn had accepted.

When they arrived and he was introduced to Lady Wycombe, he mentioned that he, too, was a writer and by chance had his latest essay in his pocket. Lady Wycombe had taken him up immediately and graciously invited him to present it.

Ann had not quite liked how he had put himself forward, but she had been impressed with his essay on the merits of a classical education, though she thought perhaps many of his ideas were derivative and resolved to check two or three points in the works of other authors. However, even if the arguments were not his own, he had organized and presented them well.

"Well, Ann, what did you think of the poet who is taking literary London by storm?" Lady Emily Gwent took Ann's elbow and guided her a little away from the crush around Mr. Faris.

"Why, everyone seems to have enjoyed his performance enormously," Ann replied carefully. "I imagine Lady Wycombe's reputation as a literary hostess is enhanced by her coup in persuading him to read here this evening."

"Ah, but what did *you* think, my dear?" Lady Emily persisted. "Do not fear to speak your mind freely."

Ann gave her friend a questioning look, then burst forth candidly, "Frankly then, Lady Emily, his work lacks polish and subtlety. His style is imitative and hackneyed and he really has no notion of how poetry should be written. His words are all for effect; they lack imagination and flow. He seeks admiration, but conveys no real feeling for his subject."

"That is certainly candid, my dear." Lady Emily gave Ann a wry look, her green eyes sparkling with some unnamed emotion Ann could not fathom.

"Oh, good heavens! My wretched tongue. Forgive me, Lady Emily. You—you did invite me to be frank. I am sorry if I have insulted your opinion."

Lady Emily laughed with delight, a deep, musical sound. "On

the contrary, my dear Ann! You have confirmed my own assessment. Our opinions and taste march in similar vein, it seems."

Ann smiled in relief. "Oh, I am glad I have not offended you."

"Nonsense, my dear. We two think alike. Have you not noticed?"

"I had trusted my aunt's judgment until tonight," Ann confided, "but she recommended Mr. Faris to me so highly and now that I have heard him, well . . ."

"Do not blame her for getting a little carried away. Mr. Faris is a sensation at the moment. It seems everyone has been carried away by his charm, and—well, you can see why he has attracted all the ladies. He *does* have an angelic countenance. With his white-gold hair and wide blue eyes framed by long golden lashes and boyish smile, the ladies all cluster round him, like bees drawn to pollen. And then his story is so sad. He is an orphan, you know, with no means of support except for the generosity of his patrons. He had just started at Oxford when his clergyman father died, leaving him penniless and forced to earn his living by writing poetry. Does it not wring your heart, my dear?" Lady Emily asked with a droll look.

"Well, it would, if he were truly talented, or even if he were truly *trying* to write well."

"Oh, he is talented, indeed." Lady Emily bent nearer to whisper, "Talented at pulling the wool over everyone's eyes."

"But not quite everyone's," Ann returned. Both ladies laughed.

"Good night, my dear." Lady Emily patted her hand. "You must come to *my* next literary evening. I shall send you an invitation. Now I must dash. My son is arriving home from school for the term break this evening and I must be there to greet him."

Lady Emily went to bid Lady Wycombe farewell and Ann turned to Mr. Allenthorp, who did not have such a large group gathered round him.

They conversed on a variety of topics until her aunt approached, telling Ann that it was time to leave.

"Tomorrow is not one of the days you go to Uncle Müller for

your lessons, but may I call and take you walking in the Green Park in the afternoon, Miss Forester?"

Ann looked to her aunt for her approval and, receiving a rather grudging nod, said, "Thank you, Mr. Allenthorp. I should enjoy that. At half past four, then?"

The arrangement was made and she was glad. She would enjoy conversing with an intelligent, sober gentleman. She needed distraction from her troubled thoughts—thoughts that, despite her best efforts to banish them, still centered on a tall and darkly handsome rogue.

The lovely May day was a perfect embodiment of spring, exactly as the poets said it should be. Birds chirruped in the newly leafed trees, flowers bloomed profusely, wafting their soft scents on the light breeze, ducks floated on the lazy Serpentine, leaving small ripples on the glassy surface of the water in their wake. The sky was the hue of winking blue sapphires and the sun was warm enough to put off heavy cloaks and topcoats.

It was a perfect day for a walk in the park and Ann was enjoying it. She was on the arm of Mr. Allenthorp.

"There is nothing I enjoy so much as talking with you, Miss Forester," he was saying, recalling her attention from the scenery.

"That is a compliment, indeed, sir, but I would have thought that your writing gives you greater pleasure," she replied.

"Is that your way of telling me that your music gives you greater pleasure than conversing with me?" he asked in that familiar way he had adopted of late.

Ann fidgeted uncomfortably. He was becoming very particular in his attentions recently. She was not sure what she felt about him. He was a well looking young man. Handsome even. Compactly formed with sandy-colored hair and pale blue eyes, with a rather white complexion, he was barely taller than she, but he carried himself with assurance. It seemed to her at times that he tried to emulate an air of fashion that he could not afford.

She admired his writing talent, of course, and his serious cast of mind so strangely at odds with the garish waistcoats and strong cologne he affected. But she disliked the air of proprietorship he had adopted toward her, holding to her elbow if they were in company, wanting to know all her plans, and offering to accompany her everywhere. She very much feared he was courting her and she had no wish to take their relationship to a warmer level.

"May I say that your walking dress suits you admirably? Is it new?"

She murmured that it was fairly new and thanked him for the compliment.

"And what are your plans for this evening? It would be my pleasure to escort you and your aunt, if you are going out."

It was a perfect day for a walk in the park, but Lord Robert was not enjoying himself. Miss Tennyson, the young lady on his arm, was deeply bashful and almost frightened of him. He could not extract a word from her but a barely audible, "Yes, my lord," when he ventured on a topic of conversation. He suppressed a sigh and gave it up. Georgie should be along any minute now and would release them both from this uncomfortable arrangement.

His eyes scanned the lane ahead and he came to a dead halt, alarming Miss Tennyson. He paid the girl no heed. Not Georgie, but *Ann* was there in the preappointed meeting place beneath the spreading copper beech.

There was a man with her. She was leaning on his arm and listening intently to something he was saying.

Rage surged through him. Hell and the devil, but he wanted to plant the fellow a facer! He set off in motion again as abruptly as he had stopped, almost dragging a startled Miss Tennyson with him.

"Good day, *Miss* Forester."

"Oh!" She paled. "Good—good day, Lord Robert. I did not expect to see you here."

"I am quite sure you did not. Is it not a lovely spring day? A perfect day for a walk in the park." His words were strangely at odds with his furious expression darkening his eyes and curling his lips into a sneer.

"Yes, indeed. We were only saying so just now," she said, meeting his glare with one of her own.

His jaw clenched at that "we." "Miss Tennyson," he said turning to the young lady on his arm, "are you acquainted with Miss Forester?"

"How—how do you do, Miss Forester?" Miss Tennyson got out in a croak. She was almost paralyzed with shyness and alarm at the tense undercurrents vibrating from this unlooked-for meeting.

"Are you not going to introduce me to your *friend?*" Lord Robert asked, turning the word into an insult.

Ann made the introduction, but flushed in angry surprise when Lord Robert said, "Have you known Miss Forester long, Allenthorp? She and I are old acquaintances. Is that not right, *Ann,* my dear?" His eyes caressed her intimately.

"A few months is not a long-standing acquaintance, Lord Robert," she corrected, ready to engage him in battle if he were indeed drawing the lines.

"No, not long. But we knew one another *well* enough for it to have seemed like a lifetime's acquaintance."

Allenthorp's eyebrows rose. "That is odd. Miss Forester and I have spoken almost daily for many weeks now and she has not once mentioned *your* name, Lyndhurst."

These words acted like a spark on dry kindling. Almost snarling, Lord Robert took a step closer to them, while Miss Tennyson pulled helplessly on his arm. "Who *are* you, Allenthorp?" he asked arrogantly, looking down his aristocratic nose.

"Hallo, Susan," Georgie called to Miss Tennyson as she appeared round a bend in the path, right on cue. "And Robin, you are here, as well. Why, there is Ann with you, too! May we join the party?" she asked merrily, coming up to them on the arm of a rather well-muscled, scowling young man whom she introduced as Mr. Thomas Cunningham, a friend and neighbor from home.

Lord Robert looked at Georgie blankly, forgetting that she had bade him flirt brazenly with Miss Tennyson when she brought Cunningham in their way. She gave him a conspiratorial look. Recollecting his orders, he decided his doing so now would serve a double purpose.

"Miss Tennyson and I were just remarking on the beauties of the day," Lord Robert said fulsomely, "which I was telling her pale in comparison to her own charms. I am the most fortunate man in London, to have the loveliest lady of my acquaintance on my arm today to help me admire nature's delights." Bending his dark head toward the girl, he turned the full strength of his devastating smile on her.

Susan Tennyson blushed furiously, as he had known she would, making a charming picture.

He flicked a glance at the rest of the group to see Georgie look approving, Cunningham jealous, and Ann stricken. It had been almost too easy.

"Why do we not all walk together?" Georgie exclaimed, as if the idea were just then occurring to her. "We cannot go six abreast. We would not fit on the pathway." She laughed. "I have it! I shall join Ann, if her gentleman friend does not mind, and Tom shall go with you and Lord Robert, Susan."

"It will be my pleasure," Lord Robert said with a smoldering look down at the girl on his arm.

He grimaced but could make no objection when he heard Ann politely decline the arrangement, pleading the excuse that she had to return home in order to practice her music.

"In that case, I believe I shall walk with Robin, while Susan can tell Tom all about what she has been doing since she came to London," Georgie said.

Ann and Allenthorp bid the others a rather stiff farewell.

As he set off with Georgie, Lord Robert saw Ann glance back at them at a bend in the path. He turned to Georgie and smiled into her eyes, exchanging a confidential look.

* * *

"Oh, hello, Miss Forester. Are you choosing a book, too?" a light girlish voice asked.

Ann looked up from the shelves she was perusing in Hookam's circulating library to see Miss Elspeth Gleason standing beside her.

"Good morning, Miss Gleason. Yes, indeed, I am trying to decide between a volume of Mr. Wordsworth's poetry or a copy of the play I am to see at the theatre, Sir George Etherege's *The Man of Mode.* I believe I shall be extravagant and take both."

"Oh, my! Poetry and plays? You are ever such a bluestocking, are you not? I could not read such dull stuff were I to spend ever so long looking at it."

Ann concealed her regret at the girl's foolish pride in her own ignorance. "And what have you chosen?"

"Oh, it is a book by Mrs. Radcliffe, *The Mysteries of Udolpho.* Have you heard of it?"

"Yes, indeed. Not only have I heard of it, I have read it, too. It is quite, ah, thrilling."

"A friend said it was enough to give her the shivers, but I thought I would be brave and try it anyway," Elspeth Gleason explained with an anticipatory shiver of her own.

"Well, I expect you will enjoy it, Miss Gleason."

"Have you heard the latest scandal?" The girl leaned forward with a look of open excitement on her face.

"Er, no," Ann replied warily. She did not want to be trapped into listening to a lot of frivolous, time-wasting, mean-spirited gossip.

"Well, you must know that Lord Robert Lyndhurst was seen kissing Georgie Carteret on a dark balcony at Sarah McIntyre's engagement party last night. But then Georgie came back into the ballroom on Lord Sedgemoor's arm and nothing more was seen of Lord Robert all evening."

Ann's hand went to her heart to press against the sharp pain there.

"Can you credit it?" Miss Gleason asked. "Such a gorgeous gentleman kissing Georgie Carteret? She is hardly the most attractive girl around this spring. But what I would not give to have been in her shoes, if Lord Robert was indeed kissing her!" Miss Gleason let out a long, gusty sigh, a look of moonstruck infatuation on her face.

"What do you think it would be like to be kissed by such a handsome and dangerous rake, Miss Forester? Oh!" A little gloved hand went up to her mouth and she looked over it at Ann out of wide eyes. "I should not ask such a question of a maiden lady. Do say that you will forgive me?"

Ann's heart thudded against her ribs, then her whole body went dead. Her knees sagged beneath her and she put out a hand on the bookshelf to steady herself.

"Oh, dear. I have shocked you," Miss Gleason said.

Taking bracing breaths through her nostrils, she replied, "Really, Miss Gleason, I have no wish to hear about such things. I believe we should spend time improving our minds, not repeating silly, mindless gossip."

The girl looked stunned at this piece of plain speaking. Stammering, she backed away, then turned and fled down the otherwise deserted aisle.

Still supporting herself on the bookshelf with one hand, Ann bowed her head and compressed her lips, willing the faintness to abate. She had known it! Oh, she had known it!

Even two weeks ago when she had seen him walking in the park with the lovely Miss Tennyson and flirting with her outrageously, his eyes had lit up when Georgie had come on the scene. Ann had not missed the fact that they had eventually gone off with their heads together, looking pleased with one another.

Why did she feel so devastated? He had tried to speak with her, had begged to be allowed to visit her. She had turned him away. Could she blame him if he had finally accepted her rejection and turned his attentions elsewhere?

He would have turned to other women eventually, anyway, she rationalized, a dull, heavy feeling making her suddenly very tired.

The charming and dashing Lord Robert Lyndhurst would never devote himself to one woman. She knew that. He would never stay true to a wife, even if he and Georgie—

No. She would not think about that!

She would think about how she had been neglecting her watercolors and her music lately. Yes. She would concentrate on improving the Beethoven piece she had started working on so Herr Müller would be better pleased with her—and on painting the newly budding leaves she could see outside her bedchamber window, coming into bloom in her aunt's garden below.

And she would distract herself with Mr. Allenthorp's company. He was a worthy gentleman, unlike—

No! She absolutely refused to think of *him* anymore.

Thirteen

"What happened to your face, R-Robin?" Chubby asked in astonishment as he walked unannounced into the dining room of his cousin's bachelor establishment to find his relative at breakfast two mornings after Lord Robert had suffered a double disaster.

"Chubby! Where did you spring from, old man?" Throwing aside his serviette, Robin got up from the table to welcome his cousin. "Didn't know you ever came up to London."

"C-came up to town with Betsy, m'fiancée, you know. She did not want to buy a trousseau before we were m-married. Said she could do just as well with the things she already had. But I insisted." Chubby puffed out his chest and looked almost redoubtable for a moment.

"This forcefulness is a new come-out for you, is it not, Chub?" Lord Robert hid his smile, thinking how his relative had previously been cowed by his rather intimidating mama. Was Betsy wise enough to see that Chubby should be encouraged to make his own decisions? Sight unseen she met with his approval, if so.

"What the d-deuce happened to you, Robin? Look like you've been through a m-meatgrinder."

The words *I was proposing to a lady and another suitor objected rather violently* ran through his head, but he rejected them as reflecting too little to his credit, saying instead, "Er, I ran into a rather solid and quite powerful object in the dark. Comes of having my eyes closed and not seeing it coming at the time," he confessed ruefully, thinking that Sedgemoor's fist had indeed been rather powerful, and as he had been kissing Georgie with closed eyes at the time, he had not seen it coming.

He had been blind, too, to the strong attraction Sedgemoor had lately exhibited toward Georgie. He had not taken into account how much Georgie had been in Sedgemoor's company that spring. Why had he never considered the possibility that there might be something between the pair? Enough to cause them to marry postehaste the very day after his own disastrous proposal to Georgie.

His precipitous proposal had been a mismanaged business all round. He had thought that Georgie would make a lively little companion and help forget his lingering feelings for Ann.

He supposed Georgie had been right all along. She had insisted that he was still in love with Ann and that his feelings for *her* were only of the friendly variety.

"Impressive, is it not?" Lord Robert said aloud, fingering the purple and yellow bruises on his face.

"R-rather!" Chubby exclaimed. "But how c-came you to be so careless?"

He sighed. "It is a long—and not very edifying—story that does not redound to my credit. I was rather blind . . . Come and sit down and have some breakfast. Ah, you have already eaten? Well, just a cup of coffee, then."

Although agreeing only to the coffee, Chubby absently filled his plate and sat eating his way through a second breakfast as he expounded on the many worthy attributes and virtues of his beloved. Robin leaned his chin on his fisted hand and listened with a wry smile as Chubby chattered on.

"I say, R-Robin. You *will* come to my wedding next autumn and stand up with me, will you not? That's why I have come to call on you, but it slipped my m-mind until just now."

"You unman me, my boy. You want me to stand up with you and lend you support? Me, who has been such an opponent of marriage? Are you sure you are asking the right chap?"

" 'Course I am. Always admired you. And I d-didn't think you were so opposed to matrimony anymore. Goin' to marry Miss Forester, ain't you?"

Lord Robert leaned back in his chair, took a long sip of coffee and looked at his relative through half-closed lids. " 'Fraid you are out there, my boy. Miss Forester is an acquaintance merely."

"Eh? But you was k-kissing her at Aunt Lydia's—and you had that m-moonstruck look on your face for days after. Everyone said so."

"No," Lord Robert said with a hard edge to his voice as he sat up straighter in his chair. "You—and they—are mistaken. Let it be clear. There was absolutely nothing between Miss Forester and me."

Chubby regarded him skeptically. "Well, if you say so, Robin."

Chubby left, eventually, with the promise to introduce his Betsy to Robin at the first opportunity. Lord Robert watched him go with a bemused smile, thinking that the boy had finally grown up and out of his mama's control. At only one-and-twenty, Chub seemed to be making something positive of his life. Unlike himself.

Here he was at eight-and-twenty, with two rejected proposals in four months and nothing before him but emptiness.

Well, he thought, fingering his bruised face, being knocked out by a jealous rival was hardly the answer he had expected to his proposal of marriage to Georgie. Quite content with his bachelorhood, despite being forced to live somewhat strapped for funds, he had once thought to maintain his freedom forever. Now in the space of a few months, he had proposed to two very different women—with equally unpleasant results.

He supposed he should be thankful that it was only his pride, rather than his heart, that was bruised this time.

Impatiently, he threw down the newspaper he was staring at and stood up, trying to throw off his morose mood. He needed a brisk ride in the park to blow away the bluedevils and to Hades with his bruised face! It would not be too visible from a distance. Seated atop a horse he should not cause too many ladies to faint, he decided sardonically, though he had cancelled plans to attend a play that evening. To be seen at the theatre with his still colorful phiz would never do!

Taking his hack from the mews, he proceeded to the nearby Hyde Park at a fast clip. He had just circled the park's riding track once when his eye caught a tall lady whose familiar way of holding her head caused his heart to beat faster.

Ann! He was sure it was she. And on the arm of that same shabby-genteel fellow she had been with when he had last seen her several weeks ago.

What the deuce? Did the damned mawworm live in her pocket, then?

He rode forward to investigate. Once he was level with the pair, he slowed his horse and glanced across at them. Sweeping off his hat, he inclined his head, deliberately catching Ann's eye and forcing her to look at him. "Good afternoon, Miss Forester."

Ann nodded once stiffly, then turned her head away, refusing to further acknowledge his greeting, then her eyes, wide with alarm, jerked back in his direction.

Damnation! She had noticed his face. He had forgot about it and the shock it might cause a lady of tender sensibilities.

His lips curled as he replaced his hat on his head. Ignoring Allenthorp, he touched his hat briefly with his crop to Ann and rode on.

Hell and the devil take it! he swore under his breath as he put his spurs to his horse and scandalized the passersby by sending his mount into a full gallop, she would think he had been involved in some scandalous doings. And there was no way he could explain the matter to her that would reflect to his credit.

He rode on to his sister Emily's in a foul mood, more angry and upset than he had been by Georgie's visit the previous day to inform him that she had married Sedgemoor.

"Heavens, my dear, will you not sit down and have some tea? You are making me giddy with all this pacing about," Lady Emily said to her brother, whose long strides were taking him from one side of her small parlor to the other and back again in quick succession. "What has you so restless, anyway? And will you not tell me about the mill that has left these fading bruises on your face?"

"They are nothing to signify . . . Do not worry. I am not about to create another scandal," he said with the travesty of a smile.

"Well, what is it then that has you pacing like a caged tiger?"

Picking up a paperweight from the delicately-fashioned lady's escritoire set against one wall, Lord Robert turned to face his sister. "I am thinking of going to Coniston, Em."

Lady Emily's teacup clattered in her saucer as she set it down abruptly. "Are you, my dear? You are finally going to take up your duties at the property Grandfather Belvoir left you?"

He tossed the paperweight up and down in his hands. " 'Tis time. I have felt very unsettled in town this spring. I should like to feel that I have done something to put my life in some sort of order before I am thirty. That is less than two years off now."

"You—a sheep farmer? I cannot believe it! Will you not be lonely in the Lake District? The area around Lake Coniston is not very highly populated, I believe."

"That makes no matter. I shall have my friends—and family—" he smiled at her "—to stay from time to time. Once the place is habitable, that is."

"Well, Papa will be pleased—as will Dick . . . We all will. But this is all so sudden."

"Yes, well, I am not doing it for them." He put down the bibelot, stuck his hands in his pockets and walked to the window.

"Do you feel like talking about it, my dear?" Lady Emily murmured. She knew enough about men not to push too hard for confidences, though she was consumed by curiosity. This come-out was not at all like her younger brother. Was there a woman at the bottom of it?

"Nothing to talk about." He grinned. "Women are always imagining secrets. Did you know that Chubby is about to get married?" he asked, abruptly changing the subject.

"Is he? How wonderful. He has long needed to step from behind Lavinia's skirts. Who is he marrying? Do we know her?"

"A widow named Betsy, with two children. Er, she is several years his senior, I believe."

"Not a fortune hunter, I hope?"

"I do not know. Chub does not really have much of a fortune, anyway . . . But, even if she is, perhaps she will make old Chub happy."

"Let us hope so," Lady Emily said dryly. "I shall have to investigate this matter further. I shall have him to tea. Where did you say he is staying?"

Robin gave her Chubby's direction as he walked over to her tea table and allowed her to give him some of the souchong tea she favored.

While she poured him a cup from her blue and white china pot decorated with pagodas and willow trees, she asked casually, "Robin, my dear, were you thinking of leaving town soon?"

"Fairly soon, yes."

"Please. Do not leave town until after my salon next week."

"What is this, Em?" He squinted at her, trying to decipher what was going through her mind.

"As a widow, you know, I sometimes find the lack of a man's support at my salons rather awkward. I—I require *your* support. I am having some interesting people and I wish you to be there. Promise now."

He hooted. "Require my support? Since when, Em? You have been making your own way close on nine years ago now," he teased her, but after more wheedling from her, he eventually gave the required promise.

"And how do you like this naughty play, my dear Henrietta?" Lady Wycombe was saying to Mrs. Jermyn as they stood outside their boxes during the interval of the evening performance at Drury Lane Theatre. The play in question was a revival of Sir George Etherege's Restoration comedy, *The Man of Mode.*

"I am quite scandalized," Lady Wycombe pronounced in stentorian tones before Mrs. Jermyn could open her mouth to give her opinion.

Ann stood beside her aunt, thinking over her impressions of Harriet and Dorimant, the play's battling lovers, and smiling to herself. Harriet was a woman after her own heart. One who would stand up to her rakish suitor and keep him in line, verbally besting him time after time.

She wished she could share her thoughts with someone of like-minded disposition. Lady Emily Gwent came to mind. Her eyes scanned the crowd, unconsciously looking for her friend. They widened a moment later when she spied someone quite different.

"Oh! There is Georgie—I mean Lady Sedgemoor, Aunt Henrietta. I should offer my felicitations on her recent nuptials." Mrs. Jermyn absently waved her away.

"Lady Sedgemoor, I congratulate you on your recent marriage," Ann said as she approached Georgie. "I must say, you took us all by surprise."

"Oh, Ann, call me Georgie, do. I shall not know to whom you are speaking, if you address me as 'Lady Sedgemoor.' I doubt if I shall ever recognize myself by that name." Georgie laughed merrily.

Ann laughed, too, relaxing under Georgie's friendly charm.

She watched as Georgie glanced back over her shoulder. Ann followed her gaze and saw that Viscount Sedgemoor, Georgie's husband of two days, was speaking with two members of Parliament and a government minster.

Georgie took her elbow and pulled her aside to exchange a few private words.

"I hope you will soon find it in your heart to forgive Robin, Ann," Georgie said boldly, coming straight to the point. "I've had the whole story of the misunderstanding that occurred between the two of you last Christmas from the poor boy, and he really does regret the incident that led to your estrangement most sincerely."

"Georgie, it is all over and done with now. No need to open old wounds. I'm sure we have both gone on with our normal pursuits, and have put the incident behind us," Ann said somewhat haltingly, feeling her heart break at the subject being reopened and by one, too, whom she had thought was romantically involved with Lord Robert.

"Oh, Ann. I am sorry you feel so, my dear. Come, can you not forgive him? He *is* suffering, you know. And I think you are, too . . . I *do* hate to see my friends suffering."

Ann did not deny it. "Georgie, my dear, you have too kind a heart," she said instead. "I—I saw them together you know. He was holding her. Kissing her—I think."

"But perhaps he never intended to seduce the woman. He was just holding her to console her, not wanting to embarrass her too much by rejecting her out of hand."

Ann laughed mirthlessly. "Oh, Georgie. You would defend the devil himself, I believe."

"It was not Robin's fault, you know."

"It *was* his fault. Even if he weren't trying to seduce Lady—ah, the woman in question, such activities are not unknown to him. He is a famous rake," Ann explained patiently, as though Georgie were completely unaware of that fact.

"He loves you, you know."

"Do you think so? I doubt he knows what love is."

Georgie looked at her, her expressive eyes pleading Lord Robert's case in his stead.

Ann sighed. "Georgie, Georgie. I am a plain woman. There are so many beauties to catch his eye."

"You are not! Or, you would not be," Georgie amended candidly, "if you changed your hairstyle and wore more modish gowns—the pink muslin you are wearing tonight does not sit well with your dark coloring. You should make the most of your assets."

"My assets? I did not think I had any."

Georgie clucked her tongue. "Your eyes have quite an unusual almond shape and their warm amber color is glorious. Striking, with your smooth olive skin. You should wear hues that compliment your unique coloring. Cream and dark blue—perhaps dark green, too," Georgie said, considering Ann's face. "And you are quite tall and willowy—regal looking, in fact. And you carry yourself so elegantly. How I envy you! I am such a dwarf there is no doing *anything* to make me appear taller."

"It is kind of you to take an interest, Georgie, but it is really of no use. Even if I were as pretty as you, my—my personality is rather dull."

"Me, pretty! No, I am not in the least." Georgie scoffed at the notion. "And with your kindness and wit and refinement of mind, not to mention your brilliant musical and artistic talents, you are the opposite of dull, Ann. You are just a bit reserved. But everyone who comes to know you, loves you," Georgie said sincerely to Ann's great embarrassment. "Will you not speak with Robin? Be friends with him again?"

Ann shook her head. "How could I ever trust him? Could you trust a man who was a notorious lover of many women? A man who might continue to pursue his rakish proclivities even after you had become his wife?"

"But, my dear Ann, that is exactly what I have done," Georgie answered, her eyes gleaming with a touch of humor and a touch of something else as she referred to Viscount Sedgemoor, her new husband.

"Oh, Georgie, forgive me!" Ann said, her eyes full of contrition.

Georgie hugged her. "Never mind, my dear. I can handle Gus. His philandering days are over, believe me."

"Thank you for your concern, Georgie. I confess that I had quite thought that perhaps you and Robin—"

Georgie looked back at her wide-eyed, shaking her head.

"Well, no. I suppose I was being overly fanciful. For all he is so charming, so appealing—and I do not mean just because he is so very handsome—I can never allow myself to fall completely in love with Robin. I cannot bring myself ever to trust him entirely. We are from such very different worlds, you know . . . our ideas, our values are so very dissimilar," Ann said sincerely, trying to make Georgie see that a match between Lord Robert Lyndhurst and herself would never come to pass. "You do understand, Georgie? And you will not continue to press me?"

"Yes, I do understand, my dear. I wish—well, I wish you all the best, and I will only press you to one thing. Will you not come to the party Gus and I are giving to celebrate our recent marriage with all of our friends?"

Touched by being included among Georgie's legion of friends, Ann smiled and agreed that she would try to come for a brief while. She realized as she walked back to her aunt that she had accepted out of curiosity more than anything else. She was intrigued by Georgie's marriage to the arrogant and aloof Viscount Sedgemoor. He was a strikingly handsome man with his thick blond hair and clear grey eyes that seemed to penetrate right into one's thoughts. But with his perfect manners and his reputation as a stickler for propriety, the viscount was a complete contrast to the lively, unconventional Georgie with her red hair and freckles and vivacious, effervescent personality. Their marriage could not but excite everyone's interest and curiosity.

Fourteen

Ann ducked under a low-hanging garland festooning the well-proportioned room and gazed in some wonder at all the gaily-costumed people standing about laughing and talking, flirting and eating, grabbing drinks and food from trays being circulated by costumed servants.

She had come to the masquerade alone. Mrs. Jermyn was visiting elderly friends in Richmond for several days, and although she disapproved of masquerades in principle, she was mollified by the stellar reputation of Viscount Sedgemoor's family, the St. Regises. And when Lady Emily Gwent had offered Ann her chaperonage and a seat in her carriage, Mrs. Jermyn had reluctantly given her permission for Ann to attend the affair.

Unfortunately, Lady Emily had sent round a note that morning saying that she was laid down on her bed with a sick headache and could not accompany Ann after all, although she would still send her own carriage at eight o'clock as promised.

Ann had sat down to write a note to Georgie excusing herself from the party, but as her pen moved in precise strokes over the vellum, she had changed her mind. The curiosity that had burned in her when Georgie had mentioned the masquerade at the theatre was still burning brightly. And so she decided to go. Alone.

It was not quite the thing, but she was five-and-twenty, no longer a young girl. Why not be daring for once in her life? she asked herself. She had never been to so risqué an occasion as a masquerade and she wanted to go. She tried to tell herself it was *not* because Lord Robert Lyndhurst might be there.

Ann looked about her in some trepidation as she moved about the grand room. Her own costume was in stark constrast to the exotic and gorgeous raiment of many of the other guests. Despite Georgie's rather outrageous idea that she dress as a wild maenad, a follower of the god Dionysus, and wear an exotic, revealing costume, Ann had dressed simply—as a prioress.

She was glad to hide behind the concealing white robes and veil that effectively covered her from head to foot. That way she could better observe others.

Many guests were garbed in half masks and dominoes of a staggering number of colors, brown, white, black, red, blue, pink, and green among them. Shepherds and shepherdesses cavorted, King Henry VIIIs and Anne Boelyns danced, Queen Elizabeths and Sir Francis Drakes flirted, one-eyed pirates and cutthroat buccaneers circled one another, noble Romans and Greek gods and goddesses reclined regally on the chairs set up along the walls, and a host of other characters milled about, laughing, flirting, talking, dancing.

She looked around at all the glittering costumes, marveling at the variety and richness that met her eye. Velvet and satin, silk and lace, some rich with gold and silver embroidery, some subtle and witty, some blatant and profane, some filmy, scanty and revealing, scandalously showing off the figures of their wearers, both male and female—all shocked or amused her by turns.

"Good evening, oh most holy prioress. My queen and I hope that you will enjoy the festivities," a deep voice said at her side.

Ann looked up and gasped. Realizing that the man standing before her behind the glittering golden mask was indeed her host, the dignified Lord Sedgemoor, welcoming her to the party, she had to stifle her urge to laugh. "G-good evening, my lord," she got out with a somewhat straight face.

Her dignified host was garbed as Oberon, king of the fairies from Shakespeare's *A Midsummer Night's Dream.* He was clad in a skimpy though richly patterned brown, green, gold, and rust knee-length chiton that barely reached his knees, with a crown of leaves and twigs in his rich blond hair, and golden sandals on his feet, bound with long leather thongs round his calves. He looked almost ridiculous—except he was so handsome in his revealing costume that he did not really look ridiculous at all, but very masculine and extremely attractive. She had to avert her gaze and was glad of her concealing veil to hide her blush.

"Oh, Ann! Is that you?" Georgie asked with a happy smile under her mask of blue and green feathers as she came dancing up. "I am so glad you have come." Spangles glittered in her red hair as she sneezed. She reached to readjust her feathered mask. "Pardon me. These feathers tickle my nose."

"I must not admit my identity until midnight, oh Queen Titania," Ann said in a low voice. "Is that not the rule at masquerades, your majesty?"

Georgie chuckled. "I knew Ann would recognize us, Gus. Did I not tell you so?" she said to her husband. "You are only the second person who knows who we are meant to be, Ann. Heigh ho, I suppose no one reads Shakespeare these days."

Georgie was dressed as Titania, Oberon's consort. She wore a shimmering blue and green silk undershift over one shoulder, covered by a gauze overdress of spun gold that caught the light and glittered whenever she moved. Soft, flesh-colored kid slippers covered her feet, making them appear bare. She looked an enchanted woodland creature, indeed, Ann thought.

"And now some of my magic potion for you," Georgie said, gaily sprinkling sparkling golden dust over Ann's head and shoulders.

"What in the world, Georgie?" Ann asked laughing.

"Magic dust," Georgie whispered, leaning near. "A love potion to enchant recalcitrant lovers."

"Oh, no—you promised you would give up that scheme!"

"I never give up," Georgie said with a bewitching smile for her husband as she danced off, scattering her dust over everyone in sight as she went, her laugh floating back to them on the air. Off she went spreading gaiety, literally and figuratively sprinkling her magic dust, hoping that love would bloom.

"Tell me, Madame Prioress, do you feel that my consort has

got above herself?" Sedgemoor asked rhetorically. "Shall I have my servant Puck enchant her so that she becomes enamored of an ass?"

"I am sure, my king, that Titania would give all her love to any creature who caught her eye."

"Your wisdom undoes me. I commend you, holy lady," he said. "Feel free to move about outside, if it grows too stuffy in here. Georgiana has had all the paths lighted." So saying, the viscount bowed and moved away, leaving a trail of golden dust in his wake.

Feeling unlike herself, Ann's heart beat faster with excitement. The atmosphere all around her was wildly exciting—and just a bit wicked. She felt liberated, and a bit wicked herself. She was glad to be concealed as she was, but in some ways she wished she had worn a different costume, one that would allow her to express the sense of fun and freedom she felt tonight.

When Georgie had suggested the maenad's costume, she had shaken her head and laughed in exasperated amusement. "You know that I am far too sensible a person for that."

The new viscountess had cocked her head and Ann had recognized her expression. It was full of devilment. "Well, if you insist on dressing as a holy nun, you can be Heloise," was Georgie's inspired suggestion.

"And I suppose Lord Robert is to be Abelard. Well, you know what happened to him!" Ann had riposted with an uncharacteristically mischievous grin. Then she had sobered. "Georgie, you must abandon your plans to reconcile me with Rob—Lord Robert."

"You are being foolish beyond permission, Ann, but I will abandon the two of you to your fate—for the time being. If all goes according to plan, Gus and I will be leaving town in the next day or two to spend part of our honeymoon at the Oaks, Gus's estate in Gloucestershire, you know."

"Oh! How delightful!" Ann had exclaimed, sensing that there had been some trouble between the newly wedded pair recently.

From what she had seen of them this evening, it looked as though all was on the way to being resolved.

A couple Ann had met at a musicale she had attended with her aunt approached and she exchanged a few words with them. Out of the corner of her eye, she noticed a bold cavalier from the court of King Charles II lounging negligently against the mantelpiece. One leg covered in thigh-high black leather boots with deep cuffs was cocked up behind him, resting against the marble surround. His whole pose was casual and relaxed, and utterly confident. He was laughing with a suitably rotund, disreputable-looking Falstaff in a long red wig under his outrageous feathered hat.

A familiar feeling of breathlessness came over her as she beheld the way the cavalier's costume of black velvet and silver lace became his tall figure. A black half mask outlined with silver spangles covered his eyes, while a shoulder-length French periwig of gleaming black curls concealed his own dark locks. A short black cape edged with silver was flipped over one broad shoulder and a pair of thick gloves was tucked in his wide, sash-like belt. Silver lace edged his full-skirted black jacket that ended at mid-thigh and cascades of frothy white lace at his neck and jacket sleeves caressed the darker skin of his throat and hands. One beringed hand rested lightly on the hilt of a lethal-looking rapier slung low at his waist.

Unlike the revealing garb of several gentlemen at the masque, his costume covered him completely. Nonetheless, he looked striking and mysterious and . . . well, her mind struggled to admit the word—vitally masculine.

And almost indecently attractive.

Would she ever be able to free herself of his hold on her heart? she despaired.

The pair she was speaking with moved off. Unable to help herself, Ann continued to watch her cavalier surreptitiously. Circling the room, she moved closer, drawn by his compelling presence like a moth to the flame.

Her cavalier turned to an Elizabethan gentleman distinctively attired in doublet and hose. Sir Francis Drake laughed. The sound, low and throaty, assailed Ann's ears, sending a chill through her. This Sir Francis was a woman! A woman whose tall, elegant figure and long, shapely legs were enhanced by the daring costume.

Lord Robert reached forward and flicked the woman's false moustache, flirting with her outrageously.

Ann turned her shoulder and walked away, her thawing heart freezing once more.

Lord Robert watched appreciatively as Diana, Lady Carstairs swaggered away. She had chosen a daring costume, dressing as an Elizabethan courtier. Not all women could get away with wearing doublet and hose. Undoubtedly the tall and lithe, delectable Diana was one who could. He wondered suddenly what Ann would look like garbed thus. He grinned, then frowned, thinking that he should not like her to make such an exhibition of herself for all the world to see. If she ever wore such a thing, it would be for his eyes only.

Good God!

His eyes followed the woman clad in the ghostly white robe and coiffed headdress, sailing away from him with stiffened back, her hands crossed in front of her and folded inside her long, draping sleeves. That was Ann, or he was a tinker's tailor!

Georgie had hinted that Ann would be there and admonished him to make the most of the opportunity.

He lifted his shoulders away from the mantelpiece and prepared to follow his prioress, then relaxed back again when he saw Sedgemoor approaching, giving him a black look.

His teeth gleamed in the semblance of a smile under his half mask while he touched the hilt of his French rapier lightly with his fingertips.

Robin was rewarded for his bit of brazen provocation when he saw the viscount's lips tighten in a ferocious scowl, but Sedgemoor did not take up the subtly offered challenge. The viscount passed on by, seemingly searching for someone. Undoubtedly his lady wife, Robin thought with a touch of wry humor and a touch of melancholy. Would that he were searching for his own wife! Ann.

As he searched the rooms for his bride, out of the corner of his eye Sedgemoor saw the nun garbed in white from head to toe disappear behind the curtains drawn across one of the deep window embrasures at the side of the room. He walked on, taking no further notice of this bit of impropriety. He had more urgent matters to attend to.

"Let me go, my lord! It is not at all proper that you have pulled me back here behind this curtain with you."

Her tormentor had just boldly reached out and pulled her into this concealed window embrasure with him. Furious and confused, Ann held her breath and tried not to let his physical proximity overwhelm her.

"Ho! Miss Prim and Proper, are you? Dressed as a holy nun . . . That's a bit rich after last Christmas, Ann," he drawled, his green eyes glittering through the slits in his mask.

"How dare you!"

He caught her hand as it flashed toward his cheek and held it in a strong grip. "No. You shall not hit me again. I carried the imprint of your hand for days last time."

"Let me go, Lord Robert, or I shall call out."

"Promise you will not hit me."

She nodded warily, the coif of her nun's headdress dipping down low over the white mask covering her eyes.

He flicked the headdress with a long finger. "Why have you covered all your glorious hair with this monstrosity, Ann?"

"My hair is not 'glorious' in the least."

"It *is* glorious. When it's all loose and spread about your shoulders."

She took two steps back from him. "What do you want?"

All evening, she had been fighting her attraction for him, trying to banish the thought that he was the most dashing man in the room. She had alternately wanted to speak with him, hoping that he would seek her out, and then deliberately avoided him. Now, his very real, very masculine, and very *threatening* presence scattered her thoughts like so much chaff in the wind. She felt hot and suffocated again.

"A few words. A few *kind* words, perhaps?" One side of his mouth quirked up in a half smile under his mask.

"There is nothing more to be said, my lord."

"There are *volumes* more to be said." He reached out and took her hand, holding it gently in his, playing with her fingers, making swirling motions with his thumb against her ungloved palm.

Ann looked up at him and saw the softened look in his green eyes as he gazed down at her. They stood speechless for a long moment.

"Forgive me," he whispered contritely, looking directly into her eyes.

"I—" Ann began, wavering. It was so tempting to do so. To have him take her in his arms once more and tell her that she was important to him.

As he was to her.

She gazed up at him mutely, words of forgiveness hovering on her lips, and saw his eyes drop to her mouth. His head slowly descended toward hers. His eyes closed behind his mask and her lips parted.

Someone pushed the curtain back, exposing the tableau to the view of the whole room. "Oh, ho! What have we here? A lover's tryst? A naughty nun and the Earl of Rochester, if I mistake not," the intruder exclaimed. "How intriguing!"

Ann pulled her hand from his and fled.

"Devil take it! Devil take it! Devil take it!" Lord Robert swore, pounding one fisted hand into the palm of the other as his long strides carried him along the fashionable London thoroughfares, now dark and almost deserted, that separated the Sedgemoors' townhouse from his own more modest quarters.

An eerie, smoky haze had begun to rise as cooler air floating up from the river collided with the still warm streets.

A patch of mist floated in front of his eyes and he swiped at it with a gloved hand, glowering the harder and sending forth a more spine-tingling imprecation as he slapped the silver-chased handle of the rapier at his side.

So strange did he look in his outdated costume with his black cape billowing behind him in the slight breeze, and so forbidding his expression and glittering his eyes behind his silver-edged half mask, that the few passersby who ventured along the dark pathway could be forgiven for thinking he conjured his familiar.

The few who passed him gave him a wide berth, eyeing askance the rapier gleaming in its silver scabbard at the side of the mysterious, tall, dark gentleman garbed all in black and silver whose silver spurs were ringing on the pavement as he passed.

He paid the passersby no mind, making his way home at that midnight hour.

His thoughts were all directed inward. It had been a disappointment when he learned that Georgie was married. But it was really Ann. Always Ann.

Georgie had simply been an amusing diversion for a brief span.

He had had his opportunity that evening to speak privately with Ann. Been on the point of explaining himself and begging forgiveness at long last when some bore had interrupted them and she had fled.

And he had lost his chance.

He could not take much more of this emotional upheaval. The lady would not take him back. It was just no use.

No use at all.

He could not enjoy himself in town any more. He was not the same carefree buck he had been since the upheaval in his life at Christmas.

He would leave for Coniston and his farm there in the Lake District by the end of the week. Perhaps there among the lakes and mountains and fells he could find some peace of spirit. But first there was this deuced salon of Emily's to attend on Thursday. He had solemnly given his word that he would look in. His sister had promised him some interesting company and lively conversation and a very special musical performance, but despite his love of music, his heart was not in it.

"Devil take it!" he growled once more.

Fifteen

In the days after Georgie's masquerade ball, Ann retired from social life, keeping a low profile. She had her aunt's butler turn Mr. Allenthorp away when he came to ask her to walk in the park with him. And she even cancelled her lessons with Herr Müller for a week, knowing that his nephew would insist on accompanying her home, whether she walked or took a hackney carriage. She did not wish to see Mr. Allenthorp, or any other gentleman.

She did not wish to go out at all. Even the park was not a safe destination. She did not want to chance another encounter with Lord Robert.

She did not want to think about how he had almost had her saying that, yes, she would forgive him. Nor did she wish to be reminded of how she had been longing for him to kiss her again, hoping desperately that he would do so. She did not want to think about how she had risked breaking her heart all over again for one mad moment there at the masquerade.

And so she kept to her aunt's house, devoting herself to her music and her art. She would practice on the pianoforte in the morning, then after luncheon she would set up her easel outside where the sun-warmed garden beckoned. She would forget the world beyond the garden's secluded green boundaries as she tried to capture nature's subtle colors and textures and outlines in her watercolors.

Trying to transfer the impossible passion that was eating away at her heart into something positive, she imbued her playing and painting with all the passion in her soul, pouring it out into her art.

Ann lifted her face to the sun. It was a lovely, warm day, less than a week after the masquerade. She had ventured outside today with only an old smock over her gown. A bee flitted by, making for the new-opened flowers whose strong scent was perfuming the garden.

She half closed her eyes and tried to see through the veil of her lashes the colors of the flowers just coming into bloom through new eyes.

Mixing her watercolors in deeper hues than she ever had before, she tried to capture the essence of the velvety interior of a rose petal, the green of the leaves, shading into yellow or brown in certain spots. She used a deeper green for the leaves and bolder lines to outline the veins in those leaves. For some reason today it seemed important to look deep into things, to capture their essence.

In the same way, she was trying to delve deeper into her music, trying to master the new Beethoven piano sonata that she had been working on with Herr Müller. It was one of the sonatas Beethoven himself had called *Sonatas quasi una fantasia*—sonatas like a fantasy. Herr Müller told her that Heinrich Friedrich Rellstab, a distingushed German music critic, had christened it the "Moonlight Sonata" because it reminded him of moonlight reflected on water.

She had loved it from the first moment Herr Müller had played it for her. It moved her in a way no music ever had before. It was unutterably romantic. In playing the piece over and over again, she had come to understand that it was the very essence of Romanticism in music, combining wild outbreaks of passion with the most delicate lyricism.

She was to play the piece at Lady Emily's salon on Thursday. She had been hesitant about giving so public a performance, but Lady Emily had persuaded her that it was not fair to hide her talent from those who would so greatly appreciate it.

"And my brother is to attend," Lady Emily had mentioned. "I

have been trying to persuade him to come to one of my little gatherings this age. I know he would greatly enjoy hearing you play."

"Your eldest brother?" Mrs. Jermyn had asked with interest.

"Oh, no. One of my younger brothers. Indeed, this brother is the music lover of the family. He has loved music since he was a child. Always nagging to be allowed to learn the piano along with me and our other sisters. In much the same way that I nagged to be allowed to learn Latin and Greek with my brothers." Lady Emily had laughed and shared a look of mutual understanding with Ann.

"Oh, do say you will play for Lady Emily, my dear," Mrs. Jermyn had urged. "I am sure you have worked hard enough to have perfected the piece so that you could give a command performance before the king himself! That is, if he were not quite mad, poor fellow."

And so Ann had reluctantly agreed.

When Ann and Mrs. Jermyn arrived at Lady Emily Gwent's drawing room on Thursday evening, the atmosphere in the crowded room in George Street was electric. At first Ann thought that her frisson of excitement was caused by her nervousness about performing.

She soon realized the reason for the charged atmosphere a few minutes later when Lady Emily introduced her to Miss Fanny Burney.

"My dear Fanny, here is someone after our own hearts. Let me make you known to Miss Ann Forester. She is a firm believer in the full and *equal* education of women," Lady Emily said with a warm smile.

"Is she, indeed? Then I am glad to know her." Miss Burney extended two fingers to Ann.

Thrilled to have a private word with the famous authoress, Ann told Miss Burney that she had read *Evelina, Cecilia, Camilla,* and *The Wanderer,* and thoroughly enjoyed them all.

Basking in the glow of Ann's praise for her books, Miss Burney unbent enough to reminisce about a few of the intellectual women she had known. When she mentioned the intriguing personality and brilliant conversationalist, Madame de Staël, Ann eagerly asked for her impressions of the woman.

"Yes, Miss Forester, I did meet Germaine—Barone de Staël-Holstein, as she was then—at Juniper Hall in Mickelham, near London. In 1793, it was. She was with Narbonne—Louis de Narbonne-Lara, an extremely handsome and gifted gentleman, who had been Minister of War in France before the Revolution in 1792. They had both of them come to England to escape the troubles in their own country.

"She was very plain, while he was extraordinarily handsome. I believe her intellectual endowments must have been her sole attraction for him . . . I refused to believe the gossip that Narbonne and Germaine were living in adultery," Miss Burney continued. "As I wrote to my father, I believed it to be a gross calumny. She loved him very tenderly, but so openly, so unaffectedly, and with such utter freedom from all coquetry that I believe they shared a pure but exalted friendship."

Ann blushed at this plain speaking of relations between persons not married to one another, but she was fascinated despite herself. Could a handsome man love a plain woman for accomplishments alone? she wondered.

Miss Burney moved on and Mr. Allenthorp joined Ann with a compliment on her appearance.

"You are looking well tonight, Miss Forester. Better than well—elegant, I should say," he said fulsomely.

She smiled with pleasure. She *had* taken special pains when she dressed that evening in anticipation of having the eyes of Lady Emily's guests on her while she played.

Although she had long claimed that she took no interest in her appearance, Georgie's words at the theatre had worked on her; she had consulted a London dressmaker and had had a few new dresses made up. Tonight she wore a new gown of pale ivory cream silk embroidered with delicate willow green leaves outlined with gold threads. Her only ornaments were a small emerald pendant suspended on a thin gold chain around her neck and matching emerald drop earrings in her ears.

She had tried not to remember Lord Robert's opinion of the colors that would suit her when she had chosen it.

In a spurt of impetuosity which she tried hard to regret afterward—but could not quite bring herself to do—she had had a French coiffeur in to style her hair. He had cut it shorter at the sides, applied a curling iron to form a fringe of curls around her face, and fashioned the rest of it into a loose knot, tied with sprigs of small flowers on top of her head.

When she had gazed at herself in the looking glass before setting out that evening, she had been quite surprised at the difference in her appearance. Her fashionable gown had been cut so that she actually showed some cleavage, despite her small breasts and, all in all, her tall figure looked elegant. Her eyes had glowed and the way they slanted had seemed pleasing rather than odd, as she had always thought.

She had been secretly pleased that she really did not look so very plain, after all.

But she was feeling a bit self-conscious now, especially at the warm look in Mr. Allenthorp's eyes. She was quite in charity with him, however. It was agreeable to have an admirer. It boosted her confidence.

"I have not seen you for a week," he was saying. "Have you been unwell?"

"Er, no. I have been quite busy." She distracted him by asking about how work was progressing on his latest essay. He was expansive on the subject and she was almost regretting that she had given him such an opening. Wishing she could escape from his exclusive company for a time in this rather isolated corner of Lady Emily's drawing room, her eyes darted to other groups conversing nearby.

"And you know, Miss Forester, Wordsworth says in the *Lyrical Ballads* that poetry is emotion recollected in tranquillity. I think that precept applies to all literature. I know I try to follow that rule when I am composing my essays," he pronounced rather self-importantly.

"I am not sure that I agree entirely with Mr. Wordsworth. I believe poetry especially can be written in the heat of emotion also, or when looking at an object that moves or inspires one—a ruined cathedral, for example, or a ghostly ship wrecked and foundering in the pounding waves, the glory of nature all around us, mountains and hills, lakes and forests—oh, so many things."

"The sound of a piano sonata being played to perfection?" A familiar deep voice at her shoulder startled Ann and caused her to spill some of the wine in the glass she held.

"My dear Robin, let me present you properly before you barge into the conversation of strangers," Lady Emily remonstrated. "Ann, may I present my brother, Lord Robert Lyndhurst? Robin, Miss Forester is a dear friend of mine. And here is Mr. Allenthorp, too." Lady Emily smiled at them all.

Ann felt her heart leap up into her throat, and her pulse take wing. She could only stare dumbly as she realized why Lady Emily's features had looked so familiar. Brother and sister resembled one another to a remarkable degree. That resemblance was enhanced by the emerald green velvet gown trimmed with gold lace that Lady Emily wore, complimented by the darker green jacket and gold-threaded waistcoat over a dazzling white shirt Lord Robert affected.

"*Miss* Forester?" He bowed but did not attempt to take her hand. Grateful for that at least, Ann expelled the tiny breath she was holding.

"Lord Robert," she replied through lips that felt as if they were not working properly. She gazed up at his sardonic smile and half closed eyes, the green barely visible through the forest of dark lashes and felt the familiar weakening of her limbs.

Allenthorp bowed stiffly in the face of so much sartorial magnificence and rakish reputation. Seeing Lyndhurst's arrogant glare directed his way, he remembered seeing that same menacing stare in the park and recollected that there was some prior acquaintance between Miss Forester and the tall, dark lord.

"You were discussing the relative merits of how best to compose poetry, I believe. And you were extolling Mr. Wordsworth's *dictum* about emotion recollected in tranquillity, were you not?" Lord Robert directed his question to Allenthorp in a deceptively deferential tone.

Agreeing that that was indeed so, Allenthorp again praised Wordsworth's advice on the composition of poetry.

"I have always found *that* a particularly difficult concept to understand. When I recollect emotion, it is seldom in tranquillity. If I am tranquil about it, then I have forgot what it was that touched my emotions in the first place. On the other hand, I believe Miss Forester was arguing for *passion* as the governing force behind composing good poetry. As she puts so much passion into her music, I believe we must assume she knows of what she speaks. I bow to her superior knowledge."

Lady Emily gave a gurgling laugh. "Why, Robin, I have never heard you argue the merits of 'passion' before. This is a new come-out for you."

"No, Em," he said with a wicked smile, "I have always extolled the merits of passion."

Lady Emily gasped. "Heavens, Robin, you will be having our guests think you speak of improper things," she scolded.

"No, indeed. I speak of things that move the heart—and the soul. Like poetry and music—and love. What could be more proper and admirable?" He gazed directly at Ann and her blush was fiery.

Sensing Lyndhurst's animosity and feeling himself out of his depth, Allenthorp excused himself, looking back at Ann with a frown of displeasure as he walked away.

"You must forgive me, my dear Ann, for gloating like the cat who has got at the cream. I have had little company of my brother this year, so to have him here tonight is a special pleasure for me," Lady Emily said to break the tension of the moment.

"Of course, Lady Emily," Ann agreed, though she hardly knew what she said, her thoughts were in such turmoil. "It is pleasant to have one's family around one. Especially at the holidays." Ann heard herself babbling and cringed inwardly when she realized what she had said.

"Yes, indeed. This naughty boy did not come home for Christmas this year to join the rest of us, disappointing me and Mama and Papa and all his brothers and sisters, too," Lady Emily said with a loving glance at her brother, whose arm was about her waist.

"Not *all* our brothers were disappointed, Em," he corrected, his eyes shadowed.

"You make too much of Dick's ranting and raving at all the rest of us. On occasion, he takes his position as Papa's heir far too seriously, you know, and tries to make up for Papa's laxity . . . Never mind, let us not bore Ann with our family matters. Let me tell you, instead, that Miss Forester agrees with me wholeheartedly about the equal education of girls."

"Indeed, I know that she does. Did you not tell me on one celebrated occasion, Miss Forester, that you wished to learn Greek and that you thought all females should have the same chance as us males to do so?"

"Are you and Ann previously acquainted, Robin?" Lady Emily cried in astonishment.

"Indeed, we are. Is that not so, ma'am?" Lord Robert's green eyes glinted down into Ann's, pinning her to the spot, daring her to deny it.

Feeling her cheeks heat, she admitted rather breathlessly, "Yes. We met at the Abermarles' Christmas party."

"But this is wonderful! Why did I not know? I am sure neither one of you has mentioned the other." Lady Emily laughed and linked her hand in an arm of each.

"I had no idea Lord Robert was your brother," Ann replied a trifle stiffly.

"Why, my dear Ann, you sound as though you disapprove of Robin." Sensing the tension vibrating in the air, Lady Emily glanced from one to the other with a troubled look.

"I am afraid that she does, Em," Lord Robert said, his expression inscrutable.

"What!" Lady Emily shook her brother's arm. "What have you done to give her a disgust of you, Robert Charles Lyndhurst?"

Ann's cheeks were burning now. She could not run away from him this time.

"I am afraid Miss Forester finds me an idle wastrel, Em. And she is in the right of it."

"Oh, nonsense. Is she aware of your plans to go to Coniston and put your affairs in order?"

"As you have just told her so, I daresay she is aware of it now, Em," Lord Robert said with a glint of humor that relieved the tension of the situation somewhat.

Ann searched for something innocuous to say. "I am sure that that is a most worthy goal, my lord."

Lady Emily lowered her dark brows and looked from one to the other of them, a new idea of the nature of the acquaintance between them dawning. "I believe—yes, I really believe the two of you need to talk. Unfortunately, there is no opportunity to do so now. It is time for Ann to play for us. I must introduce her to my guests. Come along, my dear."

"Then we are all in for a rare pleasure," Lord Robert said, extending his arm to Ann with an ironic bow as his sister preceded them.

Not looking at him, but conscious that they were in a drawing room crowded with onlookers, Ann allowed her fingers to rest on the dark green superfine cloth of his jacket sleeve.

"Allow me to turn the pages for you, ma'am," he murmured, giving her no chance to protest, as he handed her to her seat at the instrument.

"I—I would really rather than you did not, my lord," she said in a low voice. The heat from contact with his arm still burned her fingers and quickened her heartbeat. She did not know how she could play with him standing so near, his very presence overwhelming her senses.

"Would I be *that* much of a distraction?" he challenged mockingly.

She lifted her chin. "I trust you will turn the pages at the appropriate time. I would not want to lose my place."

His smile was twisted. "No, indeed. We cannot have you marring your performance because of my unwanted presence. But you need have no fear on the other score. I believe I can read music well enough to perform the office."

Lady Emily quietened the crowd. "Ladies and gentlemen, my guest, Miss Ann Forester, is to favor us tonight with a rendition of the Piano Sonata 14 in C-sharp minor by Herr Ludwig van Beethoven. Miss Forester."

Ann's lips trembled as she smiled briefly at the crowd. Her nerves, already stretched thin at the thought of performing before a room full of London *cognoscenti,* were made worse by Lord Robert's nearness. She quickly looked down at the keys, trying to concentrate, to compose herself, and to put him from her mind.

That he stood near her shoulder, that she could smell his distinctive scent, and feel the heat emanating from his body, did not help her do those things.

She had no time to study his face as she began to play, but once or twice she flicked him a very brief glance and marked the tension there. And when he turned the pages, she saw that his long fingers trembled.

Finally, unable to bear his nearness, to block out his presence, she closed her eyes and played the rest from memory. When she got past the first few bars, she became oblivious to anything but the music, finding peace there.

She had practiced this piece until the usual calluses on her fingers from constant playing had been rubbed raw. Ignoring the pain, she put all the skill at her command into her music. She put her heart and soul into it.

As the notes reverberated in her head, an image superimposed itself behind her closed lids, an image of him boyish and happy as he had been last Christmas, blending and merging with the music.

Forgetting about the room full of people, she played for him.

The final chord died away and Ann rested her fingers in her lap, her head bowed and her eyes still closed.

There. She had done it. She had played it for him, putting all the passion she had discovered in her soul when she had fallen in love with him, all the emotion she had kept locked up in her heart these past months, into her music.

When she finished, there was a hush over the room that was so profound one could have heard the wind sigh.

Then the applause broke out. Wild, enthusiastic applause, and soon many of the guests crowded around the piano, amid cries of, "Brava! Bravissima!"

She opened her eyes, blinked, and looked around. There was no sight of Lord Robert.

Ann walked into the deserted, almost dark library, closed the door behind her and leaned back against its cool wooden surface. She closed her eyes. When she had finished playing, Lady Emily had taken one look at her pale face and suggested that she go there for a time to compose herself before she rejoined the other guests.

She had complied gladly, slipping away while Lady Emily prevented Mr. Allenthorp from following her.

She felt empty—as though all her passion were spent. Her long, graceful fingers smoothed over her gown. She had been proud of the way her fingers had rendered the music, the way her mind had been able to concentrate despite her emotional upheaval at the moment. She knew that she had done the music justice, despite the fact that Herr Müller felt a mere woman could never do justice to the master. She wished he had been there to hear her.

No, she did not. He would have intimidated her. She would have been a pupil playing for her teacher, trying to please him, instead of playing for herself.

Yes, it had been good. And it felt wonderful to know that she had given her best.

She felt the air stirring against her face and opened her eyes. Robin was standing before her with a tender look on his face.

He opened his arms and she walked into them without a word. Closing her eyes, she rested her forehead against his shoulder, turning her face into his neck. He rocked her for a time, his arms holding her comfortingly.

It felt so good to be there. So right.

Don't speak. Please do not speak, she prayed silently.

If he spoke, she would have to come back to reality. To remember how he had betrayed her and caused her such heartbreak. To remember that she must not allow him back into her heart to do further damage. To remember that she must send him away from her, if she ever expected to regain a semblance of peace in her life.

"I do not have the words to tell you how magnificent that was," he whispered in a voice unsteady with emotion. "Some god was with you tonight, my angel of music."

"Oh, no! Please!" she breathed, pulling away and lifting her hands to ward him off. "Do not—"

Before she realized what he meant to do, he went down on one knee before her and possessed himself of her hands. "Ann." He bowed his head over them, then slowly, reverently, without another word, raised them one at a time to his lips, kissing each finger tenderly.

He held her right palm against his warm mouth for a long time, smoothing her callused fingers with his thumb, and she could see from the way his shoulders were rising and falling that he was struggling to bring himself under control. Finally he said quietly, "You moved me."

"I am glad," she said shakily, dismayed to find her voice coming out a mere thread of sound.

He gave a brief laugh but stayed where he was, looking up at her now out of luminescent eyes. "It is laughable now to think how I dared to suggest profaning your life by joining it with mine last Christmas. We are worlds apart and it is doubtful if I could ever be worthy of you, even if I struggled for a hundred years."

He bowed his head again, still holding reverently to one of her hands as though to a life line.

Tears pricked at her eyes. She blinked them back and swallowed against the lump in her throat.

"We cannot go back, can we, Ann?" he asked brokenly after a long while.

"No," she heard herself say as though from somewhere far away. She wished desperately that they could go back. She wished that she had not come to distrust him so and that she had not learned all she had of him since coming to town and decided that he would make her life miserable rather than happy.

Biting her lip, she reached out with her free hand to touch his dark hair. Feeling the crisp ends under her fingertips, she pulled them back quickly, hoping her touch had been so light that he had not felt it.

"I am going away," he said finally, rising to his feet abruptly. "To try to make something of myself at long last. I dare not ask—" He hesitated. "I have a request to make of you. I will understand if you will not grant it." He halted briefly, then plunged ahead. "Would it be asking too much of you to send me a few words from time to time? To hear from you would give me such encouragement . . . and if I could tell you how I was going on—" He stopped and swallowed. "Well, I know this sounds foolish."

"No. Not foolish. You may write to me and I will answer. But that is all I will promise. Do not—please do not think that it would mean more."

Flicking her a brief, unhappy glance, he paced away to the fireplace, and rested his arm along the mantelpiece. "No. I could not ask you for more . . . not until I have proved that there is something of me to offer, at any rate." He turned to face her, but at the look of distress on her face he quickly amended, "And probably not ever—but let me say that my life was once crossed by an angel—and blessed by her."

"Oh, do not put me on a pedestal. I am no saint."

"You are an artist, a lovely, intelligent woman whose gifts put me to shame."

She spread her long fingers wide, then folded her arms over her waist and watched the firelight flicker over his profile that was turned away from her again.

"There is something else, Ann," he said with difficulty. "Before I go away, I want you to know that there was nothing—nothing between me and Zara Stanhill at Lydia's. I would not have betrayed your trust, our lo—*friendship,* in that way. What you saw was not what it appeared to be. She means nothing to me. She never has."

Ann said nothing as her vision blurred. She could not trust herself to speak. He sounded so sincere and she wanted so desperately to believe him.

He watched her steadily for several moments, then he took a deep breath as he seemed to come to some conclusion. "Well . . . I shall say good night now, and allow you to return to your well-deserved plaudits."

Without realizing it, Ann had walked halfway across the room toward him. Now he came the rest of the way to her. He stood inches away.

"My reform may have begun, but I am not wholly a monk as yet," he said with something of his old teasing manner. "Goodbye, my dear Ann." Reaching out, he cupped her face tenderly in his hands. He hesitated briefly, then leaned forward and brushed his lips against hers.

Once.

Sweetly.

Drawing back, he looked into her wide amber eyes. He ran his hands down her arms to lace his fingers with hers. A final squeeze of her hands, and then he was gone.

Running her fingers over her lips, Ann stood looking at the door he had closed quietly behind him for several long seconds. Tears spilled over and ran unchecked down her cheeks.

He was gone. She might never see him again. "Oh, Robin,

don't go!" she whispered. Despair tore at her insides, but she willed it down.

Yes. It was for the best. She had to believe that.

Her fingers continued to stroke her trembling lips. It had been all too brief a touch for her.

Sixteen

Ann had just returned from a walk in the Green Park with Mr. Allenthorp and was removing her straw bonnet, thinking that summer was coming on apace. The heat of London had caused the flowers in her hat to wilt, she saw without surprise.

It had been decided that she was to stay in town with her aunt into the autumn to continue her lessons with Herr Müller. She had been working hard, and she hoped improving her technique, but her spirits had not been high, despite her teacher's praise. She could not get a certain absent gentleman out of her thoughts. After asking so particularly, he had not written.

"Ahem." Ann started at the butler's approach. She had not noticed him. Her thoughts had been miles away.

"A letter for you, miss." Her aunt's austere butler presented the silver salver. A rather large packet addressed to her in a bold, flowing hand rested on its gleaming surface. It was not her mother's or Lorna's handwriting.

"Thank you, Wilcox," she said, trying to contain her excitement. Removing the letter from the tray with trembling fingers, she turned it over and studied it pensively.

At the butler's curious stare, she summoned a brief smile, then turned toward the staircase. Hastening up the stairs, she ran along the landing to her bedchamber, clutching the letter in her hand. When she was behind her closed door, she lifted it to her face.

Dear Lord! He had finally written! After so long. Just when she had given up all hope.

Closing her eyes, she pressed the letter to her lips and breathed in. She could detect the scent of him still lingering on the paper. Outdoorsy. Spicy. Male.

"Stop behaving like a silly schoolgirl!" she chided herself a moment later. Crossing the room, she propped the letter on her dressing table and told herself she would not open it until she got herself under control.

She paced about her chamber for some three or four minutes, then gave up trying to suppress her excitement. She tore open the letter with eager fingers. Her eyes flew down the paper to find that he had sent her four closely-written sheets. After trying to take it all in at once, she laughed at herself, then started over. He began rather formally.

"My dear Ann,

"I trust I find you well and in good spirits. My sister Emily writes that you are to remain in town for the time being to continue your lessons on the pianoforte. I hope London does not grow too hot for you, nor too tedious now that the season has ended and many of your acquaintance will have dispersed to their country houses.

"It was my sincere intention to write to you sooner. However, when I arrived here I found everything in chaos: the house tumbling down about my ears, the servants gone, the land fallow, the barns empty, the sheep herd dissipated. There were but four ewes and a very elderly ram—long past his best, poor old chap—left in the pasture above the house. Well, I will not bore you with all the details, but things are on the way to being sorted out. The job will be a long and hard one, but I believe I have enough fortitude and determination to stick it out. Indeed, I find that I am looking forward to the challenge. It takes my mind off other matters.

"The farm runs down to the lake on one end and up into the fells of Coniston Old Man on the other. I find the area around Coniston Water incredibly beautiful, as is this entire region of the country.

"Have you ever been to the Lake District, Ann? The

mountains are as old as any on earth; the fells, the lakes, the purity of the air, and glory of the sunrise and sunset are indescribable. Perhaps one day you can see for yourself. I know that once you glimpsed it in its many moods you would long to paint it: the ever-changing sky with its rapid shifts of light and color and cloud; the mountains themselves, green and inviting at times, or dark and mysterious and dangerous, sometimes completely covered in thick cloud; the lakes with their deep blue surfaces crystal clear and still, or wild and raging in a storm, waves crashing against the banks.

"The scenery *is* glorious, though the weather is treacherous. Sometimes we have all four seasons in one day. To pit oneself against nature and the elements is a humbling feeling, indeed. Do not mistake me. I actually *like* the area, despite its isolation. There is something to be said for the solace one finds in the solitude of nature.

"Lest you think I spend all my time in lonely contemplation of the landscape, let me tell you that *that* is far from the truth, my dear girl. It is only at odd moments that I can selfishly indulge myself, like the time I was coming back from Ambleside where I purchased a new ram. I was driving the wagon with my new shepherd, Jacob Potter, on board. Rodney was trussed up in the back, protesting loudly. Rodney is our new ram—a Herdwick, who has a roving eye for the ladies.

"I was admiring the scenery around me on the return journey and trying to block out Rodney's bleating, when Jacob suddenly shouted that the ram had somehow got free of his bonds and had leapt from the wagon. I pulled the wagon to a halt, and Jacob jumped down to run after him. Young Rodney had spotted a field of ewes and was in the midst of them in no time, running this way and that, not sure which he should honor with his attentions first. By the time Jacob and I had got him back to the wagon—with no end of trouble, let me tell you—our clothes were filthy. I was ready to murder the beast, when it occurred to me that he was just like some young friends of my acquaintance, new come to town and admiring all the young lovelies, not sure which to pursue. It was as well for this young ovine that he surprised a laugh from me, otherwise I may well have decided to have him for my dinner!"

Ann dissolved in helpless laughter. She could just see the humorous scene and to imagine the immaculately groomed, sartorially magnificent Lord Robert wrestling with a sheep made her laugh even harder.

He went on to tell her of how he arose at the crack of dawn every morning to start on his many chores, usually not stopping until the sun went down, about how he spent his evenings relaxing by his fireside because even in summer he often needed to light the fire, and about how he would often think of how they said they would read Greek or poetry together in front of a cozy fire.

She smoothed out the letter to read his last few sentences. "Have I made you smile, Ann? I hope so. You should laugh more often. I smile when I think of you—as I do often."

She flushed and tingled all over. His words were a caress.

"And when I think of you, I think of music. I miss hearing any here. You will be astounded to hear that I have even been enticed into the local church to hear the choir of a Sunday even'song.

"And wonder of wonders, I have acquired a piano! A rather battered instrument, to be sure, but after we hauled it up here from Coniston village, I had the tuner in to set it to rights and—another miracle—it is now in tune and the quality is not half bad. I bang away on it to the consternation of Mrs. Braithwaite, my housekeeper, who complains that my playing reminds her of a caterwauling tomcat. I presented her with some wool for her ears as a joke, which I now find she actually uses when I sit down to play!

"My candle is guttering in its holder so I had best close now. If you find yourself with the odd moment to spare, a few words from you would be more than welcome, but I will not press you. God bless you, Ann."

It was signed with a scrawl that she took to be "Lyndhurst." Looking up from the letter with shining eyes, she realized she had misjudged him. He was no frivolous blade. He was a gentle man of hidden depths: warm and funny, business-like and competent, hard-working and struggling—and lonely. Yes, there was something unbearably lonely about the thought of him putting in a full day's work and then sitting alone by his fireside in the evening reading poetry or playing his battered piano with no one to hear.

She was consumed by her letter. It seemed he was there with her, telling her all about the farm and the funny incidents and the wonderful scenery. Wrapping her arms round herself, she hugged the knowledge to her heart that here was the real Lord Robert—the real Robin, the man she had glimpsed last Christmas.

She closed her eyes, visualizing him sitting in the small room, his chair drawn up to the fire, his booted feet resting on the fender, a glass of wine at his side and a book of poetry open on his lap. How she wished— She stopped herself.

No. He must find his way alone—for now.

But he would have an answer to his letter as soon as she could contrive it, she decided, opening her writing desk, taking out letter paper and looking about for a pen.

An hour later, she looked up from her letter with a bemused smile. After staring off into space for a few moments, she dipped the quill in the ink pot and set it to the paper once more. She ended with a warm valediction, hesitated a moment before signing it simply "Ann," then sealed it with a wafer.

Picking up Lord Robert's letter, she read it through once more.

They could never go back.

No.

But perhaps they could go forward.

* * *

"Here ye be at long last, Master Robert," his housekeeper greeted him in her thick Cumbrian accent when he stepped into the house bringing a blast of cold Lakelands air and rain with him. "Yer dinner's gone cold long since and just look at ye, all covered with mud and shiverin' with cold." She clucked her tongue and fussed about him, helping him off with his heavy sheepskin jacket and recommending that he remove his boots that were leaving dirty, wet marks all over her clean floor.

He slapped his mud-caked leather gloves down on the table. Hiding his grin, he gave her a sweet smile instead. She seemed unable to style him "Lord Robert," but he did not correct her. She reminded him of the long-suffering nurse he and his siblings had had as children, always grumpy and fussing over them, but kind at heart, really.

"I am sure you will be able to warm up my dinner for me, Mrs. Braithwaite. And I know you will be glad to hear that Jacob and I have mended the gap in the fence in the south pasture and we will not lose any more of our sheep out onto the fells."

She nodded curtly and went off to see to his dinner.

Hurriedly divesting himself of his filthy boots on the mat, he then walked into the small ground-floor lounge in his stockinged feet to rub his hands in front of the welcome warmth blazing from the fire there. He was chilled through, but it would have been beneath his dignity to let Mrs. Braithwaite know as much. Feeling the need of some fire in his stomach to warm his insides, he walked to the sideboard to pour himself some sherry. His hand checked in mid-air as he reached for the decanter. A white rectangular paper addressed to him was resting there.

"Dear Lord! Ann," he whispered. Picking up the letter with fingers that shook slightly, he raised it to his lips. Resisting the temptation to tear it open, he put it down again while he poured himself a glass of sherry, took a long sip, then eased himself into the overstuffed chair in front of the fire, casually hooking one leg over the chair arm before he opened his letter.

A piece of paper fell out. Retrieving it from his lap, he saw it was a musical score. He smiled somewhat lopsidedly, then eagerly turned to her letter.

"My dear sir,

Come forth into the light of things,
Let Nature be your teacher. . . .
One impulse from a vernal wood
May teach you more of man,
Of moral evil and of good,
Than all the sages can.

"When I received your letter with your lovely reflections on the solace you receive from nature, it put me in mind of these lines from Mr. Wordsworth's *The Tables Turned.* Have you seen him yet? I understand that he is a great rambler, walking for miles over the fells and valleys of his beloved Lake District. And as he lives in Grasmere, he is not far away from you there in Coniston."

The rest of her letter was full of how much she had enjoyed the story of Rodney the ram, unstinting praise for his hard work, news of what she was painting and what new pieces of music Herr Müller had set her to learn, and a report of having had tea with his sister, Emily. She closed by teasing him lightly about his new piano, writing that she hoped the music she had enclosed would liven things up for him, if only for a few moments. And in a closely written postscript, she mentioned some of her favorite books and poetry that she thought he might wish to dip into during his lonely hours.

When he came to the end of the letter, he saw it was signed "Ann," in a lovely feminine script. He raised the paper to his lips once more and kissed her signature. Leaning his head back against the chair, he closed his eyes.

His gambit was working! It had taken him many days, and many false starts to compose his long letter to her, to get the tone just right. She had responded to the words he had spent those long hours poring over more quickly than he had dreamed possible. Had she really forgiven him at last? He laughed at himself. He who had always used his physical charm to entice females, was now trying to charm a woman who was hundreds of miles away—with mere words. Ah, the power of language, he mused, resting his chin on his fisted hand and stretching out a damp stockinged foot to warm it at the fender. His eyes sparkled with hope in the firelight.

How beautiful she had looked at Emily's in her ivory silk gown, with her hair worn in that softer style! And how much he missed listening to her play. Through her music she had reached his soul.

God, how he missed her!

Devil take it! He frowned in frustration a moment later. Here he was hundreds of miles away, unable to look at her, to touch her, to listen to her play . . . to tell her how much he loved her.

He jumped from his chair and went to the old oak desk shoved into one corner of the small room, piled high with papers of all sorts. Searching for a sheet of letter paper, he sent bills and lists and old periodicals flying to the floor in his impatience. Then he stopped, arrested by a sudden inspiration. Walking over to the bookcase, he reached for a well-thumbed volume of poetry, and opened it to the passage he wanted. His lips widened in an anticipatory grin.

In the coming weeks, letters fairly flew back and forth between London and Coniston. Ann included musical scores and favorite passages of poetry in her letters. Lord Robert related funny incidents around the farm and described the landscape and people of the Lake District in sometimes bold and beautiful, sometimes sensitive and poignant, word pictures, quoting poetry back to her in his turn.

He hoped the verses he chose so carefully would affect her the way they affected him. Among the many verses he sent her were five selections from Wordsworth:

It is a beauteous evening, calm and free,
The holy time is quiet as a nun
Breathless with adoration.

What music in my heart I bore
Long after it was heard no more.

Sensations sweet,
Felt in the blood, and felt along the heart.

She gave me eyes, she gave me ears;
And humble cares, and delicate fears;
A heart, the fountain of sweet tears;
And love, and thought, and joy.

What fond and wayward thoughts will slide
Into a lover's head!

And one that he had always enjoyed from Congreve:

Music has charms to soothe a savage breast.

Ann sent him Byron:

There is a pleasure in the pathless woods,
There is a rapture on the lonely shore,
There is society, where none intrudes,
By the deep sea, and music in its roar:
I love not man the less, but Nature more.

And Keats:

A thing of beauty is a joy forever:
Its loveliness increases; it will never
Pass into nothingness; but still will keep
A bower quiet for us, and a sleep
Full of sweet dreams, and health, and quiet breathing.

And, of course, Wordsworth, too:

When from our better selves we have too long
Been parted by the hurrying world, and droop,
Sick of its business, of its pleasures tired,
How gracious, how benign, is Solitude.

Dreams, books, are each a world; and books, we know,
Are a substantial world, both pure and good:
Round these, with tendrils strong as flesh and blood,
Our pastime and our happiness will grow.

Their letters became a form of courtship, aided and abetted by the timeless voices of the poets.

Ann read with pleasure and eagerness of his efforts to repair the house and build his new sheep herd. He always had an amusing episode to relate, such as how he had wanted to learn how to milk the two nanny goats he had purchased, but when Jacob had patiently tried to teach him, he had succeeded only in being butted in the rear quarters by the nanny goat who objected to his technique.

And then there was Bandit, the border collie who seemed to be training *him,* rather than the other way around when they went out to round up the sheep. The dog had looked at him as though he were not altogether there in the upper works when he had spent ages looking for a gate in the fence between the south and west pastures. Bandit had barked at him and pulled him by the edge of his jacket until he had followed the dog, who led him straight to the gate that was concealed behind a clump of furze.

One of his letters related an incident that had Ann starting up from her chair, her hand to her breast.

> "I went into Grasmere to see a farmer about purchasing some of his ewes," he wrote. "The man was out on some errand or other and while I waited for him to return, I decided to walk beside the lake for a time. A tallish, grey eminence leaning on a gnarled walking stick approached from the opposite direction. When we were near enough to speak, he held out his hand, a cordial expression of welcome on his face. As he stopped to say good day, I saw a sheaf of papers sticking from his jacket pocket. It flashed into my mind that I had encountered the great poet himself.
>
> " 'I have walked five miles this morning,' he announced matter-of-factly.
>
> "I congratulated him, but he pointed out that that was a paltry ramble for him who often walked twenty miles across the fells in the roughest weather. And when he found that I was a John's man, too, well there was nothing else for it, but I must join him for tea where we talked about student dinners in the Senior Combination Room and found that we had one or two masters in common who had been young firebreathers in his day, and who had decayed into old codgers in mine."

Ann realized Lord Robert was referring to the fact that he and Wordsworth had both attended St. John's College at Cambridge.

She was enchanted by his letters. Sometimes it seemed she was there with him, so vivid and moving were his words and descriptions. She could *see* his farm set in the grandeur of the surrounding landscape, tucked in a little valley against the rising heights of the imposing Coniston Old Man behind, leading down to the lake in front. She *knew* the people and animals he worked with everyday—Jacob, Mrs. Braithwaite, Bandit, Rodney, and the villagers and farmers round about Coniston.

And always underlying his words, she could sense his deep, abiding affection for her, usually conveyed delicately and discreetly in the lines of poetry he sent, but of late she had detected a more passionate tone seeping through.

She kept his letters by her bedside and before she blew out her candle at night, she would read over a passage or two. He had sent her a fragment from the Duc de La Rochefoucauld recently: "We pardon to the extent that we love." The words had left her unable to sleep. *Did* she love him enough to pardon him?

With some surprise, she realized that she had believed his version of events and forgiven him long since for the episode with Lady Stanhill. But she was still afraid to trust him. Because her heart, her hope, and her dreams had been shattered once, she was afraid to risk such pain again.

She longed to see him one moment, then shied away from desiring such a meeting the next. What would he say when they met again? What would she say to him? She feared that the special bond they had forged would be lost. He was all hers in his letters. But if she should see him in the flesh, she would look at his handsome face and know that he could not truly want *her.*

Well, she was safe for the moment—safe with her treasured letters—for he made no mention of coming to London.

Lord Robert tramped home through the fields eagerly every day, hoping to find another letter from Ann, but if there was not one awaiting him, he would sit down and work on the one he was composing for her.

He had never realized the seductive power of words, had never before employed such a gambit in his dealings with women. But now it struck him forcibly that he was on his way to winning Ann's heart through his letters.

Her responses grew warmer, making him feel she was there with him, verbally sparring. As his confidence of winning her affection grew, his words became more teasing, the verses of poetry he sent more deliberately seductive. In his last letter, he had sent another passage from de La Rochefoucauld that he hoped would let her know the state of his heart, "Absence diminishes mediocre passions and increases great ones, as the wind blows out candles and fans fire."

But he was restless, growing tired of this long-distance courtship. And he was lonely. He missed her.

Absence and distance had only increased his deep regard for her.

He could not wait any longer. He would put his fate to the touch.

It was the first of October already and he had not seen her since May. He was due to stand up with Chubby at his wedding in London in a sennight. He sat down to write to Ann, to tell her he was coming to London, to ask if she would see him. But then he balled up the sheet and threw it into the grate to watch it crackle to ash in the flames.

He would go to London without telling her he was coming and take her by surprise.

Seventeen

Ann was lost in thought, thinking dreamily of Lord Robert's latest letter, as she strolled along with her companion under the canopy of trees bedecked in their autumnal foliage.

She had been so afraid of being hurt, afraid to trust her heart, but his letters were wearing down her resistance, soothing away her fears. She felt warm and secure in his total regard. And she was proud of him, of the way he had put his rakish past behind him and knuckled down to hard work to secure a steady future.

"If I half close my eyes, I can almost imagine you sitting across from me at my piano," he had written in his most recent letter. "Your head is bent in concentration over the keys, and if I close my eyes entirely, I can imagine the sound of your playing, for your music lingers in my heart, long after the notes have died away."

His letters were becoming ever more intimate, his words a caress. She felt bathed in his love.

And she loved him. She loved him with a passion that she would feel her whole life long. A grand passion. There would never be another man who could replace him in her heart. She wished desperately to see him again, convinced at last that they *could* share a happy future together.

"Miss Forester," Mr. Allenthorp said rather loudly, as though he had spoken before and received no response. He drew them to a halt along a little-used, tree-lined pathway at the edge of the park and possessed himself of her hand. "I have not rushed you.

You said you wanted time. But it has been over two months now, and you have not yet given me your answer."

"Oh!" Ann cried, trying to jerk herself back to the present. His words startled her, catching her offguard. "I—I do not feel—that is, please forgive me, sir. I do not feel that I can accept your proposal." She looked at him helplessly. She had become so used to his easy company that she had almost forgotten his proposal. They were friends. That was all. But it must seem to him that she had done nothing to discourage him.

"But you have encouraged me to think—" he began. "I am sorry, ma'am. 'Tis just that you have not seemed indifferent to me. We have walked out most afternoons and I have accompanied you to the theatre, musicales, exhibitions. Our minds are in agreement on so many subjects. And I thought, I *believed* you had changed your appearance, dressed and styled your hair more fashionably to please me. Was I wrong? Why can you not now accept my offer for your hand?" he pressed her.

At one time, many weeks ago when he had first asked, before she received her first letter from Lord Robert, she had tried to convince herself that she should seriously consider marrying him. He seemed to be a worthy gentleman, one whose talent she believed should be encouraged. And her dowry would do that, once they were married and it was released into his hands. She had thought about how they shared the same opinions on many subjects, and how she believed she would be comfortable with him . . . But she did not love him. Not then and not now.

He was not the tall, dark, devilishly teasing man of her dreams who made her pulse race and set her senses on fire. He was not the man whose very soul called to hers, whose thoughts, dreams and hopes seemed to mesh with hers.

Grasping her other hand as well, Mr. Allenthorp turned her fully toward him and looked at her with determination in his pale blue eyes, trying to persuade her.

Ann took a deep breath and opened her mouth to tell him, once and for all, that it was useless. She would never marry him.

" 'Afternoon, Miss Forester. M-must say, you are looking

smashing in that lavender whatsyoumacallit," a gentleman with a small, pretty lady on his arm called loudly, sweeping his hand in the direction of Ann's new fur-trimmed pelisse.

"Mr. Harwood-Jones! Where did you—?" Ann exclaimed in confusion, aware that her face was flaming and that Mr. Allenthorp was still holding her hands in an intimate fashion. She snatched them away hastily.

"Brought my Betsy up to London—oh, er, p-pardon me, Miss Forester," Chubby apologized at a nudge from the lady on his arm. "This is my fiancée, Mrs. Eggleson. Betsy, my love, this is M-Miss Forester. The one I told you of at Aunt Lydia's last Christmas. She and m'cousin, you know," Chubby whispered loudly, waggling his eyebrows at his fiancée.

"The young lady who is friendly with your cousin Lord Robert Lyndhurst, my dear?" Mrs. Eggleson clarified for him.

"That's it, Betsy!" Chubby beamed. "We've come up to London to be married, you know," he explained confidentially. "On Friday."

"Why, congratulations, Mr. Harwood-Jones." Regaining some of her poise, Ann introduced her companion.

"Seen Robin yet, Miss Forester? Believe he arrives today. Going to support me at our wedding on Friday, you know," Chubby informed her proudly.

"N-no, I did not know," Ann admitted, stunned. He had said nothing of coming to London in his latest letter. Would he come and not tell her? Not call to see her? Her throat ached at the thought.

"Oh! Thought you would," Chubby continued, lively curiosity bright in his eyes. "Thought you and Robin was thinkin' of gettin' engaged at Christmas. He was kissin' you," he reminded her.

"Oh, no, no! You are mistaken, Mr. Harwood-Jones," she iterated quickly.

"But—I saw him, both of you," Chubby reminded her.

"Oh! I meant there was no thought of an—an engagement." Feeling lightheaded, Ann was ready to skin into the ground with embarrassment.

"That's dashed too bad," Chubby said.

Almost overcome by dizziness, Ann leaned heavily against Mr. Allenthorp for a moment, compounding the misleading impression she was giving to Lord Robert's curious relative. She despised herself for her momentary weakness. Moving away from her companion's supporting arm, she brushed down her skirts, keeping her eyes averted while she tried to regain her composure.

"I believe Miss Forester is not well. If you would excuse us, I think I should see her home," Allenthorp tried to dismiss the others.

"Not feelin' well, M-Miss Forester? I'll take you home, then. Have m'carriage waitin' just over there. We just got down to stretch our legs for a bit. Betsy believes in the ef-efficacy of fresh air, you know."

"No, no, really. I am perfectly fine," Ann insisted, but she still felt unsteady.

"I believe you are unwell, Miss Forester. You are very pale. Do let us take you home," Mrs. Eggleson added her persuasion.

Ann protested but, given no choice, she had to accept Mr. Harwood-Jones's offer. It did not help matters to find Mr. Allenthorp climbing in, too, and seating himself close beside her.

When they arrived at Mrs. Jermyn's house, not only did Mr. Allenthorp insist on seeing her to her aunt's door, but Mr. Harwood-Jones accompanied her as well. She made her escape as gracefully as she could and when she was safely inside, she did not hear the conversation between the two gentlemen which would have distressed her further.

"You well acquainted with Miss Forester?" Chubby asked, turning his bright gaze on Allenthorp.

"Very well acquainted, indeed," Allenthorp answered in a clipped voice, frowning down the end of his nose. "I hope to make Miss Forester my wife soon."

"Heh? *You* goin' to marry Miss Forester?" Chubby asked, his mouth dropping open in unhappy surprise.

"I believe I had best not discuss the business with you, sir, as

I believe you are in no way connected to the lady." So saying, Allenthorp replaced his hat on his head and sauntered down the steps of Mrs. Jerymn's residence.

Chubby looked after him dejectedly. "Poor R-Robin! Guess he's goin' to have his heart b-broken." Shaking his curly head sadly, he wandered back to his carriage where Mrs. Eggleson awaited him.

Lord Robert had just dismounted, leaving his exhausted horse in the mews at the back of his townhouse, and was striding up the yard to the door. He was bone weary, but pleased to have arrived at last. He had ridden the whole way from Coniston, too impatient to see Ann to sit doing nothing inside a well-sprung chaise and four, though such a conveyance would have been a much more comfortable way to get to London.

And then when he had reached the metropolis he had had a special errand to attend to before he could ride home to his rooms in Chandler Street.

Chubby's wedding had provided a convenient excuse for coming to town. He could not have waited much longer to see Ann in any case. He throbbed with anticipation as he thought of dropping in on her unannounced, hoping to catch her offguard, wanting to see the light of welcome, the light of love in her eyes.

If he had judged the time right, he would sweep off her feet and marry her out of hand. If she still had any doubts, he was confident that he could persuade her *physically.* His eyes gleamed with pleasure as he thought of what such physical persuasion might consist.

Though he was tired, after a quick change of clothes he paid his sister a call, deciding to walk to her house in order to stretch his legs after a long day in the saddle.

"So you approve this woman Chubby is leg-shackling himself to?" he asked, sitting on the settee in Lady Emily's drawing room, one Hessian-booted foot crossed over the other. His long fingers picked impatiently at the frilly edge of one of the cushions.

"Betsy Eggleson? Why, yes, I do. When I met her, I saw that she was mature and kind. And she seems to have a care for him. Yes, I think Charles has chosen well and will be happy in his marriage," Lady Emily answered, sipping her tea and eyeing her brother with a great deal of curiosity. His long legs were accentuated by the snugly fitting buff pantaloons he was wearing, and he was looking trim and fit, all hard muscle after these past weeks of arduous work on his farm. All her brothers were handsome men, but Robin, equally as tall as Will, came nearest to beauty in his features and his physique, she decided.

"Will you be calling on Miss Forester while you are here, Robin?" she asked directly.

He looked away and she was surprised to note a dull flush along his cheekbones. After a moment he answered hesitantly, "Yes, I plan to pay a courtesy call on her."

"A courtesy call, Robin?" Lady Emily's eyes laughed at him over the top of her teacup.

"Damn it all, Em—" he exclaimed, jumping to his feet.

"Your language, Robert! I may be your sister, but this is my drawing room—"

He lifted his hands palm up in front of him. "I apologize. But dash it all, Emily, you must see that I am trying to be subtle."

"You are in love with her then?"

He gave a crack of laughter. "Far gone." He strolled to the window and pushed back the curtain to peer out into the street.

He was half turned away from her, but she could see the tight look on his profile. Emily bit her lip and frowned. "Robin, my dear . . . there is something you should know."

He turned fully toward her, eyebrows raised in query.

"There has been talk . . ." she faltered. "It is said that Ann Forester and George Allenthorp will announce their engagement soon."

"Allenthorp? What the dev—*Deuce!* No! You must be wrong! Ann's letters to me have given me great encouragement," he stated incautiously.

"She has been writing to you then? I did not know."

Mentally he chastised himself for admitting his elder sister into the delicate matter of his heart. Shrugging off his embarrassment, he told her how he and Ann had been corresponding for the past few months and of how he hoped for future happiness with her.

"I came to town determined to put my fate to the touch. I thought I had reason for confidence . . . Now you tell me of this gossip about her and some impecunious scribbler."

"Oh, my dear, I hope you are right about her feelings for you. Her writing to you does sound as though she returns your feelings," Lady Emily said sympathetically, pity and love for him swelling her heart. "I just wanted you to be aware of what is being bruited about."

"Forewarned is forearmed, heh? I thank you for the warning, then, Em," he said lightly, but her words had greatly disturbed him. He remembered Ann had mentioned the fellow *again* in her last letter, saying that she had recently read an essay of his which she thought had great merit. She had been flattered Allenthorp had asked her to offer her criticism; "Men often assume women are not possessed of minds that can think as well as a man's," she had written.

Devil take it! He raised a fisted hand to his mouth, gnawing on one knuckle.

With worry eating at him, he decided to go immediately to see Ann to find out how the land lay for himself. He could not be wrong about her feelings for him! He *knew* she felt as he did. It was there in every line she wrote to him.

He walked rapidly to Seymour Street and rapped on Mrs. Jermyn's door, only to be told by a rather giddy young housemaid who answered his knock in place of the ailing butler that her mistress was away in the country and that Miss Forester had gone out for the evening and was not expected back until later.

Swallowing his impatience, he went to pay a duty call on Chubby to finalize plans for the wedding. He soon found his hand being almost wrung off and his shoulder buffeted heartily.

"Have a care, old chap. I will need my hand on Friday to

perform my office in the wedding," Lord Robert teased, flexing his fingers when Chubby finally let go.

"Heh? Oh, yes. That's the ticket! Can't have you in-incapacitated on my wedding day, Robin," Chubby said, ushering his relative into the ground-floor lounge in the Grosvenor Square townhouse he had inherited on his father's death three years previously.

Chubby talked excitedly of the wedding plans, then removed the precious wedding ring from a locked drawer in the huge mahogany desk that dominated the room and reverently entrusted it to his cousin's care.

Robin held it up to the light to read the inscription.

"Saw Miss Forester yesterday. She looked different. Prettier. She was walkin' in the park with some dashed hedgebird name of Allenthorp."

"The devil she was!" Robin growled, a bolt of fear rocking him. "What makes you think this Allenthorp character is a hedgebird?" he asked, his brows drawn together in a ferocious frown.

"His clothes. Out of date. No style. Shifty-eyed fellow, too. Didn't like me and Betsy speakin' to her, takin' her home when she felt ill. Wouldn't let her go alone with us when offered her a ride home in m'carriage. Insisted on comin', too."

"Hell and the devil take it!" A murderous fury gripped him. Was this Allenthorp a fortune hunter, stalking her for her dowry? Nothing was more likely.

"Thought Miss Forester was goin' to marry you, R-Robin," Chubby said with a confused, sad look, "but the hedgebird says she's goin' to m-marry him!"

"*What!* Damnation. It can't be true!"

"Well," Chubby said, scratching his head, "that's what the gent told me when I asked him straight out. Was afraid you wouldn't like it, Robin."

He was staggered. Blindly reaching for the ring case, his hand shook so that he dropped it on the Turkey carpet. "Sorry. It slipped," he said. He knelt on the carpet with Chubby to retrieve the ring.

"You will not drop it at my weddin' ceremony?" Chubby asked with a worried laugh.

"Never fear. My hand will be steady as a rock, old man," Lord Robert promised, though he was so upset he hardly knew what he said.

Soon after he took his leave, promising to meet Chubby at St. George's, Hanover Square, at eleven on Friday morning. He walked for a time without knowing where he was going. It had begun to drizzle, but he paid no heed, walking on in the dark, frosty autumn night, his breath a hiss of steam before him.

It could not be true! Yet there was mention of Allenthorp in several of her letters. And now Chubby said she was to marry the man. He was worried. Hurt. Furious.

Ann! He must see her. Surely she would deny the incredible tale.

She *loved* him. He knew she did. As he loved her. It was there in her letters, in every line she wrote to him, in the ease with which they told one another everything, in her interest in every aspect of his life—as his in hers—in the snatches of poetry they had exchanged, becoming ever more affectionate, more intimate.

Surely she could not have mistaken him and turned to another man. He had confessed his love again and again in the words he had sent her.

It was late. He found himself in front of Mrs. Jermyn's house without quite knowing how he had got there or what time it was. It was too dark to read his watch in the light of the street lamp.

A carriage clattering down the street behind him caught his attention. He walked on past the house and crossed the street. Standing in the dark shadows, he looked back and watched as the carriage pulled up before Mrs. Jermyn's front door. Pushing himself back into the deeper shadows of a tree overhanging the pale of someone's front garden, he saw a gentleman descend from the carriage. A maidservant followed. The gentleman turned to help a lady down.

His heart stood still. It was Ann.

And Allenthorp.

Dear God!

She smiled at the gentleman, then ascended the steps with him. They stood before the door for a long time, seemingly engaged in earnest conversation. The maidservant went into the house ahead of her mistress while the coachman rattled away, driving the carriage round to the mews behind the house, and still they stood together. Clenching his fists, and his teeth until they almost cracked, he prevented himself from racing across the street to snatch her away and plant his fist in the fellow's face.

Finally, the man raised Ann's hand to his lips and kissed it. He then replaced his hat on his shining blond locks and set off down the path on foot.

A burning agony twisted his gut. Fury flooded him, pounding through his veins.

He closed his eyes as the pain rocked through him. Was this how Ann had felt when she had mistaken the situation between him and Lady Stanhill at Christmas? Was *he* mistaken now?

No. Although he could have misinterpreted what he saw, there were Emily's words and Chubby's to confirm his worst fears. So—she had never meant to have him, despite the warmth of her letters. She had just been taking a certain perverse pleasure in "reforming" him.

Realizing he was still clenching his teeth and his fists, he relaxed them. A deadly calm came over him. She had played him for a fool, leading him to believe that he stood a chance of regaining her affections when all the time she was planning to marry Allenthorp.

She would be sorry.

Even before Allenthorp had completely disappeared down the street, Lord Robert was rushing up the steps of Mrs. Jermyn's house and rapping urgently on the front door.

The same young housemaid who had answered the door when he had called earlier opened it now and looked up at him out of wide, frightened eyes.

"Have no fear, my dear," he said with practiced charm. "I simply want a word with Miss Forester. I believe she has returned now."

The girl stared up at him and gulped. He curved his lips into that special smile that he had found always persuaded females to do just what he wanted, while he tucked a gold piece into her bodice with one hand and chucked her under the chin with a long finger of the other. Within seconds, she was leading him to a small sitting room at the back of the house and leaving him there with a long look over her shoulder as she went back to her duties.

He quietly pushed the door open with two fingers to see Ann standing before the fire holding her shawl tightly round her and gazing absently into the flames burning brightly in the grate.

"Hello, Ann."

"Oh! Robin! What are you—? How—? Oh, my!" she cried in astonishment, letting her shawl drop to the carpet in her surprise.

He walked forward, his smile glinting down at her, and boldly possessed himself of the cold hands that she lifted to him.

"One of your aunt's servants let me in . . . Are you not glad to see me?" he asked in a low voice, gazing right into her eyes, using all the tricks perfected in his raking days.

"Mr. Harwood-Jones said you were coming to town for his wedding, but I did not expect—" she began in a voice unlike her own. His eyes were holding hers and his smile was doing strange things to her breathing—and melting her heart.

"Yes. They are to be married on Friday. Chubby seems to have made a happy choice. Fortunate man."

"I am glad. He is such a very nice person." She gazed up at him, smiling into his eyes and squeezing his hands. "Oh, I cannot believe you are actually here! You did not let me know you were coming."

"I have missed you dreadfully, Ann," he whispered. And that was the truth, a small voice of conscience whispered in turn. He put his arms around her waist. She did not resist. "I have thought about you every day. Treasured your letters. Read them over and over again . . . Tell me you have missed me."

"I have missed you so very much, my dear Robin," she murmured. Her hands were feathering through his hair, her mouth inches from his, her amber eyes aglow with tenderness. With desire.

He closed the gap, his lips brushing back and forth across hers. His heart was thundering in his chest, his breath coming short. He was almost overwhelmed by desire—and tenderness. Which surprised and confused him. This was retaliation for her betrayal, not spontaneous lovemaking. But he was feeling as hungry as a schoolboy for her touch, for her kiss . . . was feeling that he was home, at last.

Remembering her treachery, he hardened his heart and callously continued with the plan that had half formed in his mind as he had watched her and Allenthorp, beside himself with anger, hurt, and jealousy.

She was more than eager. He felt the pressure of her hands joined behind his neck as she brought his head forward. She pressed her mouth to his for a more thorough kiss. He obliged without hesitation and soon they were lost. When her lips opened, he immediately took up the invitation, opening his mouth over hers and seeking the moist heat within, first with slow strokes, his tongue lightly touching hers, then he found himself pushing into her mouth urgently, passionately.

"Oh, Ann. Ann." His hands were roaming over her body, caressing every curve, going to the opening of her gown at her nape. Still she did not protest.

Her thighs were against his. His loins ached. He wanted a closer touch. One arm went behind her hips, pulling her closer as his knee pressed between her legs, parting them. She did not stop him.

He was kissing her wildly now, her face, her hair, her neck, her mouth again, all control gone. One hand had worked its way down inside her gown and he was caressing her warm soft flesh. She moaned against his mouth and sagged against him. Looking up through glazed eyes, he saw the settee, three, four steps behind them. He began moving her slowly backward, glad he had retained the presence of mind to lock the door behind him when he entered.

"Tell me you love me, Ann. Tell me," he demanded against her ear.

"I love you! I love you, Robin. I always have," she whispered ardently.

A great tremor shook him.

He eased her down, then bent over her. "I have wanted to do this for so long."

"I don't—Oh! What are you doing? No, no. Please stop. Someone will come. We cannot—"

Jealousy and bitterness overwhelmed him. "Why not? The door is locked and it is what we both want, is it not? And then, after you are married to Allenthorp, I can come to you often. And we can do *this*."

She was squirming beneath him. Her hands were batting his face, his chest, his shoulders as she struggled, her breath coming in sobbing gasps. "Dear God, no! I thought—I thought . . . What are you doing to me?"

His chest ached with hurt. "Showing you how it feels, Ann. Showing you how I felt when you decided to punish me for the incident with Zara Stanhill. Only she meant nothing to me. You are going to *marry* Allenthorp." His voice was ragged with emotion.

"Get out!" she said in a low, shaking voice as she sat up and glared at him, ignoring her own dishevelment. "You are nothing but a wicked seducer. Dear God! I believed that you *loved* me. What a fool I was." She laughed bitterly. "Do not ever, *ever,* come near me again.

Stopping at the door, he looked back over his shoulder with a twisted smile. "Not until you are *Mrs. Allenthorp,* at any rate," he grated sarcastically. And then he was gone.

Eighteen

"Ann! Ann Forester, is that you?" a carrying, laughing voice called out, stopping Ann in her tracks. She closed her eyes briefly. She knew she was indulging herself by coming to the park one last time before she left her aunt's house for Hampshire and home in two days' time. She really did not want to see any of the people she had known in London. It was too painful, because many of them were associated in some way with Lord Robert. Especially the lady of the merry voice who was calling out to her now.

Turning toward the elegant, crested carriage that was pulling up beside her, she composed her features and smiled and waved. "Lady Sedgemoor, what a surprise to see you in town at this time of year. I thought you were quite settled in Gloucestershire for an extended honeymoon."

"Pooh. Who is this *Lady Sedgemoor* you speak of? It's only me, Ann. Georgie. As for the honeymoon, well, I believe I qualify as an old married lady now."

Looking into the laughing blue eyes of the small lady who beckoned her to climb up inside the carriage, Ann smiled with pleasure for the first time in many days. No one could resist Georgie's charm and infectious high spirits—not even someone who had recently felt she would die after the gift of her heart had been so cruelly thrown back in her face.

"Now. Let us settle one of these carriage robes over you. It is cold today, is it not? And there are hot bricks for our feet, too. Gus thinks of everything, does he not?" Georgie laughed as she helped Ann settle on the seat beside her.

"Indeed, Lord Sedgemoor is a most thorough man," Ann agreed.

"Um," Georgie muttered, her eyebrows lowering in a frown. "Most thorough. So intent on having his own way, that there was nothing else for it but we must come to London so that I could consult the leading medical man in town, when I assured him that Dr. Matthews—our doctor at home, you know—would have done as well. And although Gus's broken leg is quite well now, I did not like to think that he would have to make two such long journeys in less than a fortnight just so that *I* might have medical advice that I could just as well have got at home!"

Ann smiled and shook her head. "Georgie, Georgie! You have lost me. Of what are you speaking?"

Georgie laughed merrily. "Oh, dear, I am become a sad rattle. Forgive me, my dear." She patted Ann's gloved hand and leaned nearer to confide, "I am in an interesting condition. I am to present Gus with a son—or daughter—in March. Imagine me, a mother!" She chuckled and Ann had to smile with her.

"How wonderful! You must both be thrilled at the prospect."

"Well, I am thrilled, but Gus is such a fusspot you would think the world will come to a standstill when this child of his is born. And nothing will do for him but that *I* must be wrapped in cotton wool as though I were made of priceless porcelain!" Georgie made a disgusted face. "Men!"

"I think it lovely that he is so concerned for you," Ann said a little sadly.

"Do you, my dear? Well, I suppose it is a lovely thought. But to put that thought into action and to be forbidding me to drive and to run, and to make me lie down in the afternoons for a nap when I am not at all tired, and to eat all the special foods he considers appropriate for a preg—well, for a pregnant woman—he becomes overbearing at times. But I have ways to get round him."

Ann looked interested. It was Georgie's turn to blush. To cover her slight discomfort she said, "But his insistence on coming to London does have the advantage of allowing me to buy Christmas presents for all my friends while I am here. *And* to arrange for a Christmas house party at the Oaks when we return. I have convinced him a house party will be just the thing to keep my spirits up while I wait for the baby. You will come, will you not, Ann?" Georgie asked brightly.

"It is very kind of you, but I do not think—"

"Oh, do not hesitate in that way and look frightened. I am not planning to serve you for Christmas dinner in place of the goose!"

Ann laughed at Georgie's foolishness. "My dear Georgie, I am only just now packing up to return home to Hampshire after an extended stay with my aunt. I believe my mother is expecting me to spend Christmas with her."

"Oh, I will invite your mother, too." Georgie airily waved away this objection.

"But—but why?"

"Because I like having many friends about me at the holidays. And you are one of my friends, are you not?"

"You are very kind—"

"Kind? Is it kind to want to be with people one likes and admires? Yes, and perhaps I have an ulterior motive, too."

Ann looked at her suspiciously.

"You play the pianoforte better than anyone I have ever heard. Perhaps I want you to provide entertainment at my house party, have you thought of that?" Georgie said in a sinister voice that was so at odds with her bright blue eyes, freckled nose, bright red curls, and overall innocent appearance that Ann laughed helplessly.

"Oh, Georgie, I do not wonder that Lord Sedgemoor tries to restrict you somewhat. You are incorrigible!"

"Yes, Gus is the soul of propriety. He does not like it even if I commit the minor solecism of appearing in public without a hat! And that brings me to a question for you, my dear Ann. Why were you walking alone in the park? Where was your maid? Have all your admirers deserted you?" Georgie asked with lively curiosity. "Did I come along in the nick of time to rescue you?"

Ann blushed and laughed slightly. "Nothing so interesting as you imagine. I am five-and-twenty. Quite an old maid who does not need a servant to lend me countenance."

Georgie's eyes twinkled. "Pooh! You are a very attractive lady who will soon be married, if I do not miss my guess. How is the dear boy?"

"The—the dear boy?" Ann asked in bewilderment.

"Of course I speak of Robin. I had word of him not long ago. He is working hard, putting his farm in order there in the Lake District. And I have heard that he has hopes where you are concerned. Will you be living out in the wilds with him? How exciting!" Georgie looked at her expectantly like a cock robin sitting on a fencepost watching a gardener till the soil, hoping for a worm to turn up in the next forkful of earth.

"N-no. I am afraid that you greatly mistake the matter," Ann said heavily, realizing that Georgie would not be satisfied without some explanation. Trapped as she was in the Sedgemoor carriage, she soon found herself spilling out a part of the story into Georgie's eager, and sympathetic, ears.

"And so you see, I would not have Lord Robert Lyndhurst now if he were served up to me on a platter!" Ann summed up, her fury with him rising again as she recollected their last meeting. "And now that there is no chance that we will end up together, I wonder whether I should not accept Mr. Allenthorp's proposal after all," she added perversely.

"Oh, Ann, do not!" Georgie exclaimed, clasping Ann's gloved hand in hers. "Do not marry without great love. Oh, do not think of doing so for even a moment!"

Ann smiled sadly. "There will be no 'great love' for me, my dear. It is too late and besides, I could not—well, let me say that I believe if I do not marry Mr. Allenthorp and devote myself to promoting his literary career and that of others like him, I will go to my grave a spinster."

Georgie shuddered at the bleakness of the prospect Ann outlined for herself. "You shall not. I shall see to it!"

"Oh, no, Georgie. Please do not interfere," Ann protested.

Georgie sat back and composed her gamine features into a serious expression. "You are perfectly right. Forgive me. I am impetuous sometimes."

A smile trembled at the corners of Ann's mouth.

Georgie grinned sunnily in response. "I can see what you are going to say. It is what Gus is forever saying. I am *always* impetuous. There. I have admitted it and saved you the trouble. But wait until after my Christmas house party before you make a definite decision to accept Mr. Allenthorp. Promise, Ann." Georgie looked at her beseechingly.

Unable to resist the viscountess, Ann promised, "Very well, then." She was surprised to find that her spirits lifted after she had postponed the decision that had been weighing on her for days.

When Georgie returned to her Brook Street townhouse after dropping Ann at Mrs. Jermyn's, she went straight to her writing table, stripped off her gloves, and sat down to dash off a letter.

"Dear Robin," she began. She wrote furiously for over half an hour, smudging her fingers and one cheek with ink in her haste. When she ended with a flourish, she looked up with a gleam in her turquoise eyes that her husband would instantly have recognized as devilment, were he present. Fortunately for Georgie's scheme, the viscount was still at his club and thus the missive was closed with his official seal and sent winging on its way to Coniston with Lord Sedgemoor none the wiser.

"It is a good thing this house is so large. The little viscountess has invited over thirty guests, with more arriving for this Christmas party by the day, and neighbors coming for dinner almost every night. However, there is ample room . . . My dear, this pale blue damask wall hanging is exquisite, do you not agree?" Mrs. Forester remarked to Ann as they stood in the deserted first-floor great room or saloon at the Oaks, the ancestral home of Viscount and Viscountess Sedgemoor.

Ann, who had done her practicing on the excellent pianoforte in the music room, had come to the saloon to try the instrument there, to make sure it was in tune for Georgie's musical evening, when her mother had come to find her.

"And that plasterwork ceiling with its painted medallions of mythological scenes is simply breathtaking!" Mrs. Forester rhapsodized.

"Yes, indeed, Mama. It is all very impressive. Georgie said the room was redone by Adam in the early 1770s. Everything is in the best of good taste." Ann ran her fingertips over the Latin words engraved in the Italian marble mantelpiece: *semper cum honore.* Always act with honor. The same phrase was emblazoned on every mantelplace in the Oaks. Evidently it was the family motto. Well, Ann thought, it was an admirable guiding principle. She wondered if the family always lived up to the words.

"It must have taken the St. Regis family many generations to assemble all this fine furniture and these wonderful paintings," Mrs. Forester continued, moving about the room and admiring the furniture, art objects, and fittings.

Ann's thoughts soon strayed from her mother's comments on the elegant room to the conversation at dinner the previous evening. She had been seated next to Mr. Charles Harwood-Jones. He and his wife Betsy lived in the neighborhood and had been invited to dinner that night.

"Did—did your wedding go off well, Mr. Harwood-Jones?" Ann had asked when she found that gentleman was her dinner partner. No topic of conversation that did not touch on his relative occurred to her, and though she wished to avoid all reference to Lord Robert, she could not in all courtesy avoid asking about the Harwood-Jones's recent nuptials.

Chubby had grinned happily and told her all about the momentous day, then added, "R-Robin was not himself. Betsy said he seemed pre-preoccupied about something. It's too bad. I was hopin' that you and Robin— But I mustn't say so, Betsy said." He looked conscious as he apologized.

Ann had ducked her head to hide her blush, but Mr. Harwood-Jones's next words had her jerking round to face him again.

"D-don't see your fiancé here, M-Miss Forester. Did he not come?"

"My *fiancé?*" she had replied in surprise. "I am afraid you are mistaken, sir. I am not engaged to be married."

"B-but that's what that fellow told me in London. Allenthorp was his name." Chubby looked puzzled. "Said you had an understandin'. Expected to make you his wife soon."

"No. Indeed not. I am engaged to no one." Ann's heart had begun to beat faster for some reason. At Mr. Harwood-Jones's next words, she understood why.

Holding his fork and knife suspended in mid-air above his plate, he had screwed his head round to look at her. "I'm sure that's what the fellow told me. And then I told Robin. He didn't like it. Was d-dashed cut up about it, in fact. Almost forgot Betsy's ring at my weddin', you know. And looked like the very d-deuce, too—uh, pardon my expression, ma'am."

"Oh, I see," Ann said. So Lord Robert had truly believed she was planning to marry George Allenthorp when he had called on her, when he had—well, when he had behaved so badly. Her heart had done a somersault as she realized that he had been very upset. That did not excuse his behavior, but she understood better now why he had acted as he did.

Why in the world had Mr. Allenthorp led Mr. Harwood-Jones to believe they were engaged? She was excessively annoyed with him for saying such a thing. More than annoyed—he might have forever ruined her chance for happiness.

And then after dinner, she had had a chance for a private coze with Lady Emily Gwent, who was also a guest at the house party.

"Georgie was so insistent that I come, that I finally had to agree to stop in for three or four days on my way home, though I sent my son and daughter on ahead of me," Lady Emily was saying to Ann as they sat somewhere apart from the other ladies while they waited for the gentlemen to join them. "Our family all like to gather at Papa's and Mama's home in Cornwall for the holiday, you know."

"You are fortunate in your large family, Lady Emily," Ann had said, then lifted her teacup to her lips to hide her expression. She was trying desperately not to think of one particular member of that family.

"Oh, Ann, we are such good friends, I wish you would call me Emily."

Ann smilingly agreed, then Lady Emily continued with raised brows, "Are congratulations in order?"

"Congratulations?" Ann had asked in bewilderment.

"Before I left town I had heard that you and Mr. Allenthorp planned to announce your engagement soon. Is that not the case?"

"No. Oh, no! Not at all," Ann had exclaimed in embarrassment.

"Ah. I am glad then. You will forgive me if I exercise a friend's candor and say that I do not believe you would have suited."

Ann had looked down and fidgeted with her teacup, unable to answer.

Observing her, Lady Emily added, "It will be a disappointment if Robin does not join us at home for Christmas again this year. The family circle is incomplete without him. I do not know his plans, but he is not very happy at present, I believe," she said carefully, leaning forward and speaking confidentially. "I had quite hoped that perhaps you and he . . . ?"

"No. Oh, no, Emily. I—I cannot discuss your brother," Ann had said in some distress, clenching her hands in her lap.

"Can you not, my dear? Well, I will not press you . . . I will only say that he was very pale and bluedeviled at dear Charles's wedding. I think Charles lived in terror that he had forgotten the ring. However, he had not. He produced it the crucial moment and all went smoothly despite Charles's nervousness. Poor dear. He reminded of my own dear John at our wedding so many years ago," she said fondly, her eyes dreamy.

"I am sorry you lost your husband in the wars, Emily. Was it a long time ago?" Ann had asked sympathetically, glad to change the subject.

"John was killed at Talavera in 1809. Nine years ago now." She sighed. "We had a good marriage. So much so that I do not wish to marry again. However, I am having trouble convincing various people, including my married sisters, Catherine and Frances. And I believe Georgie has invited me here to try her hand at matchmaking," Lady Emily confided.

"Why am I not surprised?" Ann laughed, then continued in a low voice, "I believe she delights in matching as many people as she can. Though I asked her specifically not to involve me in her schemes. Who has been invited for you?"

"I believe it is Lord Cranford, the young man with the auburn hair," Lady Emily said diffidently. "Though why on earth Georgie would think to match *me,* a mother of two almost grown children, with a gentleman who must be three or four years younger than I am, I have no idea. Not that I wish to be matched with anyone," she added hastily with an abashed laugh.

They had talked on easily until the gentlemen came, at which time Lord Cranford sought out Lady Emily. Ann had excused herself, noting Lady Emily's rosy blush as the elegant Lord Cranford seated himself beside her. Ann had smiled as she walked away, thinking perhaps Lady Emily had protested a little too much. Her excessive embarrassment clearly spoke of some interest in the handsome young lord's direction.

Ann had gone to bed with much to occupy her thoughts. She had lain awake long, thinking about Lord Robert, remembering what she had learned that evening, and remembering his bitter words that had wounded her so deeply the last time she had seen him. He had said he was showing her how he had felt when she had decided to punish him for the incident with Lady Stanhill. And he had been convinced she was going to *marry* George Allenthorp.

Her own pain abated somewhat as she understood that he had been hurt—and had lashed out at her in anger and pain. It was all too human to want to strike back when one was wounded. She had cried again, though not so desolately as before, wishing that he had acted differently, that he had asked her the truth of the matter before he behaved so abominably. Now there seemed to be no hope that they could ever resume their former friendship or even their warm correspondence.

Strangely though, after her disturbed night she had awoken this morning more at peace than she had been in several weeks. She had made her decision regarding Mr. Allenthorp. She would never marry him, had never really wanted to marry him. Better to go to her grave a spinster than marry without great love. Just as Georgie had said.

"Just what the devil did you write to Lyndhurst that he is turning up here at my house for Christmas?" Viscount Sedgemoor was saying to his wife in the privacy of her dressing room as she prepared for dinner. Looking cold and fierce all at once—and as noble as a Greek god—he was waving a letter about in his hand, his classically sculpted features suffused with angry color.

His wife showed no fear of the tall, athletically-built man hovering over her so threateningly. "Now, Gus, there is no need to be a bear about it. You *know* it has long been a dear wish of my heart that Ann and Robin make a match of it. If they are here together under our roof, I think they will have no choice but to admit their love for one another."

"I am not being a bear, madam wife. I do not like the fellow. I do not wish to house that—that *rake* under my roof and be forced to make polite conversation with him."

"There will be no need for you to entertain him. We have upwards of thirty guests for you to spend your time with. Besides, I will see to it that Robin spends all his time with Ann."

"I will not have him ogling you!" he said jealously, pacing about her chamber.

"Ogling me!" Georgie laughed merrily. "Gus, I am six

months gone with child. If he ogles me it will be because I am beginning to resemble a ball. Soon I will be rolling along instead of walking."

"You look very well, Georgiana," Sedgemoor assured her, looking at her with a possessive light shining in his clear grey eyes.

"What a clanker! Still, I am glad you think so, my love . . . There is no need for you to worry your head in the least. Robin has reformed, you know."

Sedgemoor snorted.

Georgie turned on her stool to give her husband her full attention. "I have been informed by a source who can be trusted that it is indeed the case. And with his sister Lady Emily here, he would do nothing to cause concern. You do not need to brew a tempest in a teapot over it, my love. All will be well, I promise you." Pushing herself up from the dressing table stool, Georgie grasped her husband's jacket lapels and stood on tiptoe to press a kiss on his finely chiseled lips.

"Georgiana, do not think to get round me, my girl," he said severely, but his arms had already tightened round her and he was regarding her through half closed eyes.

Georgie, sensing that he was weakening, smiled impishly. "My dearest heart, Robin is in love with Ann," she explained for the thousandth time. "If my plans go aright, I believe he will carry her off and marry her out of hand before ever Christmas comes. So you will not have to glower at him for the whole time. Please, Gus. As a Christmas present to me, allow Robin our hospitality."

By now her hands had crept round his neck, where her fingers stroked through his silky blond hair. She kissed his chin, then worked her way up his firm jaw to his ear, knowing the best way to get round him.

He moved his head so that he could taste her lips with his own. The kiss lasted a considerable time, until the child in her womb objected rather violently to being pressed so tightly between its parents.

Georgie moved back laughing. Lifting her husband's hand, she pressed it to her swollen belly.

"It's the baby, Gus. Objecting to her father's attentions and kicking her poor mother to death."

"Yes. He is a vigorous soul, Georgiana," he said, smiling boyishly and looking a bit disheveled after their embrace.

"A superb athlete, like her father."

"Never still. Like his mother."

Nineteen

"Devil take it!" Lord Robert swore, swiping at the snow that was spiking his eyelashes, making it difficult to see. As he was unfamiliar with the route, he was doubly handicapped. But he was determined to reach his destination that night.

"Come on, Pericles, old boy," he said to his horse, who was struggling to pull his hooves from the thick drifts of snow already covering the ground. "We should see the house over the next rise, according to the landlord at that last tavern anyway."

It would be ironic if he got this far, this close to his destination where light and warmth—and perhaps love—awaited him, only to fail in the last mile.

The landlord at that inn he had stopped at a mile back had tried to persuade him to put up at his establishment and not attempt to reach the Oaks that evening. The snow had been falling all day, lazily at first, but was coming down now thicker and faster. But he had not wanted to stop.

He had had a letter from Georgie—Viscountess Sedgemoor, he amended, trying to think of her by her title even in his private thoughts—inviting him to spend Christmas at her husband's estate, and telling him that she had also invited Ann, to keep her safe from the clutches of her impecunious writer friend Allenthorp.

"Ann is pining for you, Robin," Georgie had written, "but if you do not make it up with her and claim her for yourself, she will likely commit herself to Allenthorp after the holidays and be lost to you forever. You must come. The matter is most urgent!"

Georgie had underlined her words for emphasis and used a superfluity of exclamation marks. All unnecessary, he thought. At her first mention of Ann, she had his complete attention.

And so here he was on the way to the Sedgemoors' estate, where he knew he would not find a warm welcome from the viscount. But Georgie's words had forced him to act with all haste. If she believed he still had a chance with Ann, he would be a fool not to take it.

He had broken his heart over her for a year now. The last few weeks had been beyond hell, days and nights of pure torture. He had relived his last scene with her over and over again, hating himself. He had reread her letters and found all over again all the affection he thought had been there when he had left for London so full of hope. He just could not understand how she could choose Allenthorp over him. He decided he must be too flawed a person to ever win her trust, as he had proved to his shame by what he had done in London.

He had sat down and tried again and again to write an apology to her. He could not find words adequate enough to excuse the enormity of his offense. Each time he had wadded up the paper and thrown it into the flames where it had flared briefly, then turned to ash.

Like his hopes.

He expected any day to hear of Ann's betrothal to Allenthorp—and in so fearing had not read any of the London papers to see his fears confirmed. He had immersed himself in the work of his small holding instead, doing most of the manual chores and hard labor himself. Many days he went out with the sheep at dawn, while Jacob complained that he had taken over his job. Other days he had walked for miles over the fells and had climbed Coniston Old Man so many times, he felt he could find his way to the summit in his sleep. His hands and his face were chapped and weatherbeaten now that winter had set in. Often he did not return to the house until well after darkness had fallen, exhausted physically, but not able to sleep.

And then Lady Sedgemoor's letter, no, *Georgie's*—the devil with it! he could not think of her as anything else—Georgie's letter arrived, giving him hope. His heart had soared at the news that Ann was not yet irrevocably committed to his rival. And Georgie said that Ann was pining for him.

Was she?

He knew he was pining for her. And he knew things could not be any worse than they were now. Though he feared she might not be able to forgive him, he would take this last chance. The last chance for any happiness for him—for them both, he prayed. Life would be unbearably dull and lonely without her.

He climbed a long, slippery hill, dragging the reluctant horse with him. When he reached the top, lights flickered before his eyes. He raised his glove to wipe the snow from his eyes once again to make sure it was not a mirage. A huge grin split his face. "There it is, Pericles. We have made it! We shall be all right now."

"Oh, Robin!" Georgie put a hand to her mouth and giggled as she entered the first-floor reception room to greet the weary traveler. "You look so different, I would not have known you if the butler had not announced you first."

He passed a hand over his face and Georgie was surprised to see a blush high on his cheekbones.

"Well, that's what hard work out-of-doors in a cold climate will do for you. But I am much too gallant to say the same of you, Lady Sedgemoor."

He grinned and Georgie saw the old Robin before her.

"You wicked boy to refer to my condition in such a way!"

"Actually, you look radiant, my dear." Bowing slightly, he took up her hand and planted a brief kiss on it.

"Ah, ah. Now you pour the butterboat over me. Well, you had

just better behave, if you wish my help in the delicate matter of your courtship—"

"Good evening, Lyndhurst," Sedgemoor said stiffly, coming quietly into the room in his wife's wake. "We did not expect you tonight. It is snowing quite heavily out now."

"Yes. It was hard going the last mile or two. I am afraid we will all find ourselves snowbound for the next day or so. I am exceedingly obliged for the invitation, Sedgemoor. I hope my presence will not inconvenience you too terribly," Robin replied dryly. He watched as Sedgemoor put an arm about his wife and eyed him with disfavor—which cheered him a little. It seemed the viscount was still jealous of his past friendship with Georgie. Well, he was glad. It just went to show that Sedgemoor was in love with Georgie, as she was with him.

"I believe that we shall contrive to keep all our guests suitably entertained, provided they behave themselves," the viscount returned levelly.

Georgie intervened hastily to prevent her husband giving the bone-weary traveler a cutting set-down. It was not so long ago that they had been at daggers drawn. "Robin, I know you are exhausted after traveling so far and in such poor conditions today, but I have a small favor to ask of you."

Lord Robert cocked a brow, noting the viscount's glower at Georgie's words.

"For you, my dear viscountess, anything," he said smoothly, enjoying the furious look on Sedgemoor's face.

"Would you mind telling Ann that we must postpone our musical evening for half an hour or so? Convey my apologies to her and explain that several of our guests want to walk outside in the snow for a time before we have our little concert."

"Of course," he replied rather tightly, trying to conceal his nervousness from the Sedgemoors. The moment of truth was at hand. He felt very ill-prepared to face her, to offer his abject apology and put his fate to the touch.

"She is in the music room practicing. I declare, she practices so much one would think her fingers would be falling off by now. The footman will show you the way." With an encouraging smile, Georgie sent him off to find Ann.

The well-oiled door to the music room opened at the footman's touch and Lord Robert stepped inside hesitantly. Ann did not see him at first. She was seated at the pianoforte, a branch of candles illuminating her music as she played with her usual concentration.

The sight that met his eyes robbed him of breath.

She looked ethereal seated there in the candlelight in a gown of Nakara-colored silk, its pearl-like luminescence lighting up her face and emphasizing her dark hair, which was gathered in a loose knot at the top of her head with curling tendrils cascading down to caress her neck and cheeks. Dear God!

How had he ever thought her plain!

He stilled and listened for a few moments. As always, her music climbed right inside him, turning him inside out, rocking him to the core of his soul.

She did not hear him over the sound of her playing as he quietly walked farther into the room holding his breath, watching her, drinking in her appearance.

Something, perhaps the flickering of the candles over her sheet of music, caused her to look up. Her fingers crashed to a halt on the keys and she surged to her feet, her slanted amber eyes aglow with amazement.

"Robin!" Her mouth formed the word, but no sound came out as she looked across at him, utterly shocked by his appearance.

"It is I, Ann. Behind all this hair on my face—I have not shaved or cut my hair since I saw you last. A sort of penance, I suppose . . . If you do not like it, I will have it off in a minute." He could hear himself babbling, but he did not know what else to do. The emotion of the moment was overwhelming. His knees were shaky and he could not seem to think coherently.

"What are you doing here?" she whispered through stiff lips. Incongruously, she thought he looked older, more solid and mature with his full beard. He gazed at her out of weary, sad eyes that held a touch of fear as well. She wanted to reach out to comfort him, and had to link her trembling fingers together in front of her to prevent herself doing so.

"Ann, to say that I am sorry for what ha—happened in London is woefully inadequate. But I am. So sorry, my dear." His voice was unsteady and he had to swallow before he could continue. "I cannot let you marry Allenthorp. Ann, I love you. I need you," was all he could manage. Tears gleamed in his eyes as he opened his arms to her.

Her vision blurred and she could not see his face. She hesitated for the merest fraction of a second, grasping the sides of her gown with trembling hands and biting her lower lip to keep from sobbing. Tears spilled over and ran down her cheeks. Then she stretched out her arms and ran to him to be folded in a crushing embrace.

"Ann, Ann. My dearest girl, I love you to the point of insanity," he whispered against her hair, his arms holding her tightly. "Please, please do not marry Allenthorp."

"Kiss me, Robin," she replied, cupping the sides of his bearded face in her hands and looking into his green eyes brimming with tears. "Kiss me!"

"Oh, Ann!" His hands shook as they moved to hold her head and his lips to cover her mouth. Emotion that had been dammed up for weeks spilled over as he ardently complied with her request.

Warm lips met trembling mouth. Fast-beating heart met pounding one. It was a kiss of lips and mouths and tongues and hearts and souls.

A long time later, she raised her face from his and said with a shaky laugh, "I am gratified in the extreme that you have come in all this haste to resuce me, my love. Quite like young Lochinvar. But I am not going to marry Mr. Allenthorp."

"But— Georgie wrote to me. And my sister Emily, and Chubby, too—they all led me to believe that you were on the point of engaging yourself to him."

"No." She shook her head, smiling lovingly into his eyes.

"Ah. I am so glad." He closed his eyes and hugged her silently for a moment.

"While I have you in my power, my love, I will show you the document I have been carrying around in my pocket for an age now . . . On second thought, I will keep my arms about you. I feel it safer not to let you go." He kissed her briefly, then continued, "If you would put your hand inside my jacket and reach into the inside breast pocket you will find a folded paper there. I think, I *hope* you will find it of interest."

She leaned back in his arms and did as he asked while he watched her expectantly. Pulling the paper out, she cried, "But this is a special license! Dated many weeks ago."

"Yes. I got it the day I arrived in London for Chubby's wedding. You see, I was hoping—" he stopped and took a deep breath. "I was hoping we could put it to immediate use and that I could carry you off back to Coniston with me as my wife, where we could read poetry by the fireside every night and I could teach you a little Greek, just as we planned a year ago."

"Oh, Robin!" She placed her hands grasping the license over his chest. Resting her head against her hands, she listened as he told her of his desperate disappointment when first Emily told him there was something between her and Allenthorp, and then Chubby confirmed it. "So, you see, I was beside myself with jealousy when I lashed out at you. But that does not excuse what I did . . . Oh, forgive me, sweetheart!"

Her hand crept up to rest against his bearded cheek, lightly stroking the soft hair there. "I do. I have. Let us put it behind us."

"You are an angel!" He took her hand to his mouth and kissed the palm. "You will marry me, then? Tomorrow, if the snow has cleared enough to get to church."

"Yes," she said and her smile was wobbly.

"Good." He rubbed his nose against hers. "I promise to do my best to make you happy, my love. For always."

"And I you, dearest heart." She spoke against his neck.

After a considerable interval, during which they somehow found themselves comfortably ensconsed on the wide, cushioned sofa, she sat up in his lap looking soft and disheveled, her lips swollen and her eyes dreamy. She was smoothing back his long hair that now fell well over his collar in back, the ends curling up crisply and enticingly, then stopped suddenly and cried, "What on earth has happened to Georgie's concert?"

"I expect it has been postponed," he drawled with a devilish grin, looking equally disheveled.

"But I—but she—Oh heavens, what will they think of us alone together all this time?"

"I expect Lady Sedgemoor will be highly gratified, as she planned this meeting almost down to the last detail." A lock of dark hair fell over his forehead.

Ann blushed but smiled radiantly nonetheless. "Yes. That is Georgie's way . . . I hope you realize that you have been lured here by an incorrigible matchmaker, my dear, and manipulated quite shamefully."

"No! You don't say?" His green eyes twinkled into hers.

"Indeed, I fear so, my lord," she murmured demurely, her hand lifting to push back that recalcitrant lock.

He chuckled. "Well, thank God for matchmakers, then!"

She laughed, too. "Matchmakers should be a rake's worst nightmare."

"A *rake's,* perhaps. But you see before you a sober, hard-working man, a sheep farmer, my sweet love, with not a rakish thought in his head."

"No?" Her raised brows teased him.

"Well, only when he looks at *you,* my darling," he said innocently as his hands played over her body.

She leaned into his hands, giving him back endearment for endearment, kiss for kiss, and love for love.